Books by David Scott Milton

PARADISE ROAD (1974)

THE QUARTERBACK (1971)

PARADISE ROAD

PARADISE ROAD

David Scott Milton

ATHENEUM NEW YORK *1974*

Grateful acknowledgment is made for the use of excerpts from the following songs:

"Stagger Lee," by Lloyd Price and Harold Logan. Copyright © 1958, 1959 Travis Music Co., 729 Seventh Avenue, New York, N.Y. Used by permission. All rights administered by United Artists Music Company, Inc.

"Making Believe," by Joe Hobson and Roscoe Reid. Copyright 1951 by Joe Hobson and Roscoe Reid. Reprinted by permission.

"A Good Hearted Woman," by Waylon Jennings and Willie Nelson, published by Baron Music Company. Copyright © 1971 by Baron Music Publishing Company. Reprinted by permission.

"Games People Play," by Joe South, published by Lowery Music Company, Inc. Copyright © 1968 by Lowery Music Company, Inc. Reprinted by permission.

TO GERTRUDE,

the best little gambler I know

". . . you are faced with the advanced paradox that within the cosmos there is no intention. There is no project. There comes about the biosphere full of systems which behave as if they had a project. This is the core problem in biology—how do we account for the fact that purposeful systems could have grown out of a universe devoid of purpose?"—JACQUES MONOD

"I was standing on the corner when I heard my bulldog bark.
He was barking at two men who were gambling in the dark."—POPULAR SONG, "STAGGER LEE"

PARADISE ROAD

I

They called him Don Porter, but that was not his name. He had assumed it somewhere along the way. He was a lean man who appeared to be in his early thirties. He was older. He had dirty blond hair and pale blue eyes. He was thin. The fingers on his hands were long and delicate looking, the nails always manicured.

He sat now on the daybed and practiced with a worn deck of cards. He dealt the cards face up—two blackjack hands, his and the dealer's. He kept track of the cards as they fell, how many tens were gone, how many pictures, how many aces and fives. He subtracted the number of cards dealt from the total in the deck. He kept a running count of the cards, and he calculated percentages.

The room he lived in was narrow and stuffy. There was no air conditioner. A small, black fan rotated weakly on the floor. It was summer. The window was partway open, but there was no breeze. The street outside was silent. It was late night.

A single lamp illuminated the daybed. The walls of the room were a dull beige. He flicked the cards out, hand after hand.

His eyes burned from the glare of the cards, the hours

spent concentrating on them. I probably need glasses, he thought. I'll probably go blind one of these days. He had spent years studying the cards, counting, calculating percentages.

He stood up now and moved to the dresser. He lifted a pair of curved sunglasses and put them on. They were cheap plastic and gave a slightly wavy, distorted cast to the room. He looked at himself in the mirror above the dresser, and a terrible feeling of loss seized him. Surely, that wasn't himself he was looking at! Sunglass lens and flaked mirror had combined to alter his image in some subtle, yet devastating way. He appeared pale, bloodless, two-dimensional. His eyes were tired. One day he would be blind. . . .

The small alarm clock on the dresser top marked the time at 11:20. He picked up a Marsh Wheeling stogie from a half dozen next to the clock, removed the cellophane wrapper, bit off the end, and lit up.

He returned to the bed and dealt the cards once more.

Why had he picked this town? He asked himself the question on his way to the diner, walking along the deserted main street. The town was nothing more than a truck stop on the Pennsylvania-Maryland border. There were a few small factories, a strip coal mine, two taverns, and the diner. It was a dying town. The people were tight-lipped, physically and mentally stunted, mean. The best of the young in the town had left, gone north to Harrisburg or east to Philadelphia. The ones who remained appeared sullen and corroded, with blackened teeth and acned skin. It was a town of decrepit filling stations, ill-functioning neon signs. (JERRY'S SER ICE S ATION, B RDER DINER), and soot (a glass factory whose furnace coughed forth a continuous cloud of black smoke).

Yet he had chosen to remain here. Why? He had been hitchhiking south and the middle of the night landed him here. He hung around the diner and pressed the truckers passing through for a ride. No one would take him on. Morning came. He approached the owner of the diner, a heavy-set Slovak called Pepik, and asked for a meal. Pepik fed him and put him to work mopping the floor. He never left. It was as simple as that. Now, three months later, he was the short-order cook.

He spoke little. He had no friends. He had his room and his deck of cards.

Ahead of him on Main Street the red neon of the diner glowed: B RDER DINER. An occasional truck rumbled by, great diesel monsters off the interstate highway, looking for food or fuel on this forlorn sidetrack.

His nostrils burned with the odor of diesel fuel, carbon soot, oil. The night was very warm.

He would be out of here soon, he reassured himself. The System needed a bit more refining. He would have to find someone to work with, someone green, someone he could train, someone without sophistication or guile. . . .

He quickened his pace toward the diner. Pepik boiled when he was late.

"We need a batch of hash fries. And scrape down the griddle." Pepik was seated at the counter in a sweaty tee shirt. He had a cup of black coffee in front of him. He was smoking a cigarette. He was a large man with a dark, brooding face. Like many stupid people he was inordinately suspicious, convinced that everyone was out to cheat him. Every night before Porter came to work, he counted out the hamburger patties and the eggs in the refrigerator. At the end of the shift he recounted them and checked the total against the slips on the spindle next to the cash register. If an egg was short he would call Porter over. "One egg missing . . ."

"It was rotten. I threw it out."

"Where?"

"In back."

Pepik would eye him narrowly, then move to the garbage

5

can just outside the rear door. He would poke with his hairy paws among the wilted lettuce leaves, eggshells, soggy fried potatoes. He would sniff with his nose like an animal, then return to the front of the diner.

"I don't steal. . . ."

"I know you don't. You too dumb to steal."

Kitty the waitress—who did steal—would watch them out of the corner of her eye. Pepik never questioned her honesty. Porter knew why. . . .

Once a night, usually between two and three, when business was slowest, Pepik would move through the doorway in the storage bin and descend the stairs into the cellar. A few minutes later Kitty would follow, closing the door behind her. She would return ten or fifteen minutes later, avoiding Porter's stare. Her yellow waitress uniform would be rumpled. Her face would be flushed. She would enter the ladies' room, and Porter could hear water running in the sink.

The former short-order cook, Sid, a pale, tattooed rummy with skin the color of flour paste, had first clued Porter in on Kitty's behavior. "She's pecker-happy. Everybody around here gets a little bit of that. The hunky, though, got it reserved during work hours."

While Kitty and Pepik were in the cellar, Sid would grab the opportunity to drink deep from a poor boy of muscatel he hid behind the workbench. A few swigs from the poor boy and Sid would turn glum. "Imagine a cute little thing like that humping that hunky," he would complain.

One morning he flew into a wino rage and began babbling and screaming. Pepik attempted to quiet him, and he threw a tin of hot grease at the big Slovak. He missed and Pepik hit him with a milk crate. He went down. Pepik kicked him two or three times, then dragged him outside. That was the last that was seen of Sid in the Border Diner. And Porter became short-order cook.

Kitty was not yet twenty. She lived in town with an older

6

sister and brother-in-law. She had a small, thin body, no behind, and only the barest hint of breasts. Her face, though, was pretty, heart-shaped, with wide green eyes. She kept her light blond hair cut short like a boy's. Around her neck she wore a small gold crucifix.

When Porter had first started at the diner, Kitty had tried to befriend him. She smiled and joked. She asked where he was from and did he like the town and did he have a place to stay. He was unresponsive and cold in his answers. He knew that he had hurt her, and he regretted it, but there was no other way he could react. After that she pretty much left him alone.

One time Porter had spied on her and Pepik. He waited for her to move down the stairs to the cellar, then gave them sufficient time to go at it. He eased the cellar door open and quietly descended several steps. Kitty lay on a sack of potatoes, her dress lifted, her legs spread. Pepik's huge body rolled and heaved between her legs. He had pulled his trousers down but had not removed them entirely. They were bunched about his calves.

Kitty was making soft animal cries of pain or pleasure, Porter could not decide which. Her eyes were open. She saw Porter on the stairway and gazed at him with moist helplessness. He moved back up the stairs. When she returned a few minutes later, she did not look at him on her way to the ladies' room.

"Two eggs over, hash fries, sausage one, bacon one . . ." Kitty called out the order to him. He finished scraping down the griddle, then went to work frying the eggs. The kitchen was impossibly hot and reeked of stale grease.

Though the diner at this hour did the barest trickle of business, Pepik, a great believer in work for work's sake, managed constantly to devise odious tasks for Porter to accomplish: scrubbing down the floorboards behind the work counter, scraping out the refrigerator, cleaning the grease traps. Somehow the really important areas were overlooked —the exhaust ducts, the broiler, the floor behind the refrigerator. Because of this neglect, no matter how much superficial cleaning Porter did, the stench in the kitchen was barely tolerable.

He was perspiring now and his mood was ugly. How had he allowed himself to get trapped here? Why hadn't he continued south as he had planned, reached Miami, perhaps made it to Puerto Rico? What was he doing *here?*

He began to play out blackjack hands in his head . . . the dealer shows a ten, the count is heavy against the house, he's multiplied his bet by five. He draws a soft eighteen . . . should he hit? What's the percentage? What does the System index say?

His hands moved with the spatula as though he were sliding aces and tens across a green felt table in Vegas. He was at the Sahara, it was the middle of the night, he's playing head-to-head with the house. . . . Covering five hands, he's built his bet up to 10 G's. Should he hit or stick against the solemn king?

"The eggs were supposed to be over, Don." Kitty had returned with the order. He flipped them back onto the griddle and fried them over.

He was aware Kitty was staring at him as the eggs bubbled on the griddle. When he handed the platters back to her, she smiled at him. It was her first attempt at friendliness in a long while. Why this morning? It dawned on Porter that she had sensed his mood, had somehow picked up the particular desperation gnawing at him. He smiled back at her.

"Well, I don't believe it!" she said.

"What's that?"

"That's the first time I seen you smile. I didn't think you had any teeth in front."

"Maybe I don't smile 'cause I'm sick of this place."

"Maybe I am, too."

"I guess we both are, then."

8

"You know something? You're a strange-o."

"What's that?"

"Like a weirdo, only worse."

"I guess I am," he said, and they both laughed.

When he finished work, Kitty was waiting for him. She pretended to be counting out her tips, but it had taken him a half hour to clean up behind the counter, and her tips—five dollars in all—could have been added together in a couple of minutes. She was stalling and Porter knew it.

"Which way you going?" she asked outside the diner. It was daylight now, and the town looked particularly ugly, gray, and dreary under a sky filled with smoke-colored clouds.

"I don't know."

"Want me to give you a ride?"

"Where to?"

"Well, let me put it this way. In this town there are only two things you can do. Drink or the other thing."

"I don't drink."

"So we'll have to do the other thing." She smiled, a vague, shy smile, and Porter suddenly found that he liked her. Despite her obvious availability, there was an innocence about her, a little-girl exuberance that affected Porter, breaching the wall of reserve he had constructed around himself. It had been a long time since anyone had touched him.

She had a car, an old Chevy, and they drove out into the countryside beyond the town. They reached an area of gently rolling hills.

Porter was not interested in sex with her, and she sensed this. They parked the car off the main road and sat listening to the radio. A woman's voice sounded a plaintive twang through the static: "You're somebody's love. You'll never be mine. Making believe—I'll spend my lifetime loving you. Making believe . . ."

Porter grew very quiet. Kitty sat watching him, saying nothing. Around the car the trees and grass were alive with

9

the hum of summer. Porter stared out the window watching the day, now bright and green after a gray beginning. Yet he had no feeling for it. As a child the summer had contained a particular excitement for him. Now the summer was dead for him. The dealer is sliding the cards across the green felt table . . . "Making believe that I never lost you. The hour that we part I'll find someone new. My plans for the future will never come true. Making believe. What else can I do . . . ?"

The song ended. Kitty said: "Do you know who that was?"

"Kitty Wells."

"My mommy named me after her."

"Is that a fact?"

"Yeah. I like Kitty Wells."

"I like her too."

"You know who else I like? Tammy Wynette. I like her real good. But I think I like Kitty Wells best."

Porter grew quiet again. The radio played on for a while. Country and Western, the old stuff, Bob Wills, Gentleman Jim Reeves.

"You been in prison, haven't you?" Kitty said at last.

"Yes," he said.

"I can always spot a man that's been in prison."

"How's that?"

"They got a shyness to them."

"Oh."

"What were you in for?"

Porter did not speak for a moment. He felt exposed and infinitely small. He regretted opening himself up to her but could not stop himself. "Stickup."

"I knew a stickup man once. He wanted to take me on the road with him for me to drive getaway for him. I told him no way, no how. Let's put it this way, I steal from the hunky 'cause, well, just 'cause . . ."

"I pulled one damn stickup. I busted out in five-card stud

and I was just so low and desperate. One damn stickup and they nail me!"

"Goll—ee! What kind of work were you doing before the trouble?"

He gazed down at his nails. They were dirty from the work in the diner. He would have to do them later. "Gambler," he said softly.

She moved in with him, and they conspired to get away from the town. Pepik continued to take her down into the cellar, and she complied, but only because she was building up a case against him. She would screw him all right, she would screw him good one of these days.

Porter began to teach her the System. In the evenings, before work, the two of them would sit on the daybed with a deck of cards. He had drawn up a number of simple charts for her. He would deal out the cards, then point out the percentages and ratios for each hand on the charts. "A man in the slammer taught it to me," he explained. "That man sure was a whiz with numbers!"

She gazed on with wide-eyed admiration while he gracefully split and riffled the cards, making them purr with the shuffle, then flicking them out in neat, precise hands of Twenty-one. His memory amazed her. He could go through half a deck and tell her how many of each card had been played. He would expound on theory: "Twenty-one is the only game of chance where you can get the edge on the house. The house, you hear, is bound by strict rules—he's got to hit on sixteen or less, stay with more than sixteen. He's nothing more than a robot following them rules. And he's right to follow them, because they generally give him the P.C."

"P.C.? What's that?"

"P.C., that's your percentage, the edge you got. Just terms you use. Like you call your bankroll the B.R., and like that. It's the System, and it's the best there ever was."

"P.C.," she repeated thoughtfully.

11

"During a run through the deck, it varies. Sometimes the edge shifts to the player. And if he knows how to bet *mathematically,* he can cut his losses when the P.C. is with the house and win when it comes his way."

Kitty, who hadn't gone beyond the tenth grade in high school, had some difficulty absorbing the basic concept. Porter was patient with her. "Here—according to the averages it's crazy to take another card when you're holding a nineteen. But supposing you been counting the cards, and there are five cards left and you're pretty sure from the count there are three aces, a ten and a deuce remaining."

"How do you know that?"

"You been counting every card that goes out."

"You can do that?"

"With one deck I can come pretty close."

"Goll-ee!"

"Now, the dealer takes one of the cards for his down card. Four cards left. The dealer's showing a nine up." He chose four cards and placed them face down on the bed. "There's a one-in-five chance the dealer's got a nineteen, one-in-five he got an eleven. But three-in-five he got a twenty. What do the percentages say?"

She answered shyly, not at all sure. "Ask for another card."

"You got three-in-five to tie him, one-in-five to beat him." He turned the card over. It was a deuce. "But I know some gamblers, you tell them the cards and they still won't vary their play. I knew a guy in the slammer would never hit a sixteen. Never. One day I purposely gave him a peek at my hole card—I had a clear twenty. He had a sixteen. He wouldn't hit."

"That's stupid."

"That's a certain type of gambler." He got up from the daybed and lit up one of his stogies. "I was something like that when I was younger. I thought the cards were controlled by destiny. I was a loser because of that thinking."

He grew silent now and puffed on his cigar. He had spent the last couple of years in prison training his mind, rethinking basic concepts. He would become a winner. He was aware of how far he had to go. Short-order cook in a truck-stop diner, cramped, ugly rented room, nothing in the world more than could be stuffed in a small canvas bag—one couldn't be judged a winner on circumstances like that. But it would all change. He had the System now. And he had Kitty to help him.

"Who figured all these things out?" Kitty asked.

"I learned it from a man named Monty," Porter said.

"Where did Monty learn it?"

"From the horse's mouth, fellow who discovered it, name of Billy Ray Walker. Ol' Monty used to buddy with him out in Vegas and Reno. Said Billy Ray'd walk into Caesar's Palace or the Sahara, buy himself a hundred dollars' worth of red chips, and before the night was over, he'd walk out with fifteen, twenty thousand dollars. That's the truth. He was a mathematical genius with cards. If ol' Monty could have stuck with Billy Ray instead of getting hung with a murder rap, he'd a-been on Paradise Road, in more ways than one."

Porter suddenly was seized by a strong feeling of dissatisfaction with himself. There was only so much of the System he had been able to absorb. He had mastered the basic strategy and some aspects of advanced strategy. He had trained himself to count the cards so well he was never more than a point or two off. Yet, he had no natural inclination for mathematics. The more complex percentages and ratios had eluded him.

Not Monty, though. Monty had mastered it all. He was like a computer. At each moment in the deal he knew the precise advantage for or against the house.

If Monty were with him now! If he and Monty were on their way to Vegas! They'd take the town and turn it upside down. They'd score millions. . . .

Sometimes at night as he lay in bed, in that thin margin between sleep and wakefulness, a vision would come to him, more vivid than any dream; a vision of such palpable richness, such incredible purity that his whole being would grow warm with it. An estate on a cliff overlooking the ocean. The sea below tumbling and roaring with incredible ferocity. A mansion—his mansion—on the lip of the precipice, halls of white marble, ornaments of gold, servants in formal attire gliding through massive chambers, rose petals snowing down . . .

He sat next to Kitty on the bed. She was staring at the cards. "Golly, it makes my head ache, all this counting and remembering!" He kissed her brow. She smiled and leaned back on the bed. He undressed her.

Her body was lithe and soft, a little girl's body. She shaved her hair all over. He had asked her why, and she had just shrugged and said, "I dunno. Don't men like it that way?"

She closed her eyes when he made love to her. She would sigh softly and murmur over and over, "Oh, Donny, Donny . . ."

He felt clumsy and dishonest. Donny was not his name. While they made love, while he gently moved within her, his mind's eye was gathering up the deal. . . .

They robbed the Slovak and headed south. While Kitty had been in the cellar with Pepik, Porter emptied the cash register. There was fourteen dollars and change. In a cigar box beneath the register he found another sixty dollars.

Kitty then joined him and told him Pepik was taking his nap—as he always did after using her. Neither one of them felt any guilt about robbing the old man. Seventy-five dollars for all those free screws—Pepik still had the best of the bargain.

They drove south through Maryland, then Virginia. Dawn came up over the Shenandoah Valley. The gently rolling hills—pastel shades of green—appeared like a great blanket

14

spread over some giant sleeping form. In the early morning light the hills seemed almost alive, to be breathing softly. Kitty said, "Did you ever see anything so beautiful, Donny? Did you ever?"

Porter laughed and shook his head and puffed on his stogie. He turned up the radio and music flooded the car. They were tuned in to WWVA in Wheeling, West Virginia. Waylon Jennings was singing "Good-Hearted Woman." "She's a good-hearted woman in love with a good-timing man. She loves him in spite of his ways that she don't understand . . ."

For the first time since leaving prison he felt genuinely free. "We're going to tear those casinos wide open! We're going to hit Vegas and own that town!"

Toward midmorning they turned off the main highway and followed a narrow two-lane road through the Blue Ridge Mountains. The day grew silent. Great dark trees overhung the road, muffling it in shadow. Kitty and Porter did not speak.

The road wound along the rim of the mountain and below them they could see somber stretches of gray trees. They saw few cars on the road. They drove for hours without saying a word.

Toward evening they crossed into Tennessee. Now they encountered the Great Smokies on the way to Knoxville. A thunderstorm was gathering as they started the ascent up into the mountains. It struck with terrifying fury, flooding the road, slowing traffic to a crawl.

Great feathery streaks of lightning shattered the night sky, followed by enormous, rolling cracks of thunder that crashed about the car, burying it in hollow sound.

The narrow road wound round and round up the black mountainside. To the side of the road, barely visible, were the slat-board shacks of the mountain people, yellowish lamps fighting the thick downpour, shimmering behind heavy curtains of rain.

15

Then these were obliterated by the downpour, then the headlights of the cars in the opposite lane, then everything. Porter pulled the car to the side of the road and waited.

Kitty was trembling on the seat next to him. He put his arm around her. She began to whimper like a frightened animal.

"What's wrong?" he asked softly. "It's just a little old rain. It'll pass."

"I'm afraid," she said. "Storms always make me afraid. My mommy used to always let me crawl into bed with her."

"Well, I'm not your mommy, but I guess I'll have to do."

She smiled at this, and he kissed her tears and pulled her in close to him. With the storm raging about them, he made love to her in the car.

They arrived on the outskirts of Memphis early the next morning. The day was muggy hot, and Porter steered the car into a small filling station to check the radiator.

As he got out of the car, he heard a loud hiss from the left front tire. He watched helplessly as the tire flatted out.

"Look like you got you a flat tire," a voice said behind him. He turned. A tall, thin country type in work shirt and Levi's, his hands in his pockets, stood next to the car. "Want me to patch her up for you?"

"This your gas station?"

"Sure is."

"All right, patch her up."

"Lucky you happened by here when she went out. That road's mighty hot."

Porter had taken an instant dislike to the man. It was his eyes. They were dull, cold, cunning. He reminded him of certain rural con artists he had encountered in prison. Lean, leathery faced, laconic. They moved with a hick-town lassitude and generally kept their eyes to the ground. But you always knew they were watching you. When they smiled, the eyes never changed expression. They'd steal the fillings out of your teeth if you'd let them. "You got a spare?" the man asked.

Kitty had come round to Porter's side. "We got a spare?"

She nodded yes. Porter opened the trunk and took out the spare tire. It was nearly bald.

The gas station man examined the tire. "Wouldn't let my worst enemy ride around on this tire."

"What do you suggest?"

"I could fix you up with a new one at a right fair price."

"Forget it."

"Well, just be sure you get out of sight of this station when she blows on you. Young fellow just last week rode out of here on a set of bald tires, blew a right rear one just round the bend. They scooped him up off the highway with a teaspoon."

"We'll take our chances."

The man didn't so much as shrug and set to work changing the flat tire. He no sooner had the front of the car jacked up when Porter noticed that the left rear tire was going flat.

He looked on in amazement and despair. Two flat tires within five minutes of each other! It defied all laws of probability. "Son-of-a-bitch, look at that," Porter said.

The gas station man barely glanced over. "Yep," he said, and continued to unscrew the lugs on the front tire.

"Won't be able to patch this one up," he said, after he had the tire off the rim. He showed Porter a three-inch-long gash in the bottom of the tire, from which he had removed a length of knife-sharp metal.

"What the hell's that?"

"Looks to me like a piece of a bearing."

"How'd it get into my tire?"

"Damned if I know. These roads, you're liable to pick up anything." He set to work putting the spare tire on the front, then turned his attention to the rear tire. A piece of very sharp glass had punctured the rear tire.

"This one's finished, too," he said. "I'll tell you what I'll do. Let me give you two new tires up front where you need 'em. Shift that right front tire to the back and put that spare back in the trunk."

"How much?"

"Seeing how you're in a bit of a fix, I figure I can give 'em to you at a discount. Forty dollars."

"Forty dollars!"

"On the other hand I got one used tire I could give you for ten, and a new tire . . . thirty dollars."

Porter shrugged, disgusted. All in all, including Pepik's money, he and Kitty had a little more than a hundred dollars. Under the best of circumstances that would just get them to Las Vegas. Now with thirty of it gone, they'd never make it.

Two flat tires at the same time! Senseless! It was like splitting deuces against a king and pulling double Twenty-one. The System says it's madness and yet somewhere, sometime a gambler tries and catches it.

Porter examined the used tire. It had a split in the tire wall. He pointed this out to the station man. "This tire's not worth two dollars."

"Guess if you're riding down the road it's not, but if you're stuck here—"

"It wouldn't get us five miles."

"Man sold it to me said it rode right fine. And he was a good ol' boy sold it to me."

Porter decided to spend the forty dollars and get the new tires. The gas station man charged him another five for labor. As they were driving away from the station, Porter glanced in the rearview mirror. The man was kneeling down on the roadway leading to the pumps, placing, with great care, the pieces of metal and glass on the surface of the drive.

"We got to get us some money! That's all there is to it!" They had taken a hotel room on Front Street in Memphis.

Porter was standing at the window, glumly puffing on his stogie. It was midmorning and the day already was steaming. The Mississippi moved slowly past the hotel, just beyond their window. Under a dull, hot sky it oozed broad and muddy toward the delta lands of the south. The Arkansas bank of the river across the way looked parched and barren.

Porter was exhausted and edgy. The drive, almost nonstop for more than thirty hours, and the aggravation over having been taken for forty-five dollars, had worn his nerves thin. He had decided they would get some sleep, then he would scour the town for a game of twenty-one.

Kitty stretched out fully clothed on the bed and within minutes was asleep. Porter moved to the bed and gazed down on her. In sleep she suddenly appeared to be no more than a child. There was an innocence, a helplessness about her that touched Porter. He sat next to her on the bed for a long time. He sat staring down at her, wondering at how people connect, how they exist in some sort of prison of their own selves, strangers always to every other person on this earth—and yet they do connect. Fragile, tentative, almost unreal—these connections seemed to him as meaningless as those two flat tires earlier, as arbitrary as which card flashed next from the deck. Kitty could be with a thousand men, yet she was with him. Why? To what purpose had they become part of each other's lives? The thought made him sad, yet also somehow warmed him.

He removed his deck of cards from his canvas bag. He spread them out face down on his side of the bed. The backs of the cards were imprinted with the name, HAROLD'S CLUB, RENO, NEVADA. They had belonged to Monty. He had brought them into the pen with him. It would be a long time before Monty would see Reno again.

He shuffled the cards, then ran through one play of the deck. The System count favored the player, but the deal pulled the winning hands. He grew disgusted and laid the deck aside. He fell into an uneasy sleep.

He awoke several times during the day. He was bathed in perspiration. The air in the room was heavy and stifling. He checked the ancient air conditioner set into the base of the window. It hummed loudly but produced only a weak flow of tepid air.

It was evening when he decided to get up for good. He shook Kitty and asked her if she was hungry. She murmured no and turned back to sleep. He rose and splashed cold water on his face.

Downstairs the lobby was humming. A half dozen cotton traders in cream-colored linen suits and broad-brimmed hats sat around smoking cigars and telling raucous stories. A group of salesmen flirted with several heavy-set, rouged women—pros, Porter had no doubt. An out-of-state siding canvasser, red-faced and perspiring, screamed at his jobber over the phone in a booth near the rear stairway.

The evening was muggy. A large ceiling fan circled slowly above the lobby. More ornament than anything else, it did little better than stir the thick air and complement the wrought-iron grillwork of the lobby.

Porter approached the black bellman, who was busy polishing a brass balustrade. The black man gazed at him with heavy-lidded eyes. "I'm looking for a card game," Porter said. He handed the man a folded dollar bill.

"Poker game running in one of the rooms," the bellman said.

"I'm looking for blackjack."

"Believe you'll have to visit Jelly Jim's place for that."

He explained to Porter how to find Jelly Jim's. "Tell 'im Josh from the Cotton King sent you."

Jelly Jim's was located in a warehouse district just east of Front Street. The street was cobblestone. It was completely deserted. The air was heavy and smelled of the river. Porter turned down an alleyway, dark except for a single bare light bulb burning above an iron door in the middle of the block.

There was a neatly lettered sign on the door: "MEMPHIS CORRUGATED BOX CO." Porter pushed a buzzer next to the door. A mirrored peek-hole clicked open, and he was conscious of a great brown eye staring at him. He mentioned Josh's name. The door opened and he was admitted to Jelly Jim's.

A large black man in a black suit, black shirt buttoned at the neck, and no tie ushered him through an archway. He entered a wide, grottolike room with flagstone floor, red brick walls, and heavy wooden tables and chairs. His nostrils were assailed by a strong odor of burning grease. Along one wall of the club ran a heavy oak bar. In a corner was a large stone grill with racks of ribs broiling over it. An enormous oil painting of a reclining nude hung behind the bar.

The place was pretty much full: cotton traders and farmers, bargemen and out-of-state salesmen, lumber and livestock workers. The women for the most part appeared to be professionals, Tennessee and Arkansas hill girls come to this river town for a variety of obscure purposes that eventually led them to the trade. They were hefty girls, who wore their cheap, skin-tight dresses, bouffant hairdos, and rhinestone jewelry awkwardly, like school kids at their first prom. The men were dressed in anything from flashy tinhorn duds, with silk shirts, string ties and custom-built boots, to plaid work shirts, Levi's and clodhoppers.

A country band, clad in purple sequined jackets, performed on a platform just beyond a cramped dance area. A short, dark-haired girl in pink dress, pink hair bow, silver sequined shoes, and a rhinestone crucifix around her neck, sang in a high hillbilly twang, "Take Me Home, Country Roads," while the men and women performed a clumsy two-step to the music.

An enormously large man in a blue velvet suit approached Porter. He had a head full of greasy curls and a drooping Fu Manchu mustache. His face disappeared into the folds of fat that formed his neck, and his belly bulged prodigiously. His whole being seemed to quiver as he moved and Porter

21

assumed this was Jelly Jim. "What can I do for you?" the man asked.

"I'm looking to do some card playing."

"What's your game? Five-card stud? Hold 'em? Draw? We got something for everybody round back."

"Looking for a little blackjack."

The man gazed around the club, then nodded. He led Porter down a narrow brick passageway to another room. A game of Hold 'em was in progress.

The dealer was a wiry, balding man with long, thin hands and dull eyes. He wore steel-rimmed spectacles. On his pinky finger he had a small, but obviously expensive, diamond ring.

Jelly Jim watched while the deal was completed, then he motioned the dealer over. A second dealer replaced him.

"Man wants to play some blackjack. How you feel about that?"

"Head-to-head?" the dealer asked. Porter nodded. "I don't mind," the dealer said.

"He may have five dollars, he may have five million, I never seen the man before in my life," Jelly Jim drawled.

"I don't mind," the dealer said again.

They moved into a room beyond the poker room. The dealer snapped on a green-shaded overhead light. There were a half dozen sealed decks of cards on the table. He passed over one of the decks, and Porter broke the seal.

"Can I send you back some ribs?" Jelly Jim asked.

"That'd be good."

"We got some fine ribs here. What would you like to drink with that?"

"Whiskey and soda."

He didn't want the drink, but he was afraid he'd arouse suspicion if he turned it down. One of Monty's principles in the System was no booze: "They'll get you so piss-ass drunk you couldn't count the toes on your feet, let alone fifty-two cards. Or they slip you a Mickey, or some damn

22

animal tranquilizer. To play the System you got to develop a powerful allergy to alcohol."

He would drink his whiskey and soda very slowly, he told himself.

Jelly Jim left the room. The dealer spread the cards face up on the green felt table-top. Then he ran his thumbnail along the edge of the cards, catching each corner with the tip of his nail. Porter nodded, satisfied they were starting with a full deck. The dealer shuffled up.

Porter laid out sixty dollars on the table and the dealer gave him ten five-dollar chips and ten one-dollar chips. He began the deal.

Some dealers are slow and methodical; others move like demons. This man had lightning hands. Porter had all he could do to keep up the count. In the pen, practicing with Monty, he had gained confidence he could stay with anyone. Monty was fast, very fast. This dealer was faster.

There was a certain elegance in the way he snapped the cards onto the table, tapping the back of the deck with his thumb while waiting Porter's play; then flicking out the next hand at the same time the cards of the previous hand were buried, still managing in some miraculous way also to scoop in or pay out chips. And all the while his eyes, hard and opaque behind steel-rimmed glasses, combed walls and ceiling, appearing to see everything but the cards, yet, of course, seeing them best of all.

Porter had two things to concern himself with: the speed with which the dealer scooped up the cards and redealt, sometimes not permitting him to fix firmly the image of the card in his mind, preventing an accurate count; and Porter's own inclination to get greedy, overbet the end of the deck, and tip the System. He warned himself to be cautious.

He started his bets off with a base at two dollars. When the edge favored the house, he would drop his bet to a dollar; when it swung to him, he would raise it to three. As they neared the bottom of the deck, with the System at its most powerful, he would double or triple his basic bet if the edge came his way.

They played the first two runs of the deck pretty much even; then, although the P.C. favored Porter, the dealer grabbed four hands in a row—two blackjacks, a twenty-one, and a twenty. Porter was down fifteen dollars.

A black waiter arrived with the spareribs and whiskey. Porter cut his bets back as the dealer reshuffled and began a new round.

He played with even greater care now, keeping his bets to one and two dollars. He ate from the plate of ribs as he played, taking an occasional sip of his whiskey, feeling more comfortable now, hooking into the dealer's style and counting the cards with greater assurance.

At one point he neglected to wipe the rib grease from his fingers and the corner of the card caught a smudge. The dealer spotted it immediately, held the card at arm's length in front of him, and made an elaborate gesture of wiping it clean.

He continued to lose. The percentages were running strongly with the house now, and all he could do was make the best of the situation, hold his bets down, and wait for the edge to shift.

His stack of chips was decreasing slowly now, going down in steps. He would lose a few, then hold even for a run of the deck, then lose a few more. An hour had gone by. He had less than twenty dollars now.

He was growing tired. The speed of the deal, the rapid flick, flick, flick, scoop! of the cards, the pressure felt gambling with bottom money, knowing there was no margin for loss, began to work on him, wearing him down. If only the percentages would turn his way!

He had learned from Monty the necessity for stamina. Mathematically you've got the edge, Monty would say. You have to win in the long run. You must stay with the cards. Never walk away a loser.

But the house could stay forever. The player was limited by his capital, his durability, his nerves, and brain.

The cards continued to spin out, while his mind ticked them off: "Three tens, four sevens, an ace, two sixes, minus two count, 42, 41, 40, plus three count, six P.C., four-to-one ratio, bet three, now eight, six showing, now four, double down . . ." Constantly, his mind winding on, a mechanical bobbin spooling up threads of information, transposing flashing plastic cards into cabalistic mathematical relationships . . . The back of his neck ached from the hunch of his shoulders over the table. His hands were wet with perspiration. He couldn't catch the percentages.

Now he was down to ten dollars, now down to eight. If he struck a twenty, the dealer blackjacked; doubling down on eleven he drew an ace.

Inside he was aware his confidence was crumbling. He began to doubt the System: fatal, Monty would say! He began to consider *luck*. How could the System operate if the P.C. constantly eluded you?

He asked for a break. He was down to his last five dollars. He walked away from the table and wiped the perspiration from his hands. He lit up a stogie and tried to clear his mind. His fingers were trembling. Had he miscalculated that last run? Was he dropping the count? How could he expect to win, *ever*, if his mathematics were off?

"Want another drink?"

"Coffee," Porter said. The dealer picked up a phone on the wall and ordered coffee.

"You from around here?"

"Traveling through."

"Well, hell, if you lose fifty, sixty bucks, that ain't nothing."

The coffee arrived—a silver pot and dainty porcelain cup—on a small plastic tray. Now, with the coffee in him, he felt better. His head cleared. The count became more accurate; he regained confidence in his calculations.

At last, the percentages began to come his way; the cards started to fall for him. On the first run through the deck, he won back twenty dollars. In a half hour he was thirty dollars ahead; within the next five hands he doubled his capital. The point count stayed with him. He pyramided his bets.

Now, it seemed he could do no wrong. The cards seemed almost to play themselves. Whenever he had the edge on the dealer, he caught his point; it happened as though marked out beforehand on one of the little charts he had drawn up for Kitty. If he anticipated a picture, a picture fell, dreamed of an ace, and there it was! His whole body seemed to be trembling inside. How had he ever doubted the System? The stack of chips in front of him sprouted and grew like a thing alive.

He was afraid to count them now, but he was sure he was ahead at least three hundred dollars. He was betting ten, fifteen, twenty dollars a hand. Occasionally, when the P.C. fell, he would cut back, but he never cut back too far. The System worked best when you were playing with the house's money. That was the time to jump in.

The dealer ran through the deck and approached the bottom. Porter's count, plus for the player, skyrocketed—the highest it had been all evening. The percentages were all to him: five cards remaining—three tens, two aces, and a nine. If he caught a blackjack, he'd pull in a buck-and-a-half on a dollar. He bet fifty dollars. . . .

He tightened his concentration, focusing only on the cards. He could feel his heart racing rapidly; he was aware of a sudden weakness in his body. A part of his mind fought to shut out his body, to apprehend only the cards.

He had counted correctly. He was certain of it. One ten, two pictures, two aces, and a nine. They were there all right, buried in the hard impenetrability of what remained of the deck.

The pattern on the back of the remaining cards, a network of thin blue lines, created a mesh into which Porter attempted to project his thought. His mind would cut their pattern. The System, as powerful as any laser, would slice right through, routing all sway of chance, obliterating the mystery in the card's plastic heart. . . .

The dealer gripped the deck lightly with one hand, while he adjusted Porter's chips with the other. His eyes behind his glasses were cold. He dealt the cards.

Flick, one card down to Porter, flick, another to the dealer. Porter glanced at his card. It was a ten. The dealer paused, straightening his spectacles. The criss-cross pattern on the back of the cards seemed to dance in his hands. Although prayer was not a part of the System, Porter found himself praying for an ace.

The next card fell, and it was not to be. He had caught the nine.

The dealer flipped his second card up—a queen—then he peeked at his hole card. If it were an ace, the dealer would immediately turn his hand up on blackjack. He fingered the corner of his hole card. A trickle of perspiration started down Porter's face. He did not breathe. He stared down at the green felt of the table-top.

The dealer leaned back. He did not turn up the card. He has a ten, Porter thought. He has a ten. . . .

Now he was in trouble. The two remaining cards were aces: of that he was certain. To beat the dealer's twenty, he must take them. Yet to take two hits on a nineteen was lunacy. The dealer would know his game then: he was either counting or marking.

He called for the two cards and pulled the aces. The dealer turned his cards up and stared at them for a long time before paying off the bet.

His eyes met Porter's as he slid the chips over to him. There was confusion in his look, and a knife-glint of anger. "Never saw anybody pull that one off," he said.

"I misread it. Thought the nine was a six." Porter laughed. The dealer did not respond.

Porter knew now that he should leave. He was ahead nearly four hundred dollars. But he did not get up from the table.

They took another break. Porter again ordered whiskey and soda. He kept his eyes on the dealer. The dealer spread the deck face down on the table and examined the backs of the cards for markings. Then he held the edges up to the light to see if they had been tampered with. He set the deck aside and selected a fresh one from the stack at his elbow.

They began to play again. Porter was aware that Jelly Jim and another man had entered the room. The second man was short, dark, and heavy-set—beefy, rather than fat. He had narrow black eyes that fixed Porter with a stare that did not waver. There was no hostility in the stare, and that somehow made it more disconcerting. It was as though he didn't regard Porter as quite human.

The dealer had signaled them; Porter had no doubt about it. They were here to watch his play.

The percentages continued to favor Porter, but he began to lose. He was worn out now, mentally and emotionally exhausted. He was distracted by the two men behind him; he was angry that he was still playing. He was blowing the count now, betting erratically. He was catching good margins, but overbetting them, then losing the cards. His pile of winning chips began to shrink.

He told himself to get up, move for the door, leave! But still he remained.

Something invidious was working deep inside him: a belief that somehow the System was beyond the laws of mathematics, that as long as he had the System he could not lose. His mind rejected this. His mind knew that, if anything, the System was a strait jacket of mathematical certainties. Yet, the excitement, the beauty of the System clicking for him, had produced a dangerous intoxication. He visualized it working indefinitely for him. He saw himself walking out of Jelly Jim's with a thousand, two thousand dollars. He and Kitty would arrive in Vegas with a stake. They would go after the great casinos backed by a powerful bankroll. They would cash in on the big ones, the hundred-dollar tables, the fifty-thousand-dollar games. . . .

He continued to lose. His pile dwindled. No matter how hard he attempted to concentrate, how he drove his mind into the heart of the deck, the tide was running the other way. It had all grown cold for him.

He was down to two hundred dollars, then a hundred and fifty. He began to cut back on his bets, but he still carried that illusion of infallibility inside him, and he did not cut back far enough.

He was misjudging the count now: he was constantly a point or two off in his calculations. He would anticipate a ten and grab an eight, look for a deuce and an ace would fall. The whole thing was coming apart. He knew it, yet he could not quit.

Now he had a hundred dollars, now seventy-five. He raged inside at the stupidity that kept him at the table. He thought back on the time when the table in front of him was piled high with chips and grew sick with disgust at himself.

Then he had what seemed to him a reprieve. It was the end-deck situation once more, and the percentage was high in his favor. According to his count there were five cards remaining—a nine, a two, and three pictures. It was a set-up ripe for the player.

He was down to his original sixty dollars. He had been playing now for more than five hours. He pushed half of his remaining chips—thirty dollars—forward.

He caught the nine and the two, and that was perfect for him. He would double down on the eleven. The dealer would have the two picture cards, and he would hit for the third. Twenty-one, and that's the name of the game, and at this point nothing could beat it.

He turned his cards face up and set the rest of his money on top of them.

The dealer slid his card to him. He could feel the two men behind him shift and move forward a bit. He lifted the corner of the card.

It was a four.

He looked up, pale and shaken. The dealer raked in the last of his money. There was a hint of a smile playing at the corners of his mouth.

Porter sat for a moment fingering the edge of the table. It was possible he had miscounted. Or the house had slipped in a bum deck. Since the power of the System resides with the tens and aces, the surest way to break the player was to have a deck salted with low cards; lessen the tens and aces, and the percentage for the house becomes unbeatable.

The dealer was sliding the deck into its case. "Can I look at the cards?" Porter asked.

"Take a walk," the short, dark man behind him said.

"I want to look at the cards."

The dark man hit him. The blow caught him on the side of the head, and suddenly the room tilted forward as he went crashing into the table. The man kicked him as he lay on the floor. "You're a wise guy, aren't you?" the man said. He had a vague Southern drawl.

When Porter got to his feet, he could feel a trickle of blood coming from the corner of his mouth. There was a dull ache in his ribs. Jelly Jim wheezed: "Don't ever come round here again, you hear? I see you again I'm gonna have your balls crushed. Now get out!"

The short, dark man pushed Porter out into the alley through a rear door. He had less than a dollar remaining in his pocket.

II

He lay on the bed in the sweltering room unable to sleep. He played over and over in his mind's eye the events of that evening. As a gambling man, he knew what it was to lose—that wasn't what bothered him. It was the fallibility of the System.

The System had taken on the weight and dimension of a religion for him. It was winning and losing, but also something more: a governing element in his life. Three years and eight months he had practiced it faithfully. He had dedicated hours, days, weeks on end to it. He had forsaken friends and family for it. . . . And now it had somehow proven fallible.

He knew somewhere that what had happened that night did not necessarily prove a flaw in the System, that the scheming hand of man might have been involved. But shouldn't the System take that into account? Or could any system take that into account?

He lay alone in the room puffing stogie after stogie until his tongue was raw from the harsh tobacco, perspiring, waiting for dawn to come.

Kitty had not been there when he had come back. He had no idea where she was. She had left no note, no message. He wondered, without much interest really, whether or not she had gone for good, taking the car with her, leaving him stranded in this hell hole of a city. And, if she had gone, why? It didn't occupy his mind very much, though.

What did matter were percentages, strategies, bets. He had made a mistake—a big mistake, no doubt about it—in grabbing the two aces to make twenty-one. The house wouldn't have minded losing; running a steady game, they had to catch an occasional beating. But having the edge turned against them—that angered them. They wanted *you* to be the gambler; they were businessmen. . . .

Porter got up off the bed and walked to the window. A faint hint of gray had begun to show above the vast gloom of the black river opposite the hotel. It would be morning soon. An occasional house light came on in the river bank area across the way in Arkansas. Cars, their headlights wavering through the somber mist shrouding the river, moved along invisible roads heading—where? Porter wondered. To work? The early shift in bankside warehouses, factories, diners, gas stations? The world before him seemed immense, dark, mysterious.

He returned to the bed. He closed his eyes, and now he saw an expanse of water without end, the ocean roiling beneath him. Now he was standing above a precipice on a cantilever of marble and gold. An exquisite woman in billowing gown moved toward him, stirring swirls of rose petals under her feet. Her eyes were bright blue, her lips parted in a hint of a smile, long blond hair flowed behind her. Her right arm was extended before her, offering Porter a gift: two cards—an ace and a queen.

Someone was kissing him. He opened his eyes. The room was flooded with daylight. Kitty leaned down over him. She kissed him again, rolling onto the bed next to him. Her breath was sour with booze.

"Hi," she said.

32

"Hi."

"Did you win us a bunch?"

"No."

"What happened?"

"I lost everything."

She curled up next to him, covering his face with kisses. "Don't mind about that," she said.

"Where you been?"

"I went out to get a bite to eat."

"It take all night?"

"Will you be angry?" she asked, timidly like a little child. He shook his head no.

"I met some salesmen from Atlanta. They took me partying."

"Did you ball with them?"

She was staring up at the ceiling. "I don't know. I guess I did something like that."

"Why?"

"It's just my nature I guess."

He got up from the bed and walked to the window. "Are you angry?" she asked.

"No." The Mississippi was now clearly visible, muddy, desolate. The parched bank across the way was barren. Porter was seized with a sudden sense of terrifying emptiness. "I think maybe we ought to split up," he said.

"But what will you do?" she asked. "You got no money . . ."

He remained quiet. The impossibility of connecting with anybody weighed on him. His whole life had seemed to go that way. What Kitty had done had no meaning, except to say they were essentially strangers. Nothing had meaning for him but a deck of cards.

"I got us some money," she said. She reached into her bra and withdrew three fifty-dollar bills. "I figured if you won this would be nice fun money."

"The men give it to you?"

She nodded yes. "Don't be angry, Donny. I did it for us. I want to stay with you. Please . . ."

He returned and sat on the edge of the bed. "I don't like you doing those things," he said.

"I won't do it again."

He kissed her eyelids and she smiled. Then her breathing deepened, and she was asleep. He made certain not to disturb her while he ran the System, hand after hand, with Monty's deck.

They left Memphis in the middle of the afternoon. They drove on through Arkansas and into Oklahoma. They didn't talk much, and when they did, it was about the System.

"There's timing involved. You've got to feel the way the cards are turning. . . ." The hills of Arkansas had given way to dry, flat, empty plains. The hot, orange-yellow disc of day was gone now, swallowed up by the horizon, and the evening was cool. The sky was immense, a huge sweep of black, pierced and mottled by great whorls of stars. Kitty leaned forward and gazed up in wonder. She felt as though they were rocketing through space toward some far distant other world.

Porter kept his eyes on the road. The white center-line formed a band, drawing him through miles of gray-black. The car hummed beneath him, the steering wheel vibrating gently in his hands. Clouds of night-bugs hit the windshield in intermittent splats, crusting the glass with the residue of their mortality. "Do you understand what I'm saying?"

"Not exactly. I mean, if the percentage gives you the advantage, what does timing have to do with it?"

"You have an advantage, but the cards don't necessarily fall for you. A man can get beat bad if he don't sense the way the cards are falling."

They drove for a while in silence. "Were you ever married?" Kitty said at last. There was a long pause. She thought at first he hadn't heard her.

34

Then: "Once, a long time ago." She waited for him to say more, but he remained quiet.

They passed through Oklahoma and into the Texas panhandle. The night had grown cold. Gusts of fierce wind jolted the car. Tumbleweed, in skittering clumps, skipped and danced across the road, performing strange, skeletal arabesques in the white beam of the headlights.

Porter turned on the radio, and Garner Ted Armstrong preached to them across miles of static-filled air, imploring them to enter "The World Tomorrow." "For the free booklet, *The World Tomorrow and What It Holds For You,* write Herbert W. Armstrong. That's Herbert W. Armstrong, Ambassador College, Pasadena, California, and let us show you what the Bible has prophesied for your future!"

West of Amarillo they stopped to eat. It was a truck diner, one long counter and a row of seats. It was empty except for the owner and two lean, weather-beaten cowboys in Levi's and western hats.

They ordered chili and coffee. They did not speak. The proprietor, a large, raw-boned woman, stood smoking a cigarette and staring out at the highway. One of the cowboys put a coin in the jukebox. A song by Eddie Arnold came on: "Make the world go away. . . ."

Porter studied the packages of Beech-Nut and Mail Pouch chewing tobaccos, beef jerky and Slim Jims, chewing gum and stomach aids, Bull Durham and wheat paper on a wire rack next to the cash register. The song continued on. Bursts of wind-blown sand exploded against the slat-board exterior of the diner.

Suddenly Porter realized Kitty was crying. Tears were streaming down her face. He put his arm around her. "What's wrong?" he asked. She shook her head. He pulled her close to him. "What's *wrong?*"

"I don't know." Then she was smiling, laughing through her tears. "I'm just crazy." She dried her eyes. "I feel bad

35

about last night," she said simply.

"Don't," Porter said. He kissed her on the cheek, brushing away the tears with his lips.

They were in New Mexico by morning. The flatlands of the Texas Panhandle were behind them now; great tables of rock, long, low blue-gray mesas, stretched against the horizon. The sky was pink, fading to lavender. The sun was just coming up. It hung, a red hot ball, in the reflection in the side-view mirror. The shadow of the car raced with them along the rocky, dun-colored shoulder of the road. Buzzards fed on carrion splattered in the center of the highway.

"Oh, Donny, look at that!" Off in the distance a dust storm was blowing. A dark swirl rose in a black smoky funnel on a plain between two giant rock formations. "Is it a tornado?" Kitty asked.

"Could be."

"Oh, goody," Kitty said, clapping her hands. "Let's see if we can catch it. I've never been in a tornado."

Porter laughed and speeded up the car. They raced until midmorning, but never seemed to gain on it. The black swirl danced on the horizon, always just beyond their reach.

They lunched in Albuquerque, in the old town plaza, and after lunch Porter went looking for a gambling joint, while Kitty napped in the back of the car. He drove around for about an hour, dropping into Indian bars, five-buck-a-night transient hotels, Mexican poolhalls—any place that looked as though it might be carrying a few card hustlers. He found poker games—stud, draw, Hold 'em—but no one willing to go head-to-head with him in blackjack.

Kitty awoke groggy from the heat. Porter passed her a Nehi orange soda. The day outside was broiling. They were on the highway heading away from Albuquerque. "How'd you make out?" Kitty asked.

"Couldn't get a game."

"Those guys in Memphis must have tipped them off," she said, and they both laughed. Paul Harvey was on the radio, talking about the effect of marijuana on family life. "Goll-ee," Kitty said. "All they do is *preach* to you 'cross country! I never did like being preached to!" Porter switched the station and picked up a program of Mexican mariachi music.

For the next few hours they rehearsed the system to the accompaniment of mariachi music. Porter acted the part of dealer, calling out the hands. They didn't concern themselves with the card count, just the basic approach to strategy.

"Ace-seven, dealer shows a ten."

"Stick."

"Wrong."

Kitty glanced down at the charts in her lap. "It says stick on seventeen or better against a ten."

"Ace-seven is a soft hand. Look at the chart for soft hands."

She began to laugh. "Soft hands! You mean that's cards that use the right soap?"

"Anything with an ace is a soft hand because an ace can be counted as one or eleven. That completely changes the mathematics of the thing."

She was reading now from the chart. "Hit a soft eighteen against a ten."

"Right."

She was learning. She might never absorb betting indexes and ratios and card count, but she'd nail down the basic stuff. And that was good enough as far as Porter was concerned. When they hit the casinos, she could take her betting lead from him. Monty explained it was always better working with someone. It was less conspicuous and easier to monopolize the table. That's the way Billy Ray Walker operated, Monty used to say.

Billy Ray Walker! Monty said he was on his way to becoming a millionaire with the System. "He got a mind on him cuts like a razor blade. He could squeeze a twenty-one out of pure bust-out cards." When he was leaving prison, Porter had promised Monty he would look up Billy Ray. "Don't go asking for him by name, you hear? And I can't describe him to you because that summabitch always disguising himself. Man, he got more looks and way of talk than Marlon Brando. Got to do it, 'cause those casino bosses'd run him right out of that town on the balls of his ass if they got on to his game. But go into Caesar's or the Dunes or the Sahara. Don't go there in the afternoon or evening, but middle of the night, early morning. Look for ten, fifteen thousand dollars on the table and a man playing the System head-to-head with the house. That'll be Billy Ray. Whisper you're a friend of Monty. You'll find him all right."

It was late afternoon now, moving into evening. They were in Arizona, nearing Holbrook, and the landscape was dry desert with stunted scrub oak and yucca, cholla and prickly pear. They passed signs for Coors beer and Honey Farms and Reptile Villages and The Cowboy Hall of Fame. They passed signs for the Petrified Forest and Painted Desert, and would have turned off if it hadn't been so late. They came to plaster tourist teepee villages, Indian curio shops, and a trading post with a sign: "SHEEP, CATTLE, PAWN, HARDWARE, SADDLE TACK, LEATHER SHOP." By the side of the road Indian women wearing canvas jackets and tight pedal-pushers, their black hair braided on either side on their wide, flat faces, squat bodies solemn in the gathering dusk, moved slowly toward the town.

It was dark when they reached Holbrook. There was an ugly, insubstantial quality to the town, as though it had sprung up overnight. Something told Porter he'd find a blackjack game here.

The main street was a carnival of neon lights—motels and souvenir shops and all-night diners—while the back streets were made up of dim, desert-town saloons and flop hotels where Chicanos, Indians, cowhands, truckers, and railroad men could booze it up and do a little whoring. Porter figured he could find *someone* looking for a little action with a deck of cards.

In a diner where Porter and Kitty stopped for a bite to eat, a toothless Chicano cowhand steered them to a local gambling joint. "It's behind the Santiago Hotel. Walk right on down the road here, you come to the railroad tracks. That dirt road there is Southwest Central Street. There's the Standard Oil of California siding there, then the lumber yard, then a row of mo-bile homes. You keep going left. You'll come to it all right. Called the Navajo Central. It's run by a Chink."

"They got Chinese in this town?"

"Damn right, amigo. Got three or four Chink restaurants here. Chinks all over the place."

"Where they come from?"

"China, where the hell you think a Chink comes from?"

"They come to work on the railroad?"

"Damn if I know. They're good people, though. They stay mostly to themselves. Live in mo-bile homes, you know. They love to gamble, amigo, believe me."

They walked to the place from the diner. Just off the highway the street suddenly became very quiet. They came to a railway embankment and turned down a gravel road. A lone streetlamp glowed dimly on the next corner.

The desert air had grown cold. A strong wind was blowing, churning up dust all around them. The air was sweet with the odor of mesquite and cholla. Far in the distance, beyond the railroad tracks, they could hear the incessant bark of a lone dog.

Porter discussed with Kitty his plan: "You'll play right along with me. Play the basic strategy and take the betting from me."

"I'm scared."

"What about?"

"I'm going to forget it all."

"No, you won't! Just keep your bets at one dollar until

you see me put down a real good bet. Then you can go up to two dollars. You need to get broken in, and I guess this place is as good as any."

At the corner, off to their left, was the Love Saloon, a whitewashed concrete building with a sign next to the door: "HOME OF INTERNATIONAL CUISINE." Sullen Chicanos and Indians in black cowboy hats and dusty Levi outfits leaned against the wall of the building and stared after Porter and Kitty with dark, impassive eyes.

They continued on down the gravel road, past a row of ramshackle frame houses with caved-in roofs and boarded-up windows. Someone had painted a sign on the warped wood siding of one of the houses: "THIS INCOME PROPERTY FOR SALE"; next to it, lettered in black charcoal, was the admonition:

                    W
                    I
                    T
                    H
        GET RIGHT
                    C
                    H
                    R
                    I
                    S
                    T

They passed a pink stucco building, dark, with boarded-up windows, called the Arizona Hotel, then they came to the Navajo Central.

It was made of wood. There was a western-style wooden porch and a sign: "LOBBY. FURNISHED ROOMS AND APARTMENTS." A row of old-fashioned school-desk chairs, joined together, lined the porch next to the entrance. There was a bare dirt yard on the side of the building with a dying palo-verde tree, several discarded tires, and a rotting 1955 Ford up on concrete blocks. A red light burned next to the entrance to the Navajo Central.

Inside was a stand-up bar, several tables, and a long bench running the length of the back wall. There was a pot-belly cast-iron stove in one corner. The coals of a dying fire glowed in the stove. Seated on the bench in semidark were four prostitutes: a Chinese girl, an Indian, and two Mexicans. They were barely visible in the heavy shadow of the room.

Two Indian cowhands stood at the bar. Three whites and an Indian were playing poker at one of the tables. A jukebox next to the bar wailed out a mournful mariachi song.

Porter and Kitty entered through the torn screen door and approached the bar. The bartender, a large Chinaman in his early fifties, looked over at them. He had a broad face and narrow black eyes. He spoke with a heavy Southwestern accent. He had a gold front tooth with an enamel star in it. "You folks want something to drink?"

"Two beers." The Chinaman set two bottles of Coors on the bar. The beer was warm. "Man at the diner said I might be able to get a blackjack game here," Porter said.

The Chinaman took his time in answering. He stared at Porter, then at Kitty. "I like blackjack," he said.

"My girl and I are on our way to Vegas."

"Yeah."

"We'd like a little tune-up."

"You come to the right place." He moved from behind the bar to the poker table and took up a fresh deck of cards. "Casino rules," he said.

The three of them sat at one of the empty tables. The prostitutes seated behind the table stared straight ahead. Porter broke the seal on the deck. The Chinaman switched on a green-shaded lamp above the table, and the prostitutes receded into gloom. "They call me Pete," the Chinaman said. "That ain't my name, but that's what they call me." He grinned. The star and gold of his tooth flashed. "I own this joint," he said.

41

"It's nice," Porter said.

"Not nice, but it serves a purpose. Which purpose is to put money in my pocket."

They began to play. It was immediately obvious that the Chinaman knew his way around a deck of cards. He handled the deal like a pro, shuffling close to his belly, riffling the cards corner in, so as to permit him a glimpse of each card if he wanted to take it. When he dealt, he held the cards in his left hand, tight in against the wrist, the back of his hand shielding the deck from the player. Porter knew the man had the tools of a mechanic; he could deal the deck anyway he chose. "You know what you're doing," he said.

"I been dealing them a long time," the Chinaman answered.

The game was straight. Porter had a good eye, going back to his stud poker days, and could spot a bum deal. The Chinaman was letting the cards fall as they came off the deck.

Porter started off easy, betting dollars, getting the feel of the game. The first couple of runs through the deck went along even. Kitty made a few minor errors—splitting nines against a ten, failing to double down with an ace-six against a three—but these were to be expected. She was nervous; Porter was sure she'd settle down.

The third round the percentage shifted heavily in favor of the player, but Porter only upped his bet a dollar. Three times in a row with two-dollar bets he won.

At the end of a half hour, Porter was ten dollars ahead, Kitty three. The Chinaman was enjoying himself. He called to one of the prostitutes to bring beer and potato chips for all of them.

The poker game broke up, and the Indian, who had been a big winner, joined the table.

He was drunk and began to bet recklessly. He sweated and breathed little bubbles of saliva at the corners of his mouth. He pounded the table and laughed very loud. He immediately started to lose, but it didn't bother him. "Pete," he yelled at the Chinaman, "I love you, Pete! I'm a Havasupai and you're a Chink and we're cousins, you know that?"

Pete grinned his gold tooth grin and agreed. "That's what they say . . ."

"Damn right. A Chink is just an Indian who was too chicken to make the trip here a million years ago!" He slapped the table with the flat of his hand. "A *million* years ago!"

Porter used the Indian as an excuse to up his bets. The Indian was pushing out twenty dollars a hand. The point count showed the deck hot for the player. Porter also laid a twenty on the table. "I'll go along with the red man," Porter said.

"Damn right!" yelled the Indian. "Got to go along with the red man! Got to do it!"

"I'll stick with the yellow man," Pete said, grinning.

"Never happen! You're chicken, Pete!" He leaned his head back and guzzled down a Coors, permitting the beer to spill out over his shirt front.

Kitty said: "I'll stick with little ol' myself." To Porter's dismay, she pushed forward her whole stack, fifteen dollars.

"That's your privilege," said the Havasupai, trying to focus on the table.

Porter tried to stop Kitty, but the Chinaman continued on with the deal. "Let the lady play her hand," he said laughing.

"Damn right," said the Indian, holding his cards up close to his perspiring face.

Porter pulled a sixteen, hit, and went over; the Indian also busted out. Kitty caught a king and queen, while Pete had to stay with eighteen.

Kitty stuck her tongue out at Porter. The Indian roared with laughter. "Son-of-a-gun!" the Indian said, pounding the table.

"She knows what she's doing," the Chinaman said.

"Better believe it, Pete!" said the Havasupai.

That was the way the game went. Whenever the edge

43

shifted to the player, Porter would bet heavily along with the Indian. Kitty would follow their example. The Indian and Porter would get clobbered, while Kitty would pull off the hand.

It galled Porter. She had disobeyed him. Most of the time she completely disregarded the System. And she was winning.

At the end of a couple of hours of play the Indian had busted out, Porter was broke, and Kitty had won a hundred and sixty dollars. The Chinaman laughed until tears came into his eyes. "That's a *good* broad to take to Las Vegas, buddy. Believe it!"

"*Better* believe it!" yelled the Indian, as he swayed in the center of the room. "Pete, you're a no-good Chink bastard and that's coming from a Havasupai, so don't you forget it!" The prostitutes leaning against the wall smiled for the first time that night. "I love you, Pete," said the Indian, lurching for the door. He hit the wall and fell back on the seat of his pants. He·sat on the floor, stunned, while the prostitutes roared with laughter.

Back in the car Porter was furious. "I gave you orders! How the hell do you expect to pull anything off if you don't follow orders!"

"Look, buster," Kitty said. "So far this trip you done nothing but lose your ass. I'm the one keeping this organization together!"

Porter pouted, while Kitty drove. After a time she realized he was truly hurt. "I'm sorry," she said. "You're the boss. It's just I never gambled before, and I guess I got carried away."

"Don't let it happen again. I mean the System's the System, and you don't mess with it."

"Yes, boss," she said. "But you got to admit I saved the day."

"The damn Chink·was dealing from the bottom of the deck."

44

"Oh, Donny, that's a big fat lie—"

He looked at her and grinned. "You done real good," he said.

"Did I really?"

He nodded and lit up a stogie and everything was fine.

III

It was well past midnight when they reached Flagstaff, Arizona. They decided to take a motel room and get a good night's rest before pushing on into Las Vegas. They had a bite to eat in an all-night Bob's Big Boy, then checked into a Holiday Inn. They were splurging with Kitty's winnings.

It was mountain country they were in now, and the air was fresh with the smell of pine. The altitude made them a bit giddy. Tall piñon trees towered above the rear of the motel, and they stood on the balcony in front of their room and stared up at the dark shadows of the trees. "You know," Kitty said, "I'm very happy I took up with you."

"I'm happy, too," Porter said.

"Before I met you, my life was pretty scurvy. You know, Donny, people can be like two things. They do one thing, and it's rotten, but they don't really feel like it's *them* that's done it. I mean they kind of stand to one side and say, 'Look what that stupid fool is doing!' Do you know what I mean?"

"I know."

"Really?"

"Sure."

" 'Cause I have a feeling I'm like a strange-o."

"It's like there's one person inside and another person—who you don't really know—walking around pretending he's that person inside."

Her face brightened. He *did* know what she meant! "Yes!" she said in amazement. "Oh, Donny, right! Yes!"

A slow, rustling rush of wind moved down from the tree-line. Kitty shivered. "Sometimes I feel real small, Donny, you know?"

"Yeah."

They entered the motel room. There was an enormous, triple-size bed, color television, thick shag rug. Kitty had never seen anything so luxurious. She bounced on the bed, then wrapped herself in the spread, and switched on the TV. A blizzard of multicolored electronic snow filled the screen. She turned off the TV and, trailing the spread behind her, proceeded to go through the drawers in the dresser.

While Porter was in the shower, Kitty studied a handful of pamphlets she found in the dresser. When he returned to the room, she had their next day planned. "We're going to visit the Grand Canyon, Donny. It's not far at all, and it's right on the way."

He unfolded his tattered Mobil road map and studied it. The idea did not excite him. "It's a hundred and fifty miles out of the way," he said.

"I want to see the Grand Canyon, please, Donny! I never seen anything in my life."

He stared at the map. He made a few measurements with his fingers.

"Please!"

"Okay," he said at last.

They kissed. Then they stretched out on the bed. They made love, and it was infinitely sweet for both of them. When they had finished, Kitty curled in close to him. Porter was strangely affected by her, and he couldn't tell why. It wasn't love, yet she *touched* him. She felt like his own heart beating against his chest. They both fell into a deep, dreamless sleep.

They didn't rise until nearly noon, then they set off for the Grand Canyon.

The drive through the San Francisco mountains was extraordinary. The sky was a white blue and it seemed to have no end. They felt as though they were traveling near the rim of the world. Broad mountain meadows, tall pampas grass stirring gracefully in the wind, stretched to the horizon. The piñon trees curved below them now in delicate ridges of deep, rich green.

Then the landscape grew more raw. The meadows gave way to red desert earth, scrub oak and Joshua, greasewood and paloverde. Porter took in deep breaths of the sweet, warm air. He grew dizzy with it. His mind relinquished, temporarily, its obsession with the System. They were speeding across the top of the world.

At the Grand Canyon, however, a change came over Porter. Among crowds of tourists moving toward the edge of the Canyon, he suddenly felt trapped, oppressed, yet terribly isolated; families and newlyweds, old folk and schoolteachers, children and foreigners—they all seemed in some way bonded to each other, all seemed part of a common, elemental experience. Only he seemed alone.

The Canyon was overpowering, limitless, but its enormity only served to increase his sense of isolation. Gigantic buttes, mesas, towers, pinnacles, sheer walls of brilliantly colored, striated rock—blood-red to the most delicate pink—seemed to encompass the horizon. The chasm below plunged more than a mile to where the Colorado River coiled insignificantly, a thin, silver ribbon. Kitty, gazing out over the Canyon, felt she could not breathe. "My God, Donny," she said softly.

He felt nothing. It seemed as though it were all cut out of cardboard, as though it were a tacky Hollywood set. He grew profoundly depressed.

48

He watched for a while, then turned and walked away. "Where are you going?" Kitty called after him.

"Into the coffee shop. I want to put in some time with the System."

He sat in the coffee shop and accused himself: He was old, he was empty, nothing moved him. He sat smoking stogie after stogie, drinking cups of black coffee, trying to discover within him some connection to other people, to the things they cared about. In order to ward off that paralyzing sense of his own aloneness, he began running blackjack hands in his mind. . . .

It was late afternoon when they returned to the road. Porter did not speak for a long while. Purple shadows pressed in on the car from dark, brooding mountains. "What's the matter, Donny?" Kitty asked.

"I don't know."

"Are you mad 'cause we took a little detour?"

"No."

"Then what is it?"

"It'll pass." But it did not pass. The System continued to drum through his brain.

He turned on the radio. A country preacher with a thick Southwestern accent was ranting on. Kitty attempted to change the station, but Porter pushed her hand away. "I want to hear what he got to say."

"It's your tongue, that you can't help but talking about your brothers and sisters," the preacher was shouting. "Bite it till it's so sore you can't talk! And every time you catch yourself talking about someone, bite your tongue until it bleeds!" The preacher's voice became soft, a whisper. "I got a letter in my hand here from a widow. She's living by herself, and she's sick and she wrote me a letter, *Glory* to God! She says here, 'God visited me while you been preaching here in Las Vegas! He made me happy like I never felt before in my life!' And in that letter I found a twenty-dollar bill, and I ask now for God to bless her. I got another letter here with a ten, *Glory* to God! Now you all out there know I never asked nobody for money in my life, but when God starts speaking, God starts blessing! And when God starts blessing, people start giving! *Glory to God!*" Now the preacher's voice was full volume again, exhorting, cajoling, conning. "Folks out there at the dice table and the roulette and the blackjack, God wants you to be a winner! Let God work a miracle in your life! Let me show you how to be successful, win and hold love, have money at all times, drive a nice car, own your own home, and live real good. Are you lonely? Do you want peace of mind? Let me pray the prayer of faith and luck for you! I am the Reverend P. Dickson, at the Sultan Motel, just below Bonanza on the Las Vegas Strip. Call me right now at 314–8485. That's 314–8485. God bless you, and good luck!"

Porter turned off the radio. "Goll-ee," Kitty said.

It was dark when they reached Vegas. The lights on the Strip appeared almost gentle from a distance, a long, colorful strand winking at them through the clear night air. Porter was not quite prepared for the assault on the senses the Strip provided close up. From the cool dark of the desert they were suddenly thrust into an angry blaze of thrashing, flashing, spinning neon, a wild, grotesque electrical eruption. He was blinded and dazed and suddenly felt as though the world were running out of control. Cars sped up and down the Strip, swerved in and out of the casinos, honking horns, screeching brakes, squealing tires, grotesque monsters lurching at them from all sides. Everything seemed to be exploding in light and metal.

He brought their car to a crawl. Kitty swiveled her head from side to side, calling out warnings: "Watch it on the right! Look out for that cab! Donny, be careful!"

He sweated and swore and prayed that they weren't creamed. Kitty was a little monkey, jumping up and down in her seat, clapping her hands, shrieking. "Donny! It's fantastic! My golly, it's bright as day!"

They drove by the Thunderbird, the Riviera, the Algiers; signs flashed: "LATIN FIRE!," "FOLIES BERGÈRE," "CAFE DE PARIS," "ALL ROOMS ONE PRICE," "WEDDING CHAPEL OPEN 24 HOURS," "DID YOU VISIT THE MILLION DOLLAR NUGGET?" They were swept along in a dizzying chromatrope of whirling color: the blue and white spinning carousel of Circus-Circus; the Silver Slipper's rotating ballet pump, glowing argent; a celestial shower at the Stardust of iridescent pinks and blues and whites; the Desert Inn, the Frontier, the Tropicana, the Sands, the Dunes, Castaways; oranges and greens and yellows and reds . . .

They came to the cool aqua of Caesar's Palace, and Porter steered the car into the drive. They rode past a great oblong pool with Romanesque statues of kneeling women spouting water from outstretched arms into the pool. This was the place they would visit first. This was Billy Ray Walker's place.

Porter had visions of finding him right off, of strolling into the casino, and there, center table, hundred-dollar chips stacked before him, would be Billy Ray Walker! Porter would recognize him immediately; he was certain of it. He had an image in his mind, cultivated over the years, of what he would look like: a gentleman of enormous elegance, with white hair and gold-rimmed spectacles. He would look like Jean Hersholt or Lionel Barrymore. Porter would sidle up to him, lean forward, and whisper in his ear: "I'm a friend of Monty's."

He parked the car in the lot, and they walked up the curved promenade to the hotel entrance. Suddenly, Porter began to lose courage. He could feel his heart surging in his chest; his hands were wet with perspiration. He hesitated partway up the walk.

"What's the matter?" Kitty asked.

"I don't know. Maybe we should get a hotel room somewhere and wash up and change to some better clothes."

"We don't have no better clothes."

"Let's wait until tomorrow—"

He had prepared himself nearly four years for this moment, and now that he was here, he felt desperately inept, somehow guilty and inferior. *They'll know I've been in prison,* he was thinking. *They'll know, they'll know. . . .*

Through the main doors to the hotel crowds of people bustled in and out. Some were stunningly attired, while others were quite shabby: men in Levi's and work shirts, women in slacks, unshaven, grizzled old-timers, hippies in tank shirts and tie-dye trousers. He felt his confidence return. "All right, c'mon," he said to Kitty. They entered the hotel.

Immediately they were assailed by a spectacular array, a whirligig of dizzying impressions: blood-red carpeting and the coruscating crystal of immense chandeliers, archways of pure white marble, huge pillars, dazzling promenades; the great domed ceiling of the casino, flashing, multifaced mirrors and parabolic festoons dripping crystal; uniformed bellhops scurrying to and fro; cocktail waitresses with incredible silicone breasts hustling trays of drinks; stony-faced dealers, and scowling, tuxedo-clad pit bosses; men and women in a bizarre diversiform of costume—elegant evening attire, oriental kimonos, saris, blue jeans, bermuda shorts, cowboy hats; hookers and gangsters, farmers and millhands, businessmen and athletes, celebrities and bust-outs—a swirling throng of people laughing, gabbing, shrieking, shouting; the whirr of the slot machines, the tickety-tick-tick-tick of the roulette wheels, the slap and riffle of playing cards. Through it all an incessant litany from the loudspeaker: "Princess Fatima . . . Princess Fatima . . . telephone for Princess Fatima . . ." Music blaring from an open lounge area; piped-in music, an insistent undercurrent—Joe South singing "Games People Play": "Oh, the games people play now, every night and every day now, never meaning what they say now, never saying what they mean . . ."

The aisle between the gaming tables was jammed with people. Kitty and Porter fought their way to the blackjack tables.

"Are you going to play?" Kitty asked.

"Not now." His head was swimming from the noise and excitement, the sheer energy of the place. He would need time to come down, to gather his wits.

At the center blackjack table—the black-chip, hundred-dollar table—they watched a small, thin man in orange cashmere sweater, white ducks, and tennis shoes drop four thousand dollars in five hands without altering his expression. Billy Ray Walker? Porter studied his play and decided not.

They moved on to the baccarat table. Coiffured and bejeweled women and impeccably tailored men shared the same game with a man in soiled khaki trousers, sweat-stained work shirt, and steel-toed boots. A Korean man at the end of the table sat with a look of heavy-lidded indifference, while controlling two great stacks of hundred-dollar bills, tossing them into the game as though they were play money. Someone at the railing whispered he was down fifty thousand; another voice added he had blown an additional thirty the night before. People moved in and out of the playing area, forwarding advice, offering consolation, assisting play. Figures were scribbled, notes were exchanged, hushed conferences were held. The whole table possessed an aura of mystery, of cabalism, of arcane divination.

Porter was exhausted. The reality of their arrival, the fact that they were *here* with the System, here in the domain of Billy Ray Walker, here ready to play and *win*, sucked at his nerves, drained him. His eyes burned and his hands trembled.

They made their way to the coffee shop, sat at the counter, and ordered sandwiches and coffee.

"My God, have you ever seen anything like it, Donny?"

He hadn't, but he wouldn't admit it. His gambling had been done in back rooms of saloons, dingy hotels, small-town pool halls. Monty had tried to prepare him for Vegas, but Porter hadn't grasped the size of the place, the splendor, the terrifying, electric energy. He shrugged and chewed on his sandwich and said, "It's just like Monty spoke. This town's ripe to be taken."

They finished their snack and walked back through the casino. It was well past midnight now, and an incredible transformation had occurred. The place was half empty. Blackjack dealers stood around at deserted tables, arms folded across their chests, faces bored and vacant. The Korean was gone from the baccarat table, as was the man in work clothes; an aging platinum-blond shill joked with the croupier. Muted, perfunctory craps continued. The roulette wheels were silent.

Monty had been right about that, too. "Wait for the late night," he would say. "Let the tourists and junketeers, showgoers and dollar players clear out. That's the hour of the System." That would be the hour of Billy Ray Walker.

They strolled around the blackjack area, moving from table to table. Nothing more interesting than a five-dollar-a-card game. No high rollers tonight. No Billy Ray Walker tonight. "Why don't you try?" Kitty whispered.

"Tomorrow," he said.

He was nervous. His hands trembled and perspired. He sat on the edge of the bed manicuring his nails.

The room was cool, but the air conditioner rattled so loudly he felt as though it would take his head off. The walls had red flowers on them, a patterned paper that was gouged and smudged with black. He thought of all the greasy heads that had leaned against those walls, of the hands that had pressed against them. The room seemed to hold evidence of every bust-out gambler that had ever occupied it.

The sagging mattress, the stained coverlet, the threadbare carpet with a giant rip down the center exposing yellow shreds of floor board. The odor of sweet perfume and disinfectant. The cigarette burns on the night table and bureau. The mirror fogged by peeling silver.

It was only temporary, this rickety hole in downtown

Vegas. One day soon they would make it up to the Strip for good. He had only to put the System into effect.

That was the problem. They had been in Vegas three days, and he hadn't yet been able to force himself to play. Somehow, now that he was here, now that they had arrived at the magical point of his imaginings, he had lost heart. The town intimidated him.

The hotel they had registered in was at First Street and Ogden, just off the Casino Center section of downtown. It was a hotel of penny slot players, broken-down old-timers, rummies, five-dollar-a-shot whores. They would do better; Porter promised Kitty that. But right now they had to conserve their resources until the time he began to play. And three days had gone by. . . .

"Goll-ee, Donny, you just got to get up off your ass and get out there. We been walking around casinos studying dealers till it's coming out of my ears. I swear if you don't go out and play, I'm going to take that old System and show you how to use it. Just like I did with that Chinaman. . . ." She was sitting on the bed sipping an orange soda while she leafed through a movie magazine.

Porter did not speak. He dug at the cuticle of his fingernail with the end of his file.

What the hell was he so nervous about? He had stood above the blackjack tables, mentally running the System down as the hands were played, and he was sure it was a winner. Everything was just as Monty had said it would be. From casino to casino rules varied a bit, but Monty had prepared him for it all: steer clear of four-deck games—the percentages are tougher, the mathematics more complex; you lose an edge at the downtown casinos where they permit the dealer to hit on a soft seventeen; the Frontier will let you double-down after splitting, Caesar's Palace will permit you to turn in half your bet on a bum hand, and so on. There was no reason in the world for him to be nervous, and yet he was. . . .

Tonight, though, he was determined to make his move. He had spent all afternoon practicing. Then he had showered, shaved; now he was cleaning his nails. He was almost ready.

They would have dinner up on the Strip at the Silver Slipper and then return downtown. He had chosen the Golden Nugget as the first place to hit. He was less intimidated by the Nugget, where they were used to dollar players, scroungers, petty hustlers, old gaffers who would hang around the blackjack table all night in the hope of picking up the price of the next day's meals.

There was an easy give-and-take between dealer and player at the Nugget, with little of the veiled hostility, the arrogance and disdain sensed in the Strip casinos. He would start out here with the System until he felt more secure.

Porter finished his nails. He held them up under the lamp. They gleamed with a dull sheen. His fingers trembled lightly.

Now he stood before the bureau mirror and smoothed his hair down. He took up a stogie and lit it. He and Kitty left the hotel room.

They traveled up to the Silver Slipper on the Strip. In the short time they had been in Vegas, he and Kitty had learned to live on very little. They ate one meal a day, a buffet at the Slipper for $2.19. The food was good, and they were permitted as much of it as they could eat. Kitty had never eaten so much in her life.

She piled her plate high with food—ribs, chicken, spaghetti, salad, four different kinds of pickles, mashed potatoes and gravy, and roast beef. "Donny, this is *fantastic!*"

"You can get seconds, you know."

"I know, Donny, but walking through that line everything looks so *good* I don't know what to take. So I take it all!"

Porter was eating one thin slice of roast beef and a spoonful of cottage cheese. "Is that all you're going to have?"

"I don't want a heavy meal on my stomach. I want to keep my head clear."

"Are you getting crazier or am I?"

"No one twisted your arm to come along on this trip."

The last few days he had begun to regret bringing her with him. She took the edge off his sense of commitment to the System; she seemed somehow to be mocking it.

That had always been his problem, securing respect. As long as people weren't permitted to get too close to you, as long as you could hide your weaknesses, you could command respect. But when they got inside you, when they knew your fears and doubts, they'd begin to tear you down. That's why for so many years he had preferred to travel alone. And now he had Kitty on his back.

With his wife it had been the same way. When she first met him, he had been hustling card games in West Virginia and Ohio. He would go from town to town and take on the local boys in stud poker. He was good at it and he managed a living. He always had a new car and fine clothes. He could afford an occasional meal in an expensive restaurant in Wheeling or Steubenville.

On a certain level he had established a reputation: lone-wolf card shark. He carried a vague aura of mystery with him into towns like Weirton and Massillon, Marietta, Athens, and Gallipolis.

It was this quality of cool, lonely impenetrability, of precise accomplishment that had attracted his wife to him.

They married, and she got inside him; and then the picking apart began. What was he doing hustling poker for twenty dollars a night? Why was he small time? If he was a gambler, why didn't he take on the big games?

He tried. For her, he tried. And failed. The big boys had it all over him in cunning and nerve. What they didn't win off you, they'd cheat you for. And that element of luck. That lack of a *system*. From the time his wife began to get on his back, his luck failed him. He became a loser.

He feared that word like he feared the plague. No one was

born a loser. He had been a winner once. With the System he would be a winner again.

"You want a cupcake with your coffee?" Kitty realized that in some way she had offended him and was trying to make it up. He shook his head.

"You didn't hardly even eat your roast beef."

"I don't want any more." He rubbed his hands together, looked down at his nails.

"I'm sorry what I said before."

"Okay," he said.

It was nearly one A.M., but the Nugget was still crowded. The old vultures were out, hovering around the blackjack area, darting from table to table, avaricious birds of prey: wrinkled old women and pasty-faced men; oriental hookers with black, dead eyes; tattooed rummies; gaunt tinhorns; Reno-style sharks, their greasy, black hair slicked flat back, pencil-thin mustaches, sideburns down to their chins; powdered and rouged dames in their sixties with sad, watery eyes, flaccid lips slashed red forming soundless imprecations—the detritus of the gambling world, floating the night, scheming, wheedling, praying . . .

In the palms of their hands they carried the currency of their dreams—fifty-cent pieces and lone gold dollar chips. If they won tonight—how much? ten dollars?—they'd leave the Nugget reborn. Tomorrow night they'd be dead once more.

"Wait at the bar," Porter said. "I don't want to arouse suspicion."

"I want to play."

"Not tonight."

In an area beyond the blackjack tables a Country and Western trio performed. Kitty sat at the bar and watched them. They sang "Apartment Number Nine": "Loneliness surrounds me . . ."

Porter had decided his initial stake would be fifty dollars. It was cutting things close. If he lost, they would have about ten dollars to last them. But he liked the roundness of the number. He would start with dollar bets, graduate to fives. He would attempt to work in multiples of five. Half a hundred, then half a thousand, then half a million . . .

He couldn't find an empty table, so he was forced to squeeze in between a fat Mexican woman and a scrawny wino. The dealer was a tall, lean westerner with milky blue eyes.

Porter started slowly, counting to himself in precise, even cadence: "Plus one, plus two, two tens, ace, plus one, minus two, minus three . . ." His nervousness was gone. His mind operated with a beautiful clarity. He was on top of the game, and the calculations came easily. He began to win.

The Mexican woman was winning also. She carefully stacked her fifty-cent pieces, rarely varying her bets, looking heavily ahead of her, seeming never even to glance at her cards. Her left eye had a gray cast to it, and it fixed the dealer with a look of unwavering malice, as though he were the devil incarnate.

The dealer remained unconcerned, snapping the cards out in a clipped, rhythmic cadence, dealing to each player an indifferent destiny, here a twenty-one, there a bust-out, giving and taking away with the same easy, relaxed lack of involvement.

The wino, who was losing, grew angry. "Don't do that to me again!" he warned, after the dealer topped his twenty with a twenty-one. The dealer, cool, detached, showing no sign he had heard him, promptly blackjacked on the next hand.

Porter's stack began to grow. He increased his bets and at the end of an hour had a hundred dollars in five-dollar chips lined up before him.

Kitty came over and stood behind him. "I'm sick of sitting at the bar," she said. "Nothing there but a bunch of hillbillies."

"Go back to the hotel."

"I'm going to take a walk."

Porter, intent on the play, made no sign that he had heard her; when he looked back over his shoulder several hands later, she was gone.

The System was working now for Porter as though the reality was penned on one of its charts. When the count was low and the advantage to the house, he cut back his bets; when the advantage was for him, he doubled and tripled the basic bets. The cards fell for him with seeming mathematical regularity. The System's promise of infallibility bloomed, an oasis, a mirage. . . .

He bet fifty dollars. The System said a ten and an ace should fall. They did. He caught a nine and a two and doubled the fifty, anticipating a ten. It fell.

Except for the Mexican woman, the other people at the table had long since blown their stake. The wino, after increasing threats to the dealer, had shouted one final curse, then slammed his cards down, and staggered off.

It was nearly five o'clock in the morning, and Porter had more than seven hundred dollars piled in front of him.

The Mexican woman was still playing her fifty-cent pieces. Occasionally she would cash them in for dollar chips, and these she would slip into a wrinkled leather purse, which she held on her lap. She seemed unimpressed by the great pile of five- and twenty-five-dollar chips in front of Porter.

A small crowd had gathered behind the table. They stood there with the dull look of deep-night losers, gazing with no special interest down at the table, remaining only because, having lost their stake, there was nothing else to do. They gazed on with a special, empty knowing. They had seen it all before.

New decks were pressed into action. Shifts changed. Dealers came and went. From time to time the only person in the casino who seemed even remotely interested in Porter's winning, the pit boss, would stand by the dealer's side and observe a hand or two. Once or twice Porter caught him staring at him from across the pit.

When Kitty returned, he had won nearly a thousand dollars. Her eyes went wide at the irregular piles of chips spilling over the table-top in front of him. "My God, Donny . . ."

And then he began to lose. The System broke down, and some bizarre anti-System seemed to take over.

Whichever way he bet, the cards fell wrong. The System told him to hit on a sixteen; he busted out. He stuck with twelve and the dealer grabbed seventeen. When he upped his bets, the cards were disastrous; cutting back—a rarity—he'd pull a blackjack.

His stack fell from a thousand to five hundred to three hundred. Built with such steady assurance, it collapsed headlong, like a routed army.

It was daylight now. His neck and shoulders ached terribly. His eyes burned with fatigue. "Donny, please!" Kitty implored. "Leave it! You still have a couple of hundred dollars."

But the System taunted, tricked, seduced. It would click for half a dozen hands, igniting hope, driving Porter on. His stack jumped up to four hundred dollars. Once again the laws of the universe were functioning. Then, in seven successive bust-out hands, the ugly underbelly of defeat would show itself, and he was down to one-fifty; then up to three hundred, followed by a sharp plummet to less than a hundred. Each gain was obliterated by precipitous loss.

He should have long since cut back his bets—even the System told him this—but defeat fed and grew on itself; the greater the loss, the more obsessive the drive to win.

He went up to a hundred and fifty again. The System said bet high: the edge favored the player. He slid out half his stack, seventy-five dollars, and pulled two nines against the dealer's six. It was the bottom of the deck; there were five cards remaining. Porter fought to remember them: four picture cards and—the last card escaped his memory. The last card. It was a low card. Which one? A plastic phantom, it slipped on by. . . .

So, though the System promised certainty, he was forced to

operate on probabilities. He anted up the last of his chips and split the nines. He drew a king and queen for double nineteen.

Now the play was to the dealer. He flicked his second card up. It was a four. Twenty. Porter was finished.

As he rose from the table, the Mexican woman spoke for the first time. "Never split nines against a six," she said. Her disfigured eye stared with blind contempt at him. He felt a wave of nausea sweep over him.

He and Kitty entered the sickly white of day. He walked to the curb and attempted to throw up. He heaved and gagged without success. His stomach was empty.

IV

They kept the window shades pulled down in the lobby of the Center Hotel. There were parking lots on either side of the hotel, and the old timers resented the tourists gawking at them on the way to their cars. The casino people in the area, at the Mint, the Fremont, the Four Queens, and the Golden Nugget, referred to the place as Hardluck Hotel.

Eddie MacRae, sitting in the lobby of the Center Hotel, considered himself anything but unlucky. He had had four professional fights in and around Fresno and Bakersfield and had won them all—three by knockouts. Tomorrow night he'd be fighting a six-round preliminary upstairs at the Silver Slipper.

He was a large man, six foot three, and had great, powerful shoulders and an enormous neck. Despite his bulk he looked intelligent. His appearance was deceptive: he was not.

This had been the curse of his life. People had expected more from him than he could deliver. They were always surprised at his simplicity. When they got to know him well, the surprise turned to ridicule.

He worked as a day laborer out of Fresno, digging irrigation canals, roadbeds, foundations. His dream since he had been a small child was to become heavyweight boxing champion of the world.

He sat now in the lobby of the Center Hotel, squeezing a rubber hand exerciser and chewing a wad of gum.

From time to time his head jerked spasmodically. He would feel a tightening in his neck, and his head would snap around. He couldn't stop it. He couldn't understand why it did that.

It had started after an amateur bout several years before. He was fighting a black golden-gloves champ. He had lost a roundhouse punch in the lights and had been beaten to a bloody pulp. The fight should have been stopped, but the referee, a former lightweight pro, took a perverse delight in seeing the large, intelligent-looking fighter take a beating. In the locker room following the fight he had developed the twitch. It embarrassed him, but he was unable to control it.

When he turned pro, the doctors checked him out. They could find no brain damage, although those things are often difficult to pinpoint. The general opinion was it was a psychological reaction to defeat. They advised him to win, and the twitch would go away.

Since that time he had trained with unswerving dedication. He had not been beaten again. The twitch, however, persisted.

He had never been to Las Vegas before. The promoters of the fights had sent him money for a bus ticket. He came up a day early to get a look at the town.

He had arrived that morning, took a room at the Center Hotel, then wandered the casinos. He lost four dollars in the slot machines and got disgusted. Now he sat in the lobby, exercising his grip and chewing gum.

He was staring at the rear wall. A deep brown water stain started in one corner of the lobby and spread down over the flowered wallpaper until it formed a great ugly blob across the wall. He was thinking of the fight tomorrow night. Who would he be facing? Would his opponent experience a fear as deep and unsettling as the one he was sure to feel before the fight? Could he *win*?

To Eddie MacRae winning was everything. This town disturbed him: there were too many losers. He would never commit his existence to chance, to cards, machines, dice. He wanted only to go up against flesh and blood. Flesh and blood you can master—if you are better trained, if you are more determined. Flesh and blood can be obliterated. Chance? Never.

Seated in the chair, he began to work his hands in a miniature approximation of his strategy: jab with the left, jab with the left, now hook with the right, again with the left, now hook with the right, again with the right, now upper-cut left, upper-cut right.

His hands jerked in short, sharp chops just above his lap. His head snapped in time with his hands.

He stopped suddenly. The deskman was looking over at him, suppressing a smile. A young girl in faded pedal pushers and sleeveless cotton blouse was moving across the lobby past him. . . .

Kitty had come down from the room. Porter and she had had an argument.

"You should have never come over to the table like that! You broke my luck!"

"But you said the System has nothing to do with luck!"

"You can hit a streak with the System just like anything else—"

"Donny, that's just plain stupid. Either the System's mathematical or it's not—"

"Don't you try to teach me about the System!"

She hated to have a man holler at her. She hated it more than anything in the world. She would prefer to have someone hit her than yell at her.

Down in the lobby she suddenly realized she had no place to go. For half the night, while Porter played, she had walked the streets and casinos in the Center. She was sick of gambling casinos and Las Vegas and Porter. She was tempted to just take the car and abandon him here, just run out on him and his damn System.

But she couldn't leave him. She needed him too much. For the first time in her life, she had become attached to a man: it had nothing to do with sex or even love. It was some sort of *need*, the way a person needs water or food, the way Porter needed his System. She had to stay with him.

She was standing by the window in the lobby, peeking out the edge of the blind. "Damn," she said. "Hey," she called over to the deskman, a short, fat black man, "why do you got these blinds down?"

"Policy of the hotel."

"Any reason for it?"

"Yeah, there's a reason for it. Reason for everything. You, me, and the bedpost might not never know that reason, but it's there. Come over here," the deskman said. She walked over to him. "Are you a working girl?" the deskman asked.

"What's that supposed to mean?"

"A fine girl like you could earn twenty-five, thirty dollars a night."

"If I wanted to sell it, I could earn more than that."

"This here is a tough town," the deskman said. He held up his right hand. His four fingers were missing. "You see that?"

"Yeah."

"They chopped 'em off." He spread the stubs out for Kitty. "Laid 'em out on a hunk of wood, took a cleaver, and chopped 'em off."

"Who?"

"You don't know nothing, do you?"

"I know some things."

"I was a blackjack dealer, doll, and the house caught me dealing the wrong cards to the wrong people, so they just chopped 'em off. That's what I'm saying about this town. It's a tough town."

66

"Where were you a dealer?"

"They call it the Paradise Hotel." The deskman laughed softly and rubbed the stubs of his fingers against his belly. "Yes, sir, a tough town. Thirty dollars a night, doll, is nice money. Yes, sir."

"I'm not interested."

She sat down in a chair next to Eddie MacRae. "Whatcha squeezing that thing for?" she asked.

He was not a man who was comfortable with women. He had a hard time looking them in the eye. The twitch of his head increased now. "It's part of my training," he said.

"Oh."

The deskman called over: "That's Eddie MacRae. He'll be fighting at the Silver Slipper tomorrow evening."

"No kidding! A boxer!"

MacRae attempted to nod, but the jerk of his head made the move ridiculous. "Why do you do it?" Kitty asked without malice. "Do you enjoy hurting people?"

Eddie MacRae squirmed in his chair. "I don't know why I do it," he said. "There's just nothing else I can do."

"Do you do it good?"

"As good as I can."

The Negro deskman laughed. "We all rise to our own level," he said. "Onliest thing I know in this life. We all rise to our own level."

Kitty and Eddie MacRae, having nothing further to say to each other, lapsed into an uncomfortable silence. The deskman dug at a rotting front tooth with a soiled toothpick. Somewhere in the recesses of the hotel a radio was playing a Spanish melody, Cuco Sanchez singing "Maria Elena."

After awhile there was a grinding noise as the elevator descended. The door opened. Porter, wearing a pair of chino trousers and a tee shirt, came into the lobby. He needed a shave. He looked to Kitty pale and suddenly old. There were dark smudges of fatigue under his eyes.

He walked to the door of the hotel and stood there staring

out into the street. He held two coins in his hand and was slowly bouncing them together in a soft, jiggling sound.

"I thought you were going to get some sleep," Kitty said.

"I couldn't sleep."

"Want to get a bite to eat?"

"I want to go back to the tables and get us some money."

"Oh, no you don't! Oh no, Donny—that's eating money!"

"I'm not hungry!"

"Well, I *am!*"

Porter turned from the door and approached Kitty. He continued to jiggle the coins in his hands. His eyes seemed dead.

"This here is Eddie MacRae, Donny. He's a boxer."

Eddie MacRae rose at the introduction and shifted his weight uncomfortably from foot to foot. "Yeah?" Porter said, nodding absently. "C'mon, we'll get something to eat."

"You want to come?" Kitty said to Eddie MacRae.

"Thank you. Thank you very much. I sure could use some company. I been sitting in this lobby so long I'm going ding-bat."

They found a coffee and doughnut shop in a penny slot arcade on Fremont. At first Kitty did most of the talking, but gradually Eddie MacRae and Porter warmed to each other.

Eddie was going on about his boxing. He's simple-minded, Porter thought. He has great dreams and he's afraid. The sincerity in his face, the pain in his eyes moved Porter. He'll be stewed, screwed, and tattooed in this life, he thought.

Porter saw an element of himself when he was that young. The world was tough. Oh, yes, it was tough. How do you get by in it?

"But why boxing?" Porter asked him.

"Because I'm good at it. Because I've never been good at nothing else."

"How do you know you're good at it?"

68

Eddie MacRae looked at him, suddenly confused. "I just know I am," he said weakly.

Porter, when young, had wanted to be a baseball player. He couldn't hit a high curve. He settled for cards.

Eddie MacRae was describing his training: "I usually get up at five o'clock in the morning, and I run six or seven miles, then I have me a *big* breakfast, a half dozen eggs, dozen slices of bacon, four pieces of toast, quart of milk—"

Kitty began to giggle. "Geemaneezers!" she said.

"Then it's off to work. Soon's I'm done work, it's down to the gym and put in a couple, three hours. Then home to a big steak and get me some sleep." He smiled. His head jerked sideways several times.

"Half dozen eggs, dozen slices bacon! Did you hear that, Donny?"

Porter shrugged. "Well, he's doing very strenuous physical work," he said authoritatively.

"That's the truth, there," said Eddie MacRae.

"Where do you live, Eddie?" Kitty asked.

"I rent me one of them mobile homes out in Sanger, not far from Fresno. Armenian guy rents it to me, real nice guy."

"That's nice," Kitty said. "Those mobile homes are nice."

"Some of them in your luxury class are real nice," Eddie MacRae said. Porter yawned. "I got me a mom and dad and five brothers down there in Fresno." Eddie MacRae paused and stared beyond Porter and Kitty. In the arcade frumpy tourist ladies were pouring pennies into the slots. "They ain't too proud of me."

"Why not?" Kitty had never met a professional boxer before. She regarded him as some sort of extraordinary creature to be questioned and explored. In a half hour she learned more about Eddie MacRae than she had gained in the months she had known Porter.

She studied the two men. Their essential dissimilarity was obvious even in their physical attitudes. The boxer sat straight up, grinning with vague embarrassment, his expression open,

69

almost childlike, while Porter, his look veiled, controlled, slouched at the counter, the stub of a stogie in his mouth, his pale eyes slowly combing the room, his gaze clouded as though shrouded behind a fine, translucent curtain.

The boxer had taken a long time answering Kitty. His head and jaw worked in painful spasms. His eyes seemed almost pleading. "They think I'm some sort of fool," he said at last, quietly, confused.

"But you're doing so well!"

Eddie MacRae began to stammer. "But—but—there's no money in the level I'm at. It costs me more for training than I've even made. And the truth is the guys I beat were some kind of bums! The last fight they dragged him off a garbage truck and put him in the ring with me. Poor guy hadn't ever a pair of boxing gloves on before!"

The boxer lapsed into silence. Kitty drank her coffee. Porter stared at his stogie end. A bell rang in the arcade behind them. Someone had hit the penny slots.

They spent the rest of the day together, the three of them. Kitty had let slip the fact that Porter was a *professional* gambler—she said it with pride, as though it were on the level with a doctor or a lawyer—and Eddie MacRae insisted they take five of his dollars and show him how a real gambler worked. "Then tomorrow you'll come to my fight and see how I operate!"

Porter worked the System easily, without strain, winning a few dollars at one casino, then moving on to the next, winning a few more, until they had visited every casino in the downtown area. By evening they had won eighty dollars.

"Wow! That's some luck!" Eddie proclaimed, deeply impressed.

"It's not luck," said Kitty. "It's skill."

"It's *something*," Eddie said. Over the boxer's protestations, they split the eighty dollars. They parted in the lobby of the hotel, after making arrangements to go to the Silver Slipper together the next night. "Hell, I ain't got no trainer or manager or no one seeing me. I should be able to get you in," Eddie MacRae said, then moved off into the ancient, scarred hotel elevator. He stood for a short moment before the door glided shut, looking pathetically huge and awkward and lost, smiling uncomfortably, his head bobbing slowly up and down.

Kitty and Porter sat for a while in the lobby. They did not speak for a long time. "Whatcha thinking?" Kitty said at last.

"I want to go back to the casinos."

"Please, Donny, I'm tired. Stay with me."

"I like that guy, Eddie," Porter said.

"I like him, too."

They returned to their room and lay on the bed. Kitty curled in close to him. "What I'm thinking," Porter said, "is maybe we can bring him into the System. The more workers we got, the more winners we got."

"That sounds good. He's a winner for sure, Donny. He got confidence in himself."

"We'll see."

Porter lay there staring up at the ceiling. He did not speak for a long while. "Do you want to make love to me?" Kitty asked. He shook his head no. "Why not?"

"I got cards on my mind," he said.

In a way she was glad. She was not really feeling sexy. She enjoyed lying there next to him, feeling the warmth of his body, knowing that he cared for her. She felt the rhythmic rise and fall of his breathing, the surge of his heart in his chest. She felt unimaginably safe in his arms.

"How do you like that Mex woman telling me I shouldn't have split those nines!" Porter said. "Damn Mex!" Kitty did not hear him. She was asleep.

Porter shifted on the bed. He tried to conjure up the image of the marble and gold castle at the edge of the sea. It would not come. Instead, he saw the casino room at Caesar's Palace, the mirrored dome, the coruscating crystal of the chandelier sprinkling brilliant facets of light over everything. He

71

is seated at the center table, going head-to-head with the dealer; the green felt of the table in front of him is covered with hundred-dollar chips. The cards are falling, falling, falling. . . . Their slap boomed in his ears. . . . The System . . . The System . . . The System is invincible. . . . Every hand a blackjack!

Eddie MacRae sat on a straight-backed chair in the service pantry off the upstairs ballroom of the Silver Slipper. He was in his blue boxer's trunks with the gold trim and his blue robe with the gold lettering on the back: "EDDIE FRESNO KID MACRAE." He was afraid. It was always like this for him before a fight—he was caught in a desperate, terrible fear that never left until the fight was over. His eyes were wide and tense, his face pale, his head quaking in embarrassing, compulsive spasms.

The pantry, used for the fights as a locker room, was filled with boxers sitting around gabbing and laughing, and it shamed Eddie that his fear should be so apparent.

His opponent, a tall, rangy black, named Freddie Hotch, was a picture of unconcern. He sat opposite Eddie MacRae restringing the laces in his boxing shoes and joking with another black fighter, a main-bouter called Bo Brown. Bo Brown's opponent, Joe Fletcher, known as the Black Avenger, stood in street clothes nearby.

Freddie Hotch flicked a shoelace at Bo Brown's belly and laughed. "Man, that gut you got there, that cat going to bust you wide open."

"Tell 'im, Freddie, tell 'im," Joe Fletcher said with a soft laugh.

Bo Brown shook his head. "Shit, don't talk that talk, baby, or I'm going to have to *revenge* the Black Avenger!"

"Shit," said Joe Fletcher, "don't even worry about your gut 'cause I'm out to do some *head*-hunting tonight!" They all laughed.

There would be three fights that evening: Freddie Hotch

72

and Eddie in a six-round preliminary, then two ten-round bouts.

The Black Avenger was rated number nine in the heavyweight division in the world. He had built up a string of fourteen straight knockouts. His fight with Bo Brown, a thirty-seven-year-old tank-job expert, was just a way of continuing to build his record.

The other ten-rounder was between two Mexican middleweights, one from Los Angeles, the other from Tijuana. The Mexicans, with flat, impassive faces and long, black hair looked enough alike to have been brothers. They stood by the door to the pantry speaking softly in Spanish.

Bo Brown's trainer, a lean, gray-haired black, would work Eddie MacRae's corner. He was occupied now taping his hands. "Don't hurt Freddie too bad," he said, cutting strips of tape from a thick roll and pressing them over Eddie's knuckles. "He ain't but had one professional fight."

Freddie Hotch was in his midthirties. It seemed strange to Eddie that he'd be just starting his prize-fighting career. "He works as a bartender in a club down in East L.A.," explained the trainer. "He's just trying to pick up a few extra bucks."

Eddie MacRae did not speak. His mouth was so thick and dry, he was certain the words would never come out. He just sat there and attempted to nod his head.

A short, dapper man poked his head in the door. "Ready for the prelim," he said, and Eddie MacRae and Freddie Hotch rose to follow him into the ballroom.

"Don't crap your pants, you hear?" Bo Brown called out to Freddie Hotch. Freddie Hotch just laughed and waved his gloved hand at the other fighter.

He put his arm around Eddie as they neared the door. "How you doing?" he said. His manner was genuinely warm and friendly, but it didn't make Eddie MacRae feel less afraid.

They entered the ballroom to desultory applause and a few hoots of derision.

The ring occupied one end of the ballroom directly in front of a bandstand area. The bandstand was set up with folding chairs, and it was here that the newsmen and local celebrities sat.

The rest of the ballroom, on a lower level than the bandstand, was the general admissions area. It was filled with people, also seated on folding chairs. A long bar ran the length of the rear wall, and a number of people stood drinking at the bar. Several casino cocktail waitresses made their way through the crowd serving drinks. A popcorn machine was in operation to one side of the pantry entrance, and the rattling sound of the corn exploding did nothing to help relax Eddie MacRae.

Making his way to the ring, Eddie searched the crowd for Porter and Kitty but could not see them. He wondered if they were even there. He had attempted to get them in free, but the man at the door was unimpressed by the fact that he was one of the fighters. "They got to pay like everyone else," he said. Eddie became embarrassed and began to stammer something, but Porter said it was all right, they would pay, and Eddie left them there. Now he could not see them.

It meant a great deal to him that they be there. He sensed deep within how terrible a thing it is to fight when you're alone.

The announcer, wearing cream-colored slacks and white shoes, moved to the center of the ring. "A preliminary bout of six rounds, in this corner weighing one hundred and ninety-two pounds, from East Los Angeles, California, Freddie Hotch!" A muffled cheer went up, and Freddie Hotch danced around in his corner and waved and smiled at the crowd.

The crowd, clean-cut, tanned, prosperous, was made up of local casino people, a smattering of tourists, and a number of old-time Vegas fight fans; for a fight crowd it was

74

unusually respectable-looking. The cheer for Freddie Hotch had gone up, not because anyone knew him, but because they were just friendly folk. He was the smaller of the two men, and he had a nice, relaxed smile.

"In this corner, weighing two hundred and twenty-four pounds, from Fresno, California, the Fresno Kid, Ernie Mac-Rae!" Someone called into the ring and corrected him. "I'm sorry," the announcer said, smiling, "*Eddie* MacRae." The crowd laughed as MacRae danced and twitched in his corner.

The referee called them to the center of the ring and offered them perfunctory instructions: "I explained the rules of the Nevada State Boxing Commission to you earlier, so I won't repeat them—" Eddie was puzzled: no one had explained any rules to him. "Just remember no rabbit punching, *et cetera*, break clean when I call break and come out fighting at the bell. Good luck."

As he shuffled to his corner, Eddie MacRae spotted Kitty and Porter seated against a side wall. Kitty was waving both arms at him. He attempted a smile, but his twitch got in the way.

The light above him shone brilliantly, blindingly, a white-hot corona, an even brighter center. He jerked his head to avoid its painful brilliance. There was no way to escape it. He was, after all, in the ring.

"He sure got a powerful build," Kitty said to Porter. "I just know he's going to murder that poor skinny malink."

"He looks scared to me," Porter said.

"What's the matter with that white guy?" a beefy man next to them called over to a friend. "He got a disease or something?"

"He doesn't got no disease," Kitty yelled out.

"He got palsy or something," the man said.

"He's a punchy," the friend called back.

"He is not!" Kitty shouted.

"Hey, Fresno," the man yelled through cupped hands. "I hope you can fight as good as you twitch!"

The crowd around all laughed. Kitty said to Porter: "That's mean, making fun of someone's condition like that."

"He ought to do something about that," Porter said. "It don't look good in front of a crowd."

Porter studied the people filling the hall. The more prosperous ones were, of course, at ringside. Each row back, the dress became less and less formal. At the rear bar area men stood in work shirts, Stetson's and Levi's.

Three people were moving into their seats at ringside, two men and a woman. The woman turned and her eyes met Porter's. She seemed surprised, as though she recognized him. She stared at him for a short moment, then looked to the ring.

The woman, strikingly lovely, had deep black hair and a pale, bony face. She wore a silver lamé gown and appeared to be about thirty, but might have been older. The expression in her eyes—quizzical, vaguely fearful—somehow got to Porter. It disturbed him. It was a look he often imagined he had in his own gaze: puzzled, desperate. He continued to stare at the back of her head, but she did not turn around.

The bell rang for the first round, and Eddie MacRae charged out of his corner. The woman at ringside was whispering to one of the men next to her. She looked back, then quickly away.

Eddie came quickly across the ring, his face tense with fear, his eyes blazing wild determination. Without a break in rhythm he began punching, hard, snapping blows that landed with shuddering accuracy. The crowd grew suddenly very quiet. The only sound was the scuffle and squeak of the boxers' shoes across the canvas, and the loud crack of Eddie MacRae's gloves exploding about the head of the amiable black man.

Freddie Hotch put his gloves up over his head and awkwardly attempted to shield himself. Eddie MacRae was all over him, chopping vicious punches to his head, arms, and shoulders, belting him in a small circle around the center of the ring. Crack! Crack! Crack! The bang of the blows echoed through the silent, awed ballroom like shots ripped from a rifle.

Eddie MacRae moved with surprising grace, even elegance, easily maneuvering the black man around the ring, snapping the punches in with speed and precision as though he were exercising on the heavy bag at the gym.

Now he shifted his attack to the body, and Freddie Hotch doubled up and tried vainly to slip away. Hotch was against the ropes. Eddie MacRae went to the head again, and a gasp went up from the crowd at the fierce power of the punches. The black man reeled along the ropes with Eddie MacRae swarming all over him. Now he put both arms forward and hung on to Eddie MacRae's waist.

It alarmed Kitty to see the change that had come over Eddie in the ring. The awkwardness, the hesitation, the gentleness were gone; they had been replaced by something wild, even insane; the pupils of the eyes were dilated, hateful; the twitch of his head was not so pronounced now and came in sharp, rapid jolts in rhythm to the slash and jerk of his punches.

Freddie Hotch was still smiling. He was hanging on and shaking his head, but smiling. Eddie continued to pound him, but he stayed in. The crowd loved it. They applauded loudly at the bell ending the first round.

Between rounds they were abuzz with admiration: impressed with the white man's punching power and the black man's ability to stand up under it. It was going to be a good fight. The old-timers, betting furiously at the bar in the rear, laughed and nodded their heads in approval, while shifting the odds and upping the ante.

A man called to his friend seated next to Porter: "A punchy, huh? Is that what you said, a punchy?"

"One round never made a fight, never did and never will," the friend said.

The woman in the first row turned and looked back at Porter. Their eyes met, then she looked away.

She was beautiful, elegant, obviously wealthy, and now Porter felt a desperate yearning to reach out to her, an exquisite ache to touch something that beautiful. She was perhaps the most beautiful woman he had ever seen. She seemed at that moment to embody all good fortune in the world; the distance between him and her was the gulf between the losers and the winners. If he could just touch her, gain a smile from her, a kiss . . .

Kitty clapped her hands as the bell sounded for the second round. "C'mon, Eddie!" she yelled. "Come on!"

The second round was a repeat of the first. MacRae moved forward ruthlessly, cracking in lefts and rights that landed with sickening, sharp thuds on the other fighter's head. Occasionally Hotch would attempt to land a blow, but the effort was pathetic and awkward. He looked like an ineffectual teen-ager in a schoolyard fight.

But Eddie could not put him down. Hotch stood up under everything that was thrown at him. Now and then, after taking a particularly telling blow, the tall, thin black would shake his head and smile in embarrassment, as though apologizing for the fact that he was being hit so often.

Eddie MacRae's expression never varied. Serious, determined, his blue eyes smoldering with deep purpose, he continued ripping off punch after punch.

It seemed to Porter, watching the fight, that in some way Eddie MacRae was not even in *that* ring. He was fighting some other fight. He was fighting a battle in a nightmare. His stare was fixed on his opponent, but *behind* his eyes the look was focused elsewhere.

"Wow, geemaneezers!" said Kitty between rounds. "Geema-neezers!" The referee was in Hotch's corner now, talking to him. Hotch was still smiling, embarrassed, assuring the referee that he could continue. At ringside and at the bar some of the bettors were paying off their bets.

Porter stared at the woman in the first row. She did not turn back to him.

The third round continued much like the first and second, although Hotch began to make a better showing of it. He had devised a method of escaping the full fury of MacRae's punches: he would dance back, then, head down, charge forward and grab hold of Eddie's waist. He still took a great deal of punishment, but many punches were wasted now, landing on the top of his head, his arms, back, and shoulders.

The round had a half minute to go. Hotch was moving back and away, when he suddenly lunged forward, driving an awkward overhand right in front of him. It caught Eddie MacRae coming in, caught him on the side of the head. The punch did not appear to be particularly hard, but it landed solidly. Eddie MacRae went down.

He was on one knee, shaking his head. His look was one of pain and confusion and disgust with himself. Kitty buried her face in her hands as the referee began the count.

The crowd, which at first had reacted with shocked silence, now found its voice and began to cheer. The man next to Porter yelled out: "Hey, punchy! Hey, punchy, get up and fight!"

Eddie was up at the count of four and took the mandatory eight count. He moved back in on Freddie Hotch, but something was missing now: his confidence was gone. The look of fear had returned to his face. He continued in control of the fight, but the knockdown had taken the spirit out of him. He looked now to Porter and Kitty much as he had when they first met him—shy, anxious, uncomfortable.

He won the next two rounds, but far less impressively. Though he continued to clobber Freddie Hotch at will, his punches lacked authority. A certain wariness had set in. He circled around. He did not drive the fight home.

79

The bell sounded for the end of the last round, and the audience applauded indifferently.

"The judges and referee by unanimous decision give the fight to MacRae!" The announcer raised Eddie MacRae's arm above his head. Although he had won, Eddie looked dispirited. He smiled and twitched and nodded without enthusiasm at the crowd. Freddie Hotch, grinning broadly, danced across the ring and hugged MacRae, and the crowd cheered loudly.

There was an intermission. People moved up the aisle toward the bar in the rear. Porter searched with his eyes for the woman in the silver gown. The two men with her were standing up now at ringside. The woman was gone.

Back in the dressing area Eddie MacRae sat with his elbows resting on his knees, his head down, staring at the floor. The pantry stank of perspiration and liniment and adhesive. Eddie was glum. How had he ever permitted himself to get tagged like that? He was hit by an amateur bolo punch and had gone down! The disgust he felt for himself was so strong he could taste it in his mouth.

Freddie Hotch was elated. One would have thought he had won the fight. He stared at himself in the mirror and adjusted his yellow nylon shirt, aqua knit slacks, and snow white sports jacket. He kept up a steady stream of laughing banter. "Man, you got two hands like sledge-hammers, felt like to take my head apart. . . . Them punches coming so fast at me all I could think of was 'Freddie, you're in some *trouble now!*'"

"How you like it out there?" Bo Brown asked languidly.

"Man, just let me collect my money and *go!*"

The promoter entered the pantry. He approached Eddie MacRae and shook his hand. "Nice fight, bub. You got a lot of power." Eddie forced an awkward grin.

The payoff was seventy-five dollars.

Now they were bringing in one of the Mexican kids. He had been slapped silly by his look-alike in the second round. His eyes were glassy, and he kept babbling something in Spanish about his mother and the tears of God, while his trainer, a gray-faced Chicano, applied ice to the back of his neck. The winner, the man from Tijuana, entered the locker area like a matador moving into the bull ring. His manner was grand, elegant, solemn. He did not speak or smile. He wiped his body with a towel and began to dress without showering.

During the intermission Eddie, in street clothes, went looking for Porter and Kitty. He found them drinking beer at the bar. "Oh, Eddie, you were tremendous! I never seen anything like it," Kitty said.

Eddie looked downcast. "I'm some kind of damned fool getting tagged by that clown—"

"You done good, Eddie," Porter said. "You got nothing to be ashamed of." He ordered a beer for the boxer. The three of them raised the paper cups in which the beer was served in a toast. "Here's to us," Porter said.

"Right," said Kitty.

"Unbeatable combination," Porter said.

"Right," said Kitty.

"Right," echoed Eddie MacRae, smiling awkwardly.

A man had moved next to them. He was a tall, lean, dapper, gray-haired man in his midfifties. He had a deep tan and wore a sharply fitted, blue pin-stripe suit. There was something quiet, almost gentle in his manner. He had large, soft, sad eyes.

A man and woman stood next to him. The second man was squat, but lean, dark, with a boxer's punched-in nose. He wore his jet-black hair long, almost down to his shoulders. The woman wore a silver lamé gown. It was the woman who had been staring at Porter.

"That was quite a fight," the older man said. His voice was light, almost lisping.

Eddie MacRae looked confused. "Should have never caught that punch," he stammered.

The man smiled and shrugged. "Those things happen," he said. "You got a terrific pair of hands, though. You got speed. You got a rugged punch. You don't see a pair of hands like that too often."

"Thank you," Eddie MacRae said. Porter was aware the woman had not taken her eyes off him.

"My wife said to me, talk to that boy. He has potential," the older man said. "I'm Matt Nathan." He paused ever so slightly, as though everyone should recognize his name. "This is my wife, Yolande, and Angel Amato. You may have seen him fight. . . ."

Eddie MacRae nodded. He had seen him fight, a few years back on television from Santa Monica. He had been a middleweight with a reputation for cunning and viciousness, a butter, kidney-puncher, and thumber. Some people compared him to Fritzie Zivic, but his career never took off. He enjoyed some success on the West Coast, then faded from sight.

Eddie attempted to introduce Kitty and Porter, but in his excitement couldn't remember their names. Porter came to his rescue. "Don Porter and Kitty," he said. Eddie MacRae stared down at the floor, his head twitching sharply.

"You have the potential to become one helluva heavyweight," Matt Nathan said. "Not often you find a white boy with that kind of potential. There was Ingemar Johansson, Jerry Quarry looked good for a while—who else?" No one answered. Mrs. Nathan smiled. She continued to stare at Porter. "If you're handled properly, you could become another Rocky Marciano."

Eddie MacRae blushed and gazed down at his shoes.

The main event had started in the ring. The Black Avenger was stalking Bo Brown around the ring. Brown was sloppy fat, and every time the Avenger hit him he shook like jelly. "I own a few fighters," Matt Nathan said. "Joe Fletcher is one of my boys." In the ring Fletcher caught Brown with a rapid combination, and Brown hugged him around the waist and held on, breathing heavily. "He's a good boy, Fletcher. Isn't that right, Angel?"

Angel Amato nodded his head slowly without looking at the ring.

"You got a manager?" Matt Nathan asked.

"Not no more, sir."

"What happened?"

"I had this guy name of Chalky—I never did know his last name—and he said he would manage me. He never got me but one fight, down in Bakersfield, and afterwards he disappeared with my share. Fifty dollars. I went looking for him and found this girl, she was a friend of his, and she said he moved to Barstow. I traveled down there, but I sure couldn't find him."

Matt Nathan said, "You're not punchy are you?"

"No, sir."

"What's that twitch about?"

"Doctor says it's psychological."

"I'd like to put you under contract. You know the Paradise Hotel?"

It was one of the larger casinos between the Landmark and the Desert Inn. "No, sir," Eddie said. Kitty remembered the black deskman with the missing fingers, but said nothing.

"I know it," said Porter. Mrs. Nathan continued to stare at him, and now it was making him uncomfortable. He felt her staring must be obvious to everyone, but no one seemed to notice.

"Well, I'm one of the owners of the Paradise Hotel. Stop by and see me there. I'll be out of town until the middle of next week. You got spending money?"

"Yes, sir."

"All right."

In the ring the second round had just begun. The Black Avenger caught Brown with an indifferently thrown overhand right. The punch appeared to have no real power. Brown fell as though chopped down by an ax. The crowd roared with laughter. Brown lay on his back, his gloved hand over his eyes, his right leg jerking slowly up and down. The referee counted him out. As the crowd began to file slowly out of the ballroom, Bo Brown could be seen still stretched out on the ring floor, his right leg pumping slowly, with no particular intent.

"Nice talking to you," Matt Nathan said with a soft smile. Then he, his wife, and Angel Amato were gone, heading back toward the dressing area to congratulate the Black Avenger.

V

"It comes and goes in waves, just like the flow of a fight does. Sometimes you get walloped and go down on your ass—just like happened to you in the ring last night. But you get right back up and keep on punching."

Porter was explaining the System to Eddie MacRae in the hotel room. Kitty had her charts spread out on the bed, and Eddie MacRae was studying them.

Porter had decided to bring Eddie MacRae into the System. With three people ganging up on the dealers, he reasoned they could multiply the percentages and drastically increase their edge. Kitty and Eddie MacRae would play the basic strategy and take the betting lead from him.

Eddie was not particularly excited by the scheme. He was a prize fighter, not a gambler. He had found himself a new manager of power and prestige, Matt Nathan. In a week or so he would be back training seriously again. The world of big-time fights was about to open to him. In addition, he was having an impossible time comprehending the ratios, percentages, and numbers Porter and Kitty were forcing on him.

They had been working all afternoon. His eyes burned and his head ached. He continued only because he did not want to offend his two new friends. He did not want to lose them. He had no one else.

"I'll never learn this damn thing!" Eddie MacRae said, fighting to recall the most simple strategy, how to play a sixteen against a ten.

"You're doing fine, Eddie," Kitty said. "It just takes practice."

Porter dealt the cards slowly, meticulously. The polished nails on his fingers gleamed under the yellow bed-stand light; light streaked the textured faces of the playing cards. Talk was muted. Kitty pointed out various aspects of the System on the charts.

The afternoon wore on. The whine of a vacuum cleaner outside the room receded down the hallway and was silent. The sunlight against the rear wall moved from brightness to gloom, exhausting itself at last on the worn carpet. Day had shifted to evening. Porter continued to deal, while Eddie MacRae struggled with the System.

The boxer squeezed his rubber exerciser and chewed on a wad of gum and pondered the play. At last a pattern began to assert itself. A soft seventeen came up, and he hit it against an ace.

"Very good, Eddie!" Kitty exclaimed.

"That's it, Eddie! Now you got it. . . ."

They broke for dinner at a luncheonette on Fremont Street, where the breakfast went for forty-eight cents and dinner, a dollar twenty-nine. They ate amid the slot machines and nickel keno.

After dinner they got in the car and rode down to East Bonanza Street, where Eddie and Porter hit baseballs pitched from a grinding mechanical monster. Kitty was surprised at how good Porter was at it. He didn't hit the ball as far as Eddie MacRae, but he hit it with more consistency, clean, curving drives that sliced into the shadows at the edge of the range. "Way to go, Don! Way to pop 'em!" Eddie MacRae called out.

Two husky teen-aged boys and their pimply-faced dates applauded when Porter came out of the cage.

"Where'd you learn that?" Kitty asked, as they drove back to Casino Center.

"Prison," Porter said. "Nothing much to do in there but play cards and baseball." He smiled. "No, I always wanted to be a baseball player. When I was a kid I was pretty good."

"What position?"

"Center field."

"Donny, you should have kept it up!"

"Yeah."

Despite Eddie MacRae's protests that he wasn't ready, Porter had decided that the three of them would sit down and play that night. He would bet the big stuff, while Kitty and the boxer followed his lead with one- and two-dollar bets. "Eddie, you stick with us, you hear? We got a combination going here that's hell to beat!"

"I appreciate you teaching me this and all, but I'm a boxer, Don. I'm not a gambler."

"Ain't no law says you can't do both," said Porter. Eddie MacRae thought about this and could not fault Porter's logic.

Porter explained the strategy for that night. He would play "third base"—the seat farthest to the dealer's right. "That's the important one, Eddie, 'cause I'll be counting all the cards as they come out, and no one can get behind me and mess us up."

They played at the Golden Nugget that night and for the first time everything in the System fell into place. Eddie MacRae made some mistakes, but on the whole he did well.

Kitty was coming along fine. She was counting the cards with some assurance now, and her play, within a certain limited confine, was impeccable.

They all won that night. When they got back to the Center Hotel, they pooled their winnings. They had come away with more than five hundred dollars.

Porter was ecstatic. "Damn, Eddie! You're Mister Luck! I knew it! I knew it!"

"I thought the System didn't depend on luck."

"It don't. But damn, a little luck never hurt no one."

"Oh, Eddie," Kitty squealed, "we're all going to be rich!"

"Better believe it!" yelled Porter.

Eddie MacRae grinned with pride.

They spent the next week immersing themselves in the System. They would practice all afternoon and late into the evening. At ten o'clock they would go out for dinner, then make the rounds of the casinos. They would never remain long in one place; they would win a pile and move on. They confined themselves to the downtown casinos for the first few days, hitting the Four Queens, the Nugget, the Mint, Binion's Horseshoe, and the Union Plaza. Then they moved up to the Strip.

On the Strip they stayed with the one-deck casinos—the International, the Silver Slipper, the Sahara, and the Stardust.

They made an incongruous trio: Eddie MacRae, shy, hulking, shuffling along, eyes blinking, head twitching; Porter, an unlit stogie held lightly in his mouth, shoulders hunched, pale eyes flitting over the gaming tables, the expression on his wan face cool and impassive; and Kitty, vaguely bedraggled, looking frail and puppylike, glowing with excitement, wide-eyed, alive to each new impression. "Donny, look at that dealer over there! He's a dwarf! My God, I never thought I'd see a dwarf dealing cards!" Or: "That girl got the most hugest breasts I've ever seen. They're unnatural. Do you think they're real?"

The System continued to perform beautifully. At the end of the first week they had won nearly five thousand dollars. They checked out of the Center Hotel and moved into a motel on Paradise Road.

Eddie MacRae hadn't forgotten about his boxing. At the end of a long night of gambling, when they returned to the motel, he would change into a pair of khakis and sweatshirt and run several miles up Paradise Road. He would pass the Paradise Hotel and think about Matt Nathan and his offer.

He would remind himself that one day he would visit Mr. Nathan. . . .

At the end of the second week they were ahead eleven thousand dollars. They took two days off and went on a spending spree. They invested in racks of new clothes: western dress for Porter and Eddie MacRae—hand-crafted cowboy boots, Stetson hats, lace shirts in pastel colors; and for Kitty, gaudy show-girl numbers, diaphanous harem pants, and skin-tight gowns with outrageous decolletage that were funny and sad on her flat, boyish figure, giving her the appearance of a little girl trying out her mother's wardrobe.

"Do I look snazzy?" she asked of Porter.

"Yes, you do," he answered, and she beamed and laughed. "Oh, Donny, we're all snazzy!"

They visited the jewelry shop at Caesar's Palace and came away wearing identical rings: a diamond-chip ace of hearts in a setting of gold. They traded in Kitty's car on a new model, an Eldorado convertible bought with two thousand dollars and easy credit.

Though outwardly affecting a look of cool, inside Porter was stunned and bewildered by the success of the System. Why hadn't it worked this way before, when he was playing alone? The System was supposed to perform in streaks— Monty had stressed how important it was to sense these mathematical tides—but since they had hooked up with Eddie MacRae, it all seemed to be going their way. Porter couldn't shake the irrational conviction that in some profoundly magical way the boxer had brought luck to the System. Eddie MacRae had taken on the proportion of an extraordinary talisman, setting everything right, ensuring success.

They were beginning to be recognized. Porter noticed it in the attentiveness of the pit bosses and the care of the dealers when they came to the tables. Certain dealers had begun to shuffle up on them early in the deck, wrecking the delicate mathematics of the System. He realized that the time was approaching when they would have to strike big in a single-deck game. After that, they would have to move on to other casinos, to the much more numerous four-deck games.

Four decks! Monty had only barely touched on the intricacies of the four-deck System. "Takes a man of genius for that. Takes a man like Billy Ray Walker to master four decks," Monty used to say with a wondering shake of his head.

With four decks, if you caught a streak, you could ride it through two hundred and eight cards. You could really make a killing. But when the cards went against you, four decks could wipe you clean, crush you. The count was terrifically taxing, the mathematics of percentage and ratio infinitely complex. It was like playing chess while doing multiplication tables. It could be mastered: Porter was sure of it. It would take a tremendous effort, but it could be done.

He had purchased a wooden dealing shoe, and a couple of hours every day he and Kitty would work with it. Kitty would deal and Porter would attempt to modify the one-deck system. He had begun a whole new series of charts, and as they would practice, he would make notes and attempt to nail down certain basic laws. He felt that he was making some grudging headway, but he still had a great deal to accomplish.

They had taken a break and were sitting around the pool at the motel. It was late afternoon, but the summer Vegas sky still burned like a furnace. Several show girls who lived at the motel were sunning themselves; a tall, blond, homosexual dancer napped on a rubber raft in the center of the pool. The air was brutally hot. There was no breeze.

Kitty sat in the sun reading a movie magazine, while Eddie MacRae worked with a deck of cards, dealing himself hands, his lips moving soundlessly with the count. Porter, lying on a canvas mat, eyes shielded behind dark glasses, puffed slowly on a Marsh Wheeling. He was plotting their next move. He had decided that tonight they would visit the Paradise Hotel.

"This damn thing is tougher than boxing three rounds with a gorilla!" Eddie MacRae said, throwing down several cards in disgust.

"You ever box a gorilla?" Kitty said.

Eddie MacRae smiled. "No, but I boxed a fella name of Patrick Busik sure smelled like one."

"What's a 'philanthropist'?" Kitty asked, picking a word out of the article she was reading.

"A what?" Porter said.

" 'Raquel Welch's advice to all young women is to avoid philanthropists.' "

"That's someone with a lot of money who likes to give it away," Porter said.

Kitty was confused. "Why should young women avoid them?"

" 'Cause in this life you get nothing for nothing."

"Hey, Don," Eddie MacRae said, "that's what we're going to be. We're going to get us so much money we're going to be philanthropists." He laughed and shuffled the cards.

"How did you get so smart, Donny?" Kitty asked.

"Prison. Best education there is."

Porter rose and began to gather up the charts spread on the concrete next to him. "Let's go," he said.

"Where?" Kitty asked.

"The Paradise Hotel."

Eddie MacRae looked up, dismayed. "Why there?" Kitty said.

"They got a one-deck game there. We ought to give it a try."

Eddie MacRae was reluctant to play at the Paradise Hotel. "I don't want to run into that Mr. Nathan. . . ." It bothered Eddie that he wasn't boxing. He kept reminding himself that this gambling interlude was only temporary. He would give it a try for a few more weeks, then get back to serious training, contact Mr. Nathan, and see if he could get lined up with a top-flight match. With Mr. Nathan behind him, who could tell what he might not accomplish? During his morning roadwork, the desert sand moving in rolling gusts across Paradise Road, Vegas behind him pale and silent in the gray dawn light, the casino signs dark now, washed out, resembling faded scraps of colored paper thrown to the wind, he would feed on his fantasies. He had reached the top, Heavyweight Champion of the World! He pictured himself returning to Fresno, the gold championship belt buckled about his waist. He would visit his father, drop in on the boys he worked construction with. Heavyweight Champion of the World! He would be pleasant with everyone: he would treat his fame and accomplishment lightly. But he would never grow shy with anyone again; he would never lower his eyes; the feeling of failure, of clumsiness, of stupidity that he always experienced in the presence of his father would be gone. He would bring his old man a box of cigars; he would take him out to dinner; they would drink martinis made with Gordon's gin, straight up with an olive—his father's favorite. He would call him by his first name, Cal. . . .

"Eddie, you got to come with me. You're my good-luck piece."

They were climbing the metal steps leading up from the pool. The railing was hot as though a fire burned beneath it. They moved up the steps gingerly, careful not to touch the railing. "Why can't we go somewhere's else?"

"They got us spotted. It's just a question of time. . . ."

"Don, I just don't want to go there. . . ."

"All right, don't go," Porter said curtly. He and Kitty entered their room. Eddie MacRae stood for a moment on the balcony overlooking the pool and stared out at the dry desert with its grotesque oases of hotels and golf courses, swimming pools, hamburger stands, car washes, gas stations and parking lots. He felt bad that he had disappointed Porter. The world suddenly seemed raw and arid to him. Why would they plant a city *here*, he was thinking? He moved off toward his room, feeling very much like he was living on the far side of the moon.

Porter decided he would play alone that evening. Eddie MacRae and Kitty would take in a movie. Kitty was certain that Porter had hurt Eddie's feelings. They would take in a cowboy movie. Eddie would enjoy that.

While they were dressing, Kitty said to Porter: "Do you enjoy being with me?"

Porter stood in front of the mirror combing his hair. The paleness of his face was concealed by the beginnings of a tan. His hair was turning a bright blond from the sun. "Yes," he said.

"You're not bored with me, are you?"

"Why should I be bored?"

"I don't know." She said nothing for a long while. She sat on the bed, a small makeup mirror propped up on the pillow before her, applying a pair of false eyelashes. "Let's put it this way—when I see all those fantastic women in this town I just begin to wonder."

"What?"

"Why you stay with me."

Porter sat next to her on the bed. He pulled her to him and kissed her. One eyelash came loose and hung from her cheekbone. He began to laugh. Kitty looked in the mirror and also laughed. Then she grew very serious. "I'm silly looking, aren't I?"

"No."

"Yes, I am. Why do you stay with me?"

"Because you know the System," he said, and meant it.

He entered the Paradise Hotel casino through the rear entrance, past a waterfall cascading into a long aqua swimming pool. It was late and the casino was quiet.

He sat at a center table and began to play. The dealer was a thin, vaguely effeminate young man with a Prince Valiant haircut and large, liquid eyes. Porter purchased a stack of twenty-five-dollar chips. "Hope you're lucky for me," he said.

"They call me old horseshoe," the dealer answered without animation. "Only that isn't the way they always pronounce it."

Bored and yawning, he dealt the cards with exaggerated slowness, as though some inner engine were running down; the cards fell with lugubrious slaps across the green felt of the table.

Porter had no complaints: he immediately began to win. He started off playing twenty-five dollars a hand. In two runs through the deck he had worked that up to a hundred dollars. When it came time to change dealers, Porter had won nearly two thousand dollars. The young dealer deftly fanned the deck flat out on the table and said with a quiet drawl: "You always hit soft eighteen?"

"Is that what I did?"

"Three times. You caught the point twice."

"No kidding?"

"Not often I see that." The dealer winked, clapped his hands softly, and was gone.

His replacement was a tall, lean, gray-haired man with a tight mouth and narrow eyes. He studied Porter with unconcealed hostility. "People like you should put your money in a bank," he said.

Porter pretended he hadn't heard him. He occupied himself rearranging the chips in front of him. The pit boss had come over to the table and was staring hard at Porter. He watched several hands then moved away.

They were trying to drive him off. When Porter busted a hand, the dealer would duck his own cards without turning the hole card up; he would shuffle up after every two or three plays. He never took his eyes off Porter.

Porter lost several hundred dollars. He should have left, but the dealer's arrogance angered him. "Why don't you just deal the cards," Porter said.

"That's what I'm doing."

"Well, I don't like the way you're doing it."

"I'm very sorry about that, sir," the dealer said with exaggerated politeness.

The pit boss moved back to the table. "What's the problem?"

"When I'm winning, he gives me a funny deal."

"I don't understand what you mean, sir," the dealer said.

"Shuffle up every hand? Don't show your hole card? That's the way you deal here?"

The pit boss and the dealer just stood there staring at him. He began to act the part of an outraged loser. "I've dropped more than ten thousand dollars in this place. . . ."

The pit boss cut him short. "You lost nothing here. . . ."

"Yesterday . . ."

"I never seen you here."

"You think you're the only pit boss in the place? You work every shift?"

"I think you ought to take your business someplace else."

"Why?"

"We don't like your type player."

Someone was standing up very close to Porter. He could feel the warmth of his body against the back of his neck. "Cash in your chips and get out of here," a soft voice said behind him.

Porter turned. Angel Amato, Matt Nathan's factotum, was standing there. He was dressed in a black business suit. His broad, scarred face, dark, hooded eyes, square, lean body created an impression not so much sinister as of cold power. He made no sign that he recognized Porter. "I'm down ten thousand dollars and they won't give me a fair deal," Porter said quietly.

"In the Paradise Hotel everyone gets the deal he deserves," Angel Amato said. His voice had the slightest hint of a Mexican accent. "Now get out of here."

Porter rose from the table and moved through the casino.

95

A large crowd was gathered around one of the crap tables, where a woman was throwing the dice, making pass after pass.

It was Yolande Nathan. She wore a tight-fitting black dress. Her face seemed extraordinarily pale, her lips a bit too red; her long, black hair was disheveled, her black eyes dull and empty. She threw the dice without even looking at them.

Porter paused and watched. She saw him and gave up the dice. She moved away from the table. "Beautiful," Porter said as she came to him.

"It makes the time go by," she said. Her face was expressionless. Porter wasn't even sure she recognized him. She had been drinking.

"They won't let me play," Porter said.

"Who?"

"The Mexican guy."

"Angel?"

"Yes."

"What are you playing?"

"Blackjack."

She led him back to the blackjack tables. She walked with a slow weave, her gaze empty. Angel was standing next to the pit boss.

"Let him play," she said.

She sat next to Porter at the table. The dealer shuffled up. She bought a hundred dollars' worth of five-dollar chips. Angel Amato stood behind them.

"How are you?" she said.

"Fine," Porter said.

"Where are your friends tonight? The prize fighter and the girl?"

She recognized him, and that enabled Porter to relax a bit. "I don't know," Porter said.

"What are you drinking?"

"Scotch."

The cocktail waitress appeared, and Yolande ordered Porter's Scotch and a martini for herself. They began to play.

Now the dealer turned up all the cards at the end of a hand; he dealt to the bottom of the deck. In an hour Porter had won another three thousand dollars. "I think I'll quit while I'm ahead," Porter said.

He cashed in his chips, and Yolande Nathan led him into the lounge area. They sat at the bar. Angel Amato stayed with them the whole time, following at a distance.

On the circular lounge stage three flat-chested girls in sequined gowns sang "Okie from Muskogee," while a twenty-piece band blasted loudly behind them, forcing the girls to cup their hands over their ears to hear themselves perform. An electric sign in flashing light bulbs winked out the name of the act: "The Rhythm Sisters."

The room was jammed with people who looked to be on their first trip to the big city. There was a boisterous gawkiness about them, a tendency to holler and laugh loudly at nothing, to spill drinks and shriek hysterically. They were dressed in gaudy sport shirts, suits with no tie, white shoes, strapless evening gowns, bouffant hairdos. They drank Tom Collinses or Sloe Gin Fizzes.

The Rhythm Sisters finished their act to great applause. The curtain to the stage swished shut. "Where's your husband tonight?" Porter asked Yolande.

"Upstairs in the penthouse, probably scoring one of the house hookers." She sloshed her drink around in the glass. She smiled at Porter.

She was a beautiful girl, but for Porter there was something more: a certain comfortable quality mixed with a palpable sexuality that touched and aroused him. He felt as though he had known her a very long time; he felt relaxed with her; it seemed as though they had already been intimate.

He sensed that she felt the same way. She looked at him and smiled in an old, familiar way. She was perfectly easy with him, and he guessed this was unusual for her. As he was uncomfortable with most people, he knew that she too must be like that. Her eyes studied Porter, and there was surprise in her look. "Who are you?" she asked, still smiling.

"Don," he said.

"I know that. I remember your name. Don Porter. But *who* are you, Don Porter?"

"Just Don Porter," he said.

"You know who I am?"

"Yes."

"That's good. I like you, Don," she said quietly.

"Why?"

"*That's* a good question," she said, and they both laughed.

They had two more drinks. Porter was getting drunk. Everything seemed warm and hazy. Yolande was extraordinarily beautiful, more beautiful than any woman he had ever known. He ached at her beauty and held himself unaccountably lucky to be sitting here with her now. Yes, he was unaccountably lucky. . . .

Now there was a loud drum roll. The curtain to the stage jerked open, and the electric light bulb sign popped out the name of the next group: "Wayne Dawson and the Hell's Angels." A man dressed in white leather strode out onto the stage, followed by five mulatto girls, also in white leather. The crowd squealed and clapped, and one man shouted out: "Do it, Wayne! Do it!" and the man in white leather called back: "I surely *will!*"

Wayne Dawson was near fifty, had dyed blond hair that hung to his shoulders, and wore a silver head band and silver boots. In a raw, whiskey voice he began to sing "The Battle Hymn of the Republic," while the girls behind him waved small American flags. The band blared so loudly that Porter's ears began to ache.

The singer's voice rose from a roar to a screech, and perspiration poured down his wrinkled, pug face. He leaped from the stage and began to circulate among the tables, kissing women and slapping hands with men. The crowd went wild, cheering and squealing. A florid-faced man with no neck called out: "I guaran-damn-tee Elvis don't put on no show like you, Wayne!" and the room roared its approval, while Wayne Dawson, his face contorted in a painful grin, sprayed the audience with saliva and perspiration as the Hell's Angels, smiling broadly, bounced their boobs and twitched their bottoms in time to the music.

Wayne Dawson completed "The Battle Hymn of the Republic," mopped his face with a silk kerchief, then launched into a slow ballad. Yolande finished her drink and rose unsteadily from the bar stool. "Why don't you take me home?" she said.

Porter gazed across the room. Angel Amato was standing at the far side of the bar, like some dark sentinel. He was not looking at them, but Porter knew he had not missed a move. "Don't worry about anything, honey," she said. She pronounced "honey" as though she had been calling him that for years.

He walked with Yolande through the casino and down a long promenade that contained a magazine counter, dress shop, jewelry store, and souvenir stand. Angel Amato followed after them. "I think we have company," Porter said.

Yolande laughed quietly. "Darling, don't worry," she said.

At the exit Porter glanced back. Angel Amato had stopped now. He was staring at them. His narrow black eyes were veiled and noncommittal. Porter and Yolande moved through the door and out into the parking lot.

Porter started up the Eldorado. "Where to?"

"Just drive."

"Any particular direction?"

"Out to the desert."

They turned off Paradise Road and onto Bonanza. After a while the buildings thinned out. The road narrowed. The city was behind them.

They were driving through a wide stretch of dark, empty land. The top of the car was down and the air was cool. The sky was brilliant and thick with stars. In the distance ahead of them a high, black wall of mountains hunched against the velvet of the night.

They turned onto a side road. They sped along into the darkness of the desert. The air was sweet with the perfume of countless desert flowers. "Park here," Yolande said, after they had driven for some distance.

He pulled the car off the unpaved road. They were in a shallow gully. Porter turned the engine off.

To their right they could see the white lights of the Vegas Strip hanging like a string of pearls in the clear night. All about them purred the steady hum of cicadas. Yolande rested her head in against Porter. He put his arm around her. Her body felt unimaginably soft and delicate under his touch.

"What's this—the local lovers' lane?"

"This is where they plant the bodies."

"What bodies?"

"Someone doesn't do the right thing, they drive him out here and put a bullet in him. Then they plant him. It's one large graveyard." She switched on the radio. Gene Autry was singing "You Are My Sunshine." "I haven't heard that song in years," Yolande said.

"Who plants bodies out here?"

"I suppose Matt has planted a few. I'm not sure. He can be a very tough man," she said.

"I'm risking my life being here with you."

"Don't worry. He'd never kill anybody because of *me*."

She turned her face to Porter, and he kissed her. Her lips were surprisingly tender. They kissed softly, tentatively, barely brushing their mouths. "Let's pretend we're in high school, Don," she said.

He smiled and she smiled back. "The first time I ever made love was in a car. His name was Barry Tolliver, and he was the quarterback on our high school football team. I don't think I've ever liked anybody as much as I liked him."

She didn't want to take her clothes off. She lifted her dress. He moved on top of her.

When they were finished, they sat for a while in the car smoking cigarettes and listening to the radio. "I like you so much," she said. She had tears in her eyes. The hum of the cicadas was like a roar in Porter's ears.

They drove back to the city in silence. She clung to him, and he sensed something desperate and fragile in her nature. He felt very close to her. He felt as though he might be Barry Tolliver and it was the evening before the big game. He would throw a seventy-yard pass and win it all. He felt sixteen years old.

She directed him to a street beyond Las Vegas Boulevard, off Rancho Road. They drove along a circular road past great stucco mansions.

The house was like a fortress. It was surrounded by a high stone wall. A black Cadillac was parked in a driveway leading up to the main gate in the wall. "I'll get out here," she said at the bottom of the drive.

She got out of the car and began to walk up the drive. The door to the Cadillac opened and Angel Amato got out. He walked with her up the drive and let her in through the gate.

VI

Yolande Nathan stood in front of her bedroom mirror. She had been standing there for a long time. She was extraordinarily depressed. Tears streamed down her face, and she didn't know why. . . .

It had something to do with an awareness that her youth was turning its back on her. She heard, in some distant corridor of her mind, a high school marching band and caught a fleeting glimpse of a spangled girl twirling a baton that flashed faster than time. . . . The girl, all firm and electric, her buttocks like steel, her back a taut arch, was high-stepping away, her smile a blinding burst of light and innocence and confidence. Her youth was marching away from her.

She was not yet thirty-five and her body was falling apart. Her once firm breasts sagged, her hips had accumulated a rubbery heaviness, her thighs had lost their tone. Years of alcohol, irregular hours, arguments, intrigues, erratic diet, lack of exercise, boredom and bitterness had extracted a certain toll. She felt used up and exhausted.

Everything seemed to be slipping by her. Las Vegas had become a prison. Her room, white and pink, trimmed in lace and silk plush, had become a prison. Tiny porcelain figurines of ballet dancers, ladies-in-waiting, smiling peasant girls, twirled and curtseyed in frozen motion on the marble top of her dressing table and seemed to her evil and invidious, Lilliputian warders that kept her locked irremediably in emptiness and futility.

Increasingly of late she was assaulted by migraine and fits of crying. A mirror was a snare to catch and crush her. Her reflected form seemed to have no will of its own, seemed to exist only to drain her. Once apprehended on silvered glass, there was nothing for her to do but stare and grow desperate, accuse herself, note every flaw and blemish, feel a tremendous revulsion at the lack of vibrancy in her body.

She stood now, weeping, trying to get control of herself. It was midafternoon. Matt had sent word up with one of the Chinese servants that he was waiting on the patio. Their son Stephen would be finishing his tennis lesson. Angel Amato would be there. Angel Amato was always there.

She took her breasts in her hands and began to massage them, trying desperately to rub some life into them. Her body felt like dead wood.

At last her tears subsided. She was aware that her headache had lessened. She entered the bathroom and washed down two Demerol, hoping to kill it entirely.

As she dressed, she thought back on the night before. Porter had reached her, inexplicably reached her, and the idea was bewildering and miraculous.

She had known many men. Over the years she had had a succession of lovers, dealers from the casino, musicians, her son's tutors, tradesmen, gas station attendants. The affairs had been short-lived, drab, and depressing. She had seen something in the men that hadn't existed. The element she sought was like quicksilver; once in her grasp, it slithered away.

She had been caught by a certain leanness, a self-containment, something cold and impersonal. When she touched the men, however, they crumbled. Their detachment was a sham. They were flawed, dependent, pathetic, and she grew to loathe them and to loathe herself.

With Don Porter she sensed it would be different. He certainly was no more intelligent nor accomplished than the others. But his isolation seemed infinitely deeper. There was a blasted look to his face that affected her; he moved coolly, but it was a cool without arrogance, and it touched her. She felt strangely close to him, as though they had been twins separated at birth, and now, years later, unknowingly, they had found each other. . . .

Matt would know what had happened. Angel would have told him. This didn't bother her: Matt always knew what she did, and it was a measure of his unfathomable nature that a man completely in control of all other aspects of his life could tolerate infidelity in his wife. Perhaps it was his indifference to her behavior that underlined his control; what his wife did with her body simply did not matter to him. *She* simply did not matter to him. He owned her and could reclaim her anytime he wanted. He held her by the strength of his acceptance.

He was the hardest human being she had ever known. He was steel throughout, without pity or remorse or concern. He loved only things that were extensions of himself. He loved her—although he didn't *care* about her—the way he loved his own hand or his ear; he loved their son in the same way. He loved his poodle dog, Princess. He loved the Paradise Hotel. They were all extensions of himself. Anything beyond the periphery of himself was an enemy to be fought and defeated.

She had seen over the years the way he had gained control of the Paradise Hotel. Terrible things had been done. Men who had considered him a friend had learned a devastating lesson.

And yet there was a contradiction. He was steel, yet he had charm. He had no sympathy or remorse, and yet he radiated these qualities. She sometimes thought he was nothing more than an inordinately skillful actor, who, because it was so alien to him, could be objective about goodness and imitate it down to its most minute detail. Or perhaps goodness was a part of him, but like a snake's skin it was something that could be shed at will.

She finished dressing and moved down the marble staircase to the floor below. She crossed through the living room, then the dining room. Everything was immaculate, quiet, cool, polished. The interior of the house was done almost entirely in white. Matt wanted it that way. He thought of his life as of an antique watch: it should be rubbed clean, oiled, kept in mint condition.

Yolande moved through the tall French doors out onto the patio. Matt was seated at a round glass table reading a newspaper. He was dressed in a pair of white slacks and a pale blue golfing shirt. He had on his tortoise-shell reading glasses. He wore a thin, delicate gold wristwatch and a diamond ring on his little finger.

Angel Amato sat opposite him staring out at the tennis courts. Princess, Matt's poodle, sat motionlessly at the edge of the patio.

Yolande seated herself, and a Chinese servant immediately set her place for brunch. They had three servants in the house, all Chinese men. They were discreet, silent, polite. Yolande had difficulty distinguishing them, although they had been with her and Matt for years. They might have been triplets, for all she knew.

She would have poached eggs, Matt a small steak with sliced tomato. It had been that way for years.

Angel Amato would not eat nor would he speak, unless prompted by Matt. He would sit there impassively, his narrow eyes constantly scanning the landscape. He would appear almost languid; in actuality he was terrifyingly alert. He had the reflexes of a cat. He carried a .32 snub-nosed revolver tucked in the waistband of his trousers.

Matt carefully folded the newspaper and placed it on the table under his elbow. His tanned face gave the illusion of vigor, but his eyes were tired. They had been married fourteen years. She had never seen his eyes look other than tired.

"What time did you get in last night?" He asked this of her with no hint of reproach in his voice, a casual question.

"Late."

"Angel tells me you've made a new friend."

"We met him at the fights."

"The blond chap?"

"Yes."

The food arrived and they began to eat. Matt Nathan focused his attention on his plate and cut the steak into small, precise squares. He seemed to be thinking of something far removed from this table or his wife's life. Still, he went through the motions of a conversation with her. "What does he do, this fellow?"

"Who?"

"The fellow you were with last night."

"Don Porter."

"Of course. Don Porter." Princess, the poodle, had approached the table and was staring with sad eyes up at Matt Nathan. He removed a square of steak from his plate and fed it to the dog.

"I don't know what he does."

"Did he mention his friend?" Matt Nathan asked.

"Which friend?"

"The prize fighter."

"No, he didn't."

"I liked that boy. Powerful kid. What do you think, Angel?"

Angel Amato turned his broad face toward Matt Nathan. He considered the question for a moment, his veiled Indian eyes narrow, noncommittal, unblinking. "Got a good punch," Angel Amato said.

"Yes, he has." Matt Nathan removed a dark Havana from a box on the table, clipped the end neatly with a cigar cutter, and lit up. "I'd like to try him in the ring with Julio Martinez."

Angel Amato smiled. His two front teeth were gold. It wasn't often he smiled. "Julio will hand him his head in his glove," he said in his light, softly accented voice.

"Will you be seeing your friend again?"

"I think so."

"Tell him I want the boxer to come and visit me."

"I'll tell him."

They sat in silence for a long while. Matt Nathan puffed on his cigar. Yolande sipped at her coffee. Angel Amato studied the landscape. "Maybe next month we'll take a couple of weeks off. Go down to Mexico. Would you like that?" Matt Nathan asked of his wife. His voice was quiet, kindly.

"Yes, I would, Matt."

"Are you happy?"

"Yes."

He took her hand in his. "I love you very much," he said quietly. He had a way of doing that, of suddenly seeming so warm and concerned, so solicitous and affectionate. He spoke to her as though Angel Amato were invisible.

"I love you, too," she said.

She could see her ten-year-old son Stephen climbing the stone steps from the tennis courts. Following behind was Lyle, his instructor. Stephen was moving at an awkward run, his thick eyeglasses askew on his nose, his right knee scraped and bleeding. He was calling out, "Mommy, Mommy," and as usual he was crying. It depressed Yolande to consider how much a burden her child seemed to her. She loved him, but she had no patience for him. The sound of his whining voice caused a tightening in the pit of her stomach. The nerves of her arms tingled with irritation.

107

Angel pulled the boy to him. "What's the matter?" he asked.

"Lyle made me fall," Stephen said. The tennis instructor, a blond man in his forties, looked uncomfortable. "He was chasing a shot. . . ."

"It's nothing," Angel said, hugging the boy to him. Angel's concern revolted Yolande Nathan. She knew he loathed the child, yet he constantly made a fuss over him.

Stephen was looking at his father. He fought his tears.

"Angel says it's nothing, little bug," Matt Nathan said. "If Angel says it's nothing, it must be nothing."

"It hurts," Stephen said.

"Oh, Stephen, don't be such a baby," Yolande said.

Matt Nathan pulled the child to him and examined the scrape. He lifted the boy onto his lap and kissed the scrape. "Better?" The boy nodded his head and hugged his father about the neck.

Yolande got up. "Put something on his leg," she said to one of the Chinese. "Then fix lunch for Lyle and the boy."

She returned to her room. Her headache had come back. She took two more Demerol, then undressed. She stood in front of her dresser, staring once more in the mirror. She stood transfixed by her own image.

After a long while she opened a drawer in the dresser and took out a bottle of brandy. Stacked next to the brandy was a pile of photo enlargements. She took the bottle and the photographs to the bed. She lay back on the bed and studied the photographs. Her image was still visible to her in the dresser mirror, and from time to time she would compare what she had once been to what she was now.

The pictures had been taken many years before. There were shots of her when she was Miss Tennessee, when she was dancing at the Copa and the Tropicana in Vegas. She had been beautiful in those days, and she now tried to arrange herself on the bed so that the mirror captured a hint of that beauty.

She began to drink. She took a long swallow straight from the bottle, and the liquor felt good burning down into her. The room became cool and soft, harsh edges lessened, her own image in form-fitted bathing suits, sequined gowns, and feathered costumes floated on the bed all around her. Her mirror image winked back at her.

She considered calling Don Porter. He had told her he was staying at the Excelsior Motel. She yearned for him, not really sexually, but with her whole being. He took on for her the quality of some palpitant teen-age fantasy, a movie star, a football hero. His presence fitted exactly some crying need in her heart, some awful, unbearable void: he was that interstitial segment that would complete the puzzle of herself. She whispered his name under her breath.

But she had no strength now. She was drowning in a pool of her own photographs. She sighed and glided off into a dream in which she was a cheerleader at a football game. She leaped into the air, and with the crowd cheering below her, she began to float away. It was an exquisite feeling: never to return to earth again.

It just wouldn't work. Don Porter was attempting to atone for the time he had spent with Yolande Nathan. He had forgone the casinos to stay in the motel room with Kitty. They had attempted to make love.

It was empty. He felt nothing, and he could tell by looking into Kitty's eyes that she felt nothing also.

They rolled together listlessly on the bed for several minutes, then gave up.

He flicked on the television. She moved into the kitchenette and poured herself a glass of milk. "Do you want anything?" she called out.

"No."

He sat up and lit a stogie. A talk show was in progress on the television. He moved his face up very close to the screen, but he wasn't really watching it. He was void of all feeling, disgusted with himself. "Where's Eddie tonight?" he asked, not really interested.

"Sleeping. He's going into serious training tomorrow."

He felt he should talk with her, but he had nothing to say. "What's wrong?" she asked after a while.

He shrugged. "I feel like doing some gambling," he said, getting up off the bed.

She stared at him, not really hurt as much as removed from him. She sensed a quiet gap between them and wondered what had happened.

"Do you want me to come along?"

He didn't really want her with him. "If you feel like it," he said.

"No, that's all right. You go alone."

Driving up Paradise Road Porter thought about Yolande Nathan. What was it that had caught him so completely? Again, he came back to that quality of *familiarity*. Even in making love they were perfectly easy with one another. They moved together as though they had been lovers for years. It was extraordinary only in how commonplace it was, how comfortable and relaxed.

And the look in her eye when she gazed on him, quizzical, vaguely ironic; and her faint half-smile, and the slightly mocking tone in her voice. They had only just met, and yet she knew him very, very well, and that warmed him and broke the sense of isolation he felt always, even with Kitty. He couldn't believe it. Was this what love was? Feeling *comfortable* with someone?

Matt Nathan sat in his office at the Paradise Hotel with Red Polikoff, his closest business associate, opposite him. Angel Amato stood by the door.

Polikoff was a fat, bald man, who had received the nickname Red years ago, when he had had a full head of wavy red hair. The hair had long gone, but the name stayed around. He had sleepy eyes, a wheeze, and he perspired a lot. "I could find out nothing about him," he said, sitting far forward in his chair. His thick thighs looked as though they might burst the seams of his trousers. Drops of perspiration had gathered at the folds of fat where his chin disappeared into his neck.

"That's peculiar, don't you think, Red?" Matt Nathan hated a mystery. A mystery could be very dangerous. He didn't care what Yolande did as long as there were no mysteries involved.

"Some people, Matt, are so insignificant they don't even carry a shadow with them."

Matt Nathan toyed with a well-shaped Havana. He studied the veins of the tobacco leaf.

"He lives with a girl at the Excelsior Motel," Angel Amato said. "He's a gambler." Red Polikoff wiped the perspiration from his chin with a silk kerchief.

"He's some half-assed gambler," Red Polikoff said.

"And the prize fighter?"

"Lives at the same motel," Angel Amato said.

"He lives at the same motel, Matt," Red Polikoff echoed.

"Where's he from?"

Red Polikoff looked back at Angel Amato. Angel said nothing. Red Polikoff shrugged. "I estimate he's some low-life hustler." Polikoff was uncomfortable. He disliked disappointing Matt Nathan.

Polikoff was the last of a close-knit group that had come to Vegas with Matt Nathan in the late forties. There were five of them. They were all from North Jersey and had grown up together. They were known as the Jersey Jews. They were tough men who had provided muscle for the Italians.

Over the years, after establishing the Paradise Hotel, they jockeyed for position. Now three of them were gone, two dead, one in retirement in Miami. Matt Nathan and Red Polikoff remained. The two dead men were part of the desert.

Matt Nathan stared at the backs of his tanned hands. He rubbed them slowly. "What do you think, Angel?"

"He's a busted valise."

"That's what I say," said Red Polikoff, nodding his head vigorously. "A busted valise."

"What would you do with him?"

"I don't think I'd worry about him," said Angel Amato.

"Nuts-and-bolts people, Matt." Red Polikoff shifted in his seat. "I wouldn't worry about him."

"You don't think so, huh?"

"I don't think so."

Matt Nathan sighed. He did worry. Despite his calm exterior he always worried. His mind was a complex of intricate circuits that transmitted a thousand worries. He had won out because he worried everything down to the smallest detail. "Red, find out more about this man. Please."

"Of course, Matt. Don't worry." He shook his head up and down; his jowls quivered pendulously. "Don't worry, Matt."

Matt Nathan rose from behind the desk and started for the door. "You can never tell with this kind of person, you know? He could be anybody."

"Don't worry, Matt. We'll find out what he is."

"I can count on you, Red. I know."

"You can count on me, Matt."

Matt Nathan smiled warmly and nodded his head. He left the office, followed by Angel Amato.

Red Polikoff went to his desk and removed a small blue bottle of digestive salts. He poured a teaspoonful of the salts into a paper cup and stirred in water from the office cooler. Red Polikoff, among other vague ailments, had a sensitive stomach.

Matt Nathan and Angel Amato took a private elevator to a suite on the top floor. It was Matt Nathan's personal suite.

There was a formal living room and dining room and a bedroom. The suite was decorated entirely in delicate shades of blue. The bedroom had a shag rug, circular bed, and two satin plush chairs. Matt Nathan took off his jacket and sat in a chair next to the bed.

Angel Amato fixed him a drink at a bar at one end of the room. The far wall was made of glass. The hotels along Paradise Road—the International and the Landmark—could be seen rising against the night sky. The lights of the Strip could be seen off to the south.

Matt Nathan stared out at the clear night and was assailed by an undefined feeling of dread. The desert night sometimes did that to him—the sense of distance and barrenness, the cold night stars: the world seemed to him a tomb. . . .

He turned away from the window. Angel Amato pulled the drapes shut across the glass wall. Then he snapped on the television set. "Fights should be coming on now," Angel Amato said.

"Get a girl up here," Matt Nathan said.

Angel Amato went to the phone next to the bed and called downstairs.

Matt Nathan lit up a cigar. The fights began. Two light-weights, a Negro and a Mexican. "Who do you like?" Matt Nathan asked.

"I'll take the black guy."

"Have we seen these guys?"

"The Mex is Reuben Sanchez."

"That's Reuben? He doesn't look so bad."

"He had some plastic surgery done. They done his ears and they done his nose."

"They did a good job."

The fighters on the television screen circled rapidly around each other. There was a soft knock at the door. Angel Amato opened it. A young blond girl entered the room.

She did not look like a hooker but rather like an attractive college coed. She had a fresh, open look on her face. She smiled perkily. "How are you?" Matt Nathan said pleasantly.

"Fine, Mr. Nathan."

"How's business?"

"It's been very good."

Matt Nathan put his arm around the girl. She snuggled next to him on the chair. "Are you happy?" he asked in a fatherly way.

She nodded her head yes. "How old are you?"

"Nineteen."

"Why did you become a whore?"

"I like money," the girl said, grinning.

"There's other ways of making money than becoming a whore."

She shrugged. "I like it 'cause it's easy."

"I'll get you a job here as a cocktail waitress. It's easy. You'll make good money."

"I like being a whore," the girl said.

"What about your mother and father?"

"What do you mean?"

"How would they feel if they knew what their daughter was doing?"

"They wouldn't like it I guess."

"All right." Matt Nathan led the girl to the bed. He began to undress her. When she attempted to assist him, he stopped her. He smiled gently. "Please," he said. "I like to do it."

When he was finished with her, he returned to the television set. "What round is it?" he asked Angel.

"Fifth."

"How's Reuben doing?"

"He looks good."

The girl was sitting on the bed, smiling. "You know something?" she said. "You're very nice, Mr. Nathan."

"Thank you."

Angel Amato now moved to the bed. He began to undress. He took off his shirt. He had a jagged scar across his midsection. The phone rang. Angel Amato answered it. "That guy Porter is in the casino," Angel said to Matt Nathan.

"We'll go down in a minute," Matt Nathan said. Angel

114

continued to undress. As he made love to the whore, Matt Nathan stood above them. The girl opened her eyes and winked at him. He smiled sadly.

He left Angel Amato and the whore in the room and took the elevator to the second level. He entered a large room where a staff of men worked around the clock watching the gaming tables through two-way mirrors.

Red Polikoff waved him over. Down below Porter was playing blackjack head-to-head with the dealer. "How's he doing?" Matt Nathan asked.

"He plays a good tight game. He knows what he's doing."

One of the staff brought a chair over to Matt Nathan. He lit up a fresh cigar and sat staring down at the table below. He was watching Porter, but he was thinking about the whore upstairs. As a youth he had had a natural gallantry toward women. He would never use a foul word in front of a woman. Then he grew up and discovered they were all whores. He sighed. That's the way it was. That was the way of the world.

Porter had no desire to gamble that evening and was playing indifferently. He had just wanted to get away from Kitty. Yolande Nathan had been on his mind, and he had come to the Paradise Hotel in the hope of meeting her.

Despite her assurances he knew the situation was dangerous: a card hustler involved with the wife of a man as powerful as Matt Nathan. She had told him her husband was a tough man; hadn't she spoken of bodies planted in the desert? Yet he felt no fear. It was something in her smile that caused him to grow very quiet and peaceful inside. . . .

"What do you want to do?" The dealer was standing above him, waiting for his decision on the hand.

He had lost the count. He hadn't even looked at his cards. He glanced down now and saw that he had a sixteen. He asked for another card and went over.

He knew that when you blew the count it was time to

walk away. Billy Ray Walker, Monty had stressed, would *never* stay in a game he didn't mentally control.

He continued to play and continued to lose. He somehow got into a discussion about which college the dealer's son should attend. "I want him to go to the Naval Academy or West Point. All they teach you in those other places is atheism and pot-smoking." Porter agreed with him, fighting to keep the count.

After a while Yolande appeared. She slid into a chair next to him.

"Hello," she said softly.

"Hello."

"How are you doing?"

"I was just getting ready to quit."

She looked unimaginably beautiful. She was dressed in a severely cut suit; she had on very little makeup. Her face was pale and her eyes watery. But her look was soft and tender, and it seemed to cut to his heart. "Play a little more," she said. "Play for me."

He pushed half his stack, five hundred dollars, out. It was the table limit. He won.

Suddenly the System caught fire. He covered three hands and bet the cards up and down according to the count. He made seven runs through the deck and won nearly fifteen thousand dollars. A crowd gathered and stood in awed silence behind him. Yolande sat next to him, smiling quietly, a little soft, sad smile. He would glance at her from time to time, and her eyes would widen at his gaze as if to swallow him up. She leaned close to him and murmured, "I love you. . . ."

"Do you?"

She nodded her head. He played awhile longer, winning more than he lost. When the count grew cold, a minus for the player, he decided to cash in. He stood up and stretched. "That's it for tonight," he said. He looked around at the crowd as the pit boss totaled up the black chips in his rack.

A man in the crowd caught his eye. He was standing directly behind Porter and, through very thick steel-rimmed glasses, fixed Porter with a pale, watery stare as though pleading with him. He was perhaps fifty years old, shabby and nondescript. He needed a shave and his brown, formless suit looked like he had slept in it. "Nice playing," the man said. His lower lip trembled. His voice was soft, a whisper, and it somehow chilled Porter. "You know how to play this game," the man said.

Porter attempted to pull away, but the man caught him by the arm. "I been running a bad streak, you know what I mean. . . ."

Yolande was moving away toward the casino exit. Porter shoved a twenty-five-dollar chip into the man's grubby hand. The man said nothing, just stared at Porter. Porter hurried away toward the exit.

The man pushed into Porter's seat. He placed the green chip in front of him and asked for change.

Angel Amato, standing next to Matt Nathan, stared down through the mirror at the table below. "Do you want me to follow them?" he asked.

Matt Nathan was weary. His eyes burned and his neck was sore from craning forward. He had been watching the table for better than an hour. "Let them go," he said.

Red Polikoff indicated the man who had taken Porter's seat. "Look who's here," he said.

"Get rid of him."

Red Polikoff lifted a phone and called down to the pit boss.

The man in the steel-rimmed spectacles had bet his first five-dollar chip and won when the pit boss moved around the table and whispered something in his ear. The man got up. His lips moved soundlessly. Mumbling to himself, he moved slowly away from the table.

Yolande Nathan wanted to take Porter home with her and make love to him on her own bed. "I don't think your husband would like that," Porter said.

She smiled and winked. "He wouldn't mind," she answered.

"Really?"

"Really."

They settled on a motel at the far end of the Strip. It was a run-down, eight-dollar-a-night spot, with a flickering neon sign in front and a chipped stucco façade. They passed a few stunted desert shrubs and a tiny, kidney-shaped swimming pool with peeling blue paint on the way to their room. A sign on the wire fence surrounding the pool read: SWIM AT YOUR OWN RISK.

The room was painted a watery green and had a sweetish smell of bug spray. The satin bedspread was stained in a dozen spots and the television did not work.

They made love, and it was very good for both of them. It was not wildly passionate lovemaking. It was simple and it was relaxed. Their bodies hugged together for a very long time, barely moving. It seemed as though they were pressing into one another, melding into the same person.

Yolande looked up at Porter, her eyes wide and puzzled. She shook her head and laughed softly. "What?" Porter asked.

"I don't understand it. . . ."

"What's that?"

"I never felt so *good* with anybody in my life."

Porter laughed. "How do you feel?" she asked. "I feel *damn* good," he said. They both laughed. He rolled off her and lay there staring up at the ceiling. "It's amazing . . ." she said.

She leaned her head on his chest and smoothed his shoulder with her hand. "Do you suppose we're brother and sister? Do you suppose we were separated when we were little and we're committing incest?" she asked.

118

"Where you from?"

"Tennessee. You?"

"Pennsylvania."

"It's still possible."

"What did your pappy look like?"

"He was fat."

"Mine was skinny."

"Maybe he's not your real pappy. Maybe he's just pretending."

Porter grew solemn. "No, that son of a bitch was my pappy, all right." His father had been a sheet-metal worker, a small, solemn man addicted to alcohol, a harsh man when he was drinking. From the time he was old enough to remember, his father had given him a regular, once-a-week beating.

Porter grew silent. He began to think of Kitty. He felt responsible for her, and he felt guilty. He had used her, and now, at least emotionally, he was throwing her away. "What do you want with me?" Porter asked.

"Why should I want anything?"

"Everybody wants something."

She smiled softly at him and shook her head. "I don't want anything from you. We just *connect*, you know?"

He nodded his head and smiled. "I know," he said.

"What are you after in this life?" she asked.

"I'm looking to take the casinos broke," Porter said.

She laughed. "If that's your main occupation, you don't have much of a future."

Porter studied the ceiling. It was covered with a network of small cracks. He had the sensation he was lying beneath a giant spider's web. "What future would you like me to have?"

She shook her head. "It's crazy," she said.

"What?"

"I'd like the two of us to be together."

"What about your husband?"

She sighed. "Yes," she said. "I know."

He began to drift off to sleep. She hugged him around the chest. She was saying to herself: "My darling, my darling, my sweet darling . . ."

"Don," she said aloud.

"Hm?"

"My husband wants to talk to your boxer friend."

The web above Porter seemed to close down on him. He was being buried in soft black strands. Now Kitty was standing before him. She was crying softly. Eddie MacRae lay dead at his feet. Porter was asleep.

Kitty had not felt this isolated since her days working in the diner for Pepik. Porter had grown away from her, and she couldn't tell why. Perhaps it was winning, the success of the System; perhaps he hadn't changed at all. Perhaps it was only in her mind.

She tossed around on the bed, alternately hot and chilled, her body soaked with cold perspiration. She was afraid. What if he deserted her? Where would she go? What would she do?

Tonight he had never seemed to her so much a stranger. It felt as though a cold, glass wall had been erected between them.

She got up from the bed. She was trembling. She put on Porter's new silk bathrobe. Even the odor of his body, which still permeated the robe, seemed alien to her tonight.

She opened the door to the motel room and stood on the balcony. Below was a small tropical garden and the swimming pool—all lit up and glowing a pale green. The air smelled sweet. The night was warm, but still she trembled.

In the distance she could see the neon of the Strip, exploding against a sky thick with stars. The sight made her queasy. Everything seemed so cold tonight, so empty.

It reminded her of when she had been a little girl and her stepfather had taken her to the country fair. They had become separated, and she had wandered around for hours amid strings of lights and strange crowds of people and a carousel with horses' heads that swung out of the night and scared her terribly. When she finally found her stepfather, he was in a ditch on the outer limit of the fair, covered with blood and puke, dead drunk. She had sat next to him on the ground trembling until morning, when her stepbrother showed up with the pickup to take them both home.

She turned from the balcony railing and approached the door to Eddie MacRae's room. She told herself she would knock once; if he did not awaken, she would return to her room.

She knocked lightly. After a short moment she heard Eddie's voice: "Who is it?" She was so happy she felt as though she would cry.

"Kitty," she said.

The door opened a crack. Eddie was standing in his shorts. "What time is it?" he asked. His face was clouded with sleep.

"I dunno. Late."

"Where's Don?"

"Gambling. Can I come in?"

"What's wrong?"

"I'm lonely is all. . . ."

He opened the door to her, and she entered his room. He switched on the light and sat in a chair. Kitty sat on the bed. They did not speak for a long moment.

She looked around the room. On the bureau was a gold statuette of a crouched boxer. There was a photograph of Eddie as a teen-ager posed in boxer's trunks and gloves. There was a Bible and a copy of a book, *Positive Thinking: Key To Success*.

"I'm sorry I woke you," Kitty said.

"That's all right. I was getting up early for some roadwork."

He picked his rubber hand exerciser off the bureau and began to squeeze it. Kitty was staring at him, and he was looking down at the floor. "Come over here, Eddie," she said.

He looked up, painfully confused. "Why?" he asked softly.

Kitty began to cry. She wanted to say something to him, but no words would come out. She wept bitterly.

He sat next to her on the bed and pulled her close to him. He stroked her hair. "What's wrong? What's wrong?" he asked over and over again.

She shook her head and bit her lip and fought to control herself. "Eddie, Eddie . . ." she said at last.

He hugged her to him. "What is it?"

"I feel like Don is just drifting away from me."

"He got the System on his mind. You know that. . . ."

She shook her head. "It's something else."

"What?"

"I don't know. . . ."

He continued to stroke her hair. She turned her face to him. They kissed.

He pulled quickly away. He got up from the bed, confused. "I can't," he said.

"Please. Just hold me."

He returned to the bed. She lay back and gathered him into her arms. After a while she opened the robe.

VII

They sat in silence in the coffee shop of the Desert Inn—Don Porter, Eddie MacRae, and Kitty—half-filled cups of cold coffee on the Formica table in front of them. Porter sucked morosely on the stub-end of a stogie; Eddie MacRae listlessly squeezed his hand exerciser. Kitty stared out the window.

It was midafternoon and the hotel patrons baked themselves beside the pool in the hundred-and-ten-degree heat. Beyond the pool the windows of the hotel, coated with a metallic veneer to reflect the sun, seemed to Kitty terrible and sinister in their blindness, as though each window concealed a spy, each room some awful secret.

She had grown to loathe Las Vegas. Everywhere it seemed people were engaged in spying, through peep-holes and two-way mirrors, across hotel lobbies and casino floors. It had become for her a city of eyes: security guards, floor managers, pit bosses, dealers. Cold, impassive, faintly accusatory.

It had been three days since she had been to Eddie Mac-Rae's room, and she still felt uneasy about it. It had been a disaster, her going there—painful, embarrassing. She had pulled him to her on the bed, and they clutched awkwardly at each other, and she had wanted him to make love to her for no other reason than to reassure her that someone *cared*, and he had tried and failed.

Afterward he had sat in a chair opposite the bed and rambled on about boxing. He seemed to be reliving certain ancient battles. Kitty lay on the bed, flushed with shame, watching him. It seemed to her that he was only vaguely aware that she was in the room. It was morning when she returned to her room.

The next day when they met, Eddie MacRae had difficulty looking Kitty in the eye. Neither one of them mentioned what had happened.

The sense of estrangement between her and Porter had increased. In the motel room he would stare at television for hours on end. She could feel his discomfort when he was with her. He was constantly yawning or rubbing his jaw or massaging his hands. He hardly spoke. At midnight he would put on his sport coat, smooth down his hair, and prepare to leave for the casinos. If she asked to come with him, he said he wanted to be alone. He was studying the casinos, he said. He was working out a big score.

She spent her time reading movie magazines or watching TV. She tried practicing four decks, but she had no heart for it now. She could hear, through the thin wall of the motel, Eddie MacRae in the next room shadowboxing or jumping rope.

She tried to explain to Porter how she felt. "Let's put it this way. We're not together no more. I mean, it's just like we're two strangers now, you know. . . ."

He stared at her uneasily, abstracted. "You got to believe in me. I'm just refining the details." The plan, the score, the big push. She didn't believe in it anymore, and she sensed that Porter didn't either. . . .

His commitment to the System had faltered since his involvement with Yolande Nathan. He spent every night with her now. Sometimes they would drive around for hours, not talking at all, the top of the car down, the radio playing softly, the cool desert air streaming over them. Other times, they would find a small bar that catered to Vegas regulars and sit in a darkened corner and hold hands and sip their drinks and babble on like a couple of kids on their first date.

She would talk about her childhood in Memphis, about how happy she had been as a teen-ager. She talked of things that had been only remotely part of his experience. She spoke about hayrides and football games and high school dances. She told him how she had been a beauty queen at seventeen; how she had then gone to New York to become a dancer.

She described her days as a Copa girl and a dancer at the Latin Quarter, how she came to Vegas with a girl friend and worked her way up to headliner at the Tropicana. She told him of her meeting with Matt Nathan. . . .

Angel Amato had not been with him in those days. His factotum had been a man named Kerry, a large Irishman who had also been a prize fighter. Every evening, after the last show, Kerry would appear at the dressing room door with a bouquet of roses for her. There would be a card inviting her to dinner with the owner of the Paradise Hotel; enclosed in the card's envelope would be a folded hundred-dollar bill.

She mailed the money back to the Paradise Hotel, and she never showed up for dinner. It was too easy to become a whore in Vegas; she had seen friends go that route, and she swore it would never happen to her.

She had a romantic idea about love. She never went to bed with a man unless she loved him, and those that she had loved had been rare: her high school sweetheart, an actor in New York, a Vegas dealer.

After the initial glamor of being a chorus girl had worn off, she wanted to get out of it; she wanted to get married, but the relationships she got into brought her just to the point of marriage before they went sour.

Every night for more than a week Kerry had visited her dressing room at the Tropicana. There was something thick, scarred, and ominous about him. He had very light hair and

125

no eyebrows. He frightened her. After a while she refused to see him and gave orders that the flowers not be accepted.

He stopped coming. She was not bothered for almost a month. Then one night, as she was crossing the parking lot to her car, a man stepped out of the shadows to talk to her. He was lean and delicately handsome. He was in his early forties. His manner was soft and hesitant, shy. It was Matt Nathan.

He apologized for having pestered her. He usually wasn't so foolish or insistent about women, but she had reached him in some deep way. He had seen her dancing at the Tropicana, had observed her around town. He had been obsessed with her since he first laid eyes on her.

He told her all this quickly, breathlessly in the parking lot of the Tropicana. It poured out of him in a soft, nervous voice. He begged her to have dinner with him.

They went out that night, to Foxy's, a delicatessen on the Strip. There, among late-night tourists, off-duty waitresses and bartenders, and bust-out gamblers with faces the color of gray ash, he had grown very quiet. She had never spent such an uncomfortable hour. He just sat there staring at her. She grew irritated and refused to manufacture conversation.

When he drove her back to her apartment, he still did not speak. It was as though their confrontation in the parking lot had completely emptied him of things to say.

He walked her to the door. As she was putting the key into the lock, he asked her to marry him. "I'm forty-two years old, I own the Paradise Hotel, I have never been married, and I want you to be my wife."

She was stunned. Her impulse was to laugh, but the expression on his face convinced her he was profoundly serious.

She saw him every evening after that. He was quiet and charming and very solicitous of her; she had never in her life been treated so well by a man. She did not love him, but his loneliness touched her. They went together for a month before they were married.

126

The marriage went well for a year. She quit her job at the Tropicana and moved into the large house off Rancho Road. She was happy.

Her relationship to Matt was like nothing she had ever imagined about marriage. They rarely went out, never entertained. They had no friends. His sexual demands on her were minimal. His whole life was tied up with the Paradise Hotel. She was aware of problems, internecine battles, but he never discussed them with her.

Gradually, painfully, she began to understand him. She realized his shyness and apparent loneliness was a screen: he was, in actuality, totally self-sufficient, wholly without fear. His charm and kindliness were a sham. He was at heart completely ruthless.

This realization was devastating. She was trapped. He would never let her go. . . .

After the first year and a half, she began to take lovers. She did this in the hope it would force Matt Nathan to turn her loose. He accepted her actions. He held onto her. Her life grew bitter; her youth began to wither. She had given up all hope of any salvation until she met Porter.

"What happened to Kerry?"

"It was after that first year of our marriage. He disappeared."

"Where?"

"I overheard some conversation. He was planted in the desert."

"Who did it?"

She did not answer for a long while. "I don't know."

Porter was torn by his involvement with Yolande and his commitment to the System. During the day, when he was away from her, he was obsessed by a sense of passing time, of opportunity trickling away. He formulated grandiose plans for one big hit.

But what to do when he made the score? Jettison Kitty and

Eddie MacRae? Run off with Yolande Nathan? Where would they go? What would they do?

The bankroll had increased to nearly twenty thousand dollars. It was a respectable amount. With twenty thousand dollars they could go head-to-head on the hundred-dollar table and stand the chance of walking away with a hundred, hundred and fifty thousand dollars. If it worked out the way he was plotting it . . .

"Never go into a big game unless you're *hungry!*" Monty used to tell him. The problem was he had lost his hunger. Yolande satisfied something in him that neither Kitty nor the System ever touched. He had made a connection with another human being.

Monty, poor, wracked Monty, futilely dreaming away the long prison days and nights with visions of Vegas and the System and Billy Ray Walker! "Billy Ray Walker'll tell you that. A man got to be *hungry*. A loser is a guy who don't have the hunger to win. . . ."

Porter drained the last bit of coffee in his cup. "In a week we're going to make the big push at Caesar's. . . ." He spoke softly, without looking at anybody, talking more to himself than to Kitty and Eddie. He had the plan now; he just needed to summon up the desire.

"I'm going into training," Eddie said.

"One night with the System, Eddie! After that you'll be able to buy the championship. . . ."

Eddie had made up his mind to see Matt Nathan. He had been pestering Porter about it all week. They had met today for that express purpose, but Porter was stalling. "Donny, you promised," Kitty said.

"Yeah, yeah."

"What do you mean, 'yeah, yeah'?"

"That's okay. We can make it some other time," Eddie said.

"Naw, that's all right."

As they moved out the front entrance to the Desert Inn,

the hot air came down on them like a blast of wind from a furnace. The steering wheel was so hot it burned when Porter put his hands on it. The hood of the car was aflame with the sun's reflection.

They drove down Desert Inn Road to Paradise, then turned into a winding drive. The Paradise Hotel rose before them, a palace of white marble in an oasis of palm and cactus, its serpentine sign strangling the alabaster façade of the hotel with coils of neon. They entered the hotel.

The bell captain escorted them down silent, carpeted corridors to Matt Nathan's office. Nathan was seated in a leather chair. A barber with a pencil-thin mustache and shiny bald head was trimming his hair, while his poodle, Princess, frolicked and nipped at his hand. Angel Amato in plum-colored shirt and avocado slacks, eyelids heavy with a certain brooding languor, sat leaning against the wall in one corner of the office.

Matt Nathan waved the barber away. His smile was dazzling. He smelled of an oppressively sweet after-shave. "You got here finally," he said to Eddie MacRae.

"I'm sorry it took so long."

"How are you?" Matt Nathan said to Kitty. His voice was quiet, his manner soft as velvet.

"I'm fine."

"You're looking very well." He stared at Kitty for a long moment, as though she were the most important person in the room. Then he shifted his focus back to Eddie MacRae. "This is what we give you: room and board at the hotel. A hundred dollars a week expense money. Two months from now you fight Julio Martinez at the Silver Slipper."

He opened a porcelain humidor on his desk-top and offered cigars to Porter and Eddie MacRae. Porter took one. "That's the real thing. Cuban," Matt Nathan said, lighting the cigar for him. "Eddie, believe me, you won't find anybody that'll look out for you the way I do. Isn't that right, Angel?" Angel Amato nodded. "Come on. I'll show you the training

129

set-up," Matt Nathan said. He hugged Eddie around the shoulders and led him toward the door. He smiled at Kitty and Porter, and his smile, radiating warmth, promised them they hadn't a better friend in the world.

Matt Nathan lifted Princess and carried her in his arms. They boarded an elevator and got off on the mezzanine level. He toyed with the dog's ears. "You're not really a dog, are you? You're a human being. You understand every word we're saying, don't you, you little devil?" He winked at Kitty, who laughed. They went through a door marked "HEALTH CLUB AND GYMNASIUM."

The area was divided into two sections: an exercise and calisthenics room for the hotel guests; and a training room for Matt Nathan's boxers. The training room was on the level below the mezzanine. It had a heavy bag, a speed bag, and a full-size ring. Casino patrons could stand on the mezzanine and watch the fighters working out. The mezzanine was lined with slot machines.

The place was like no gym Eddie MacRae had ever seen: it was done in stainless steel and plastic; there was a blue shag rug and piped-in music; an elaborate exhaust system eliminated all the familiar gym odors—perspiration, alcohol, liniments. The white canvas of the ring was immaculate.

The Black Avenger, Joe Fletcher, perspiration pouring from the sleek ebony of his body, was sparring with a large, flat-footed Indian. The Black Avenger moved lightly, gliding in wide arcs about the ring, flicking out delicate, pea-shooting jabs, while the exhausted Indian, heavy flesh painfully aquiver, plodded after him. "He's a good boy, Joe Fletcher," Matt Nathan said. "A gentleman. That's the way I like my fighters. I don't like a rowdy. You're not a rowdy are you, Eddie?"

"No, sir."

"I didn't think so."

Angel Amato was leaning on the railing, watching the action below. "He's getting those jabs in today," he said, without looking up.

"He got a nice jab. And he got a powerful right. What's more, you'll never see him abuse a woman or tell an off-color story. That's the kind of human being he is. What do you think, Eddie?"

Eddie wasn't sure what he was supposed to answer. "He's a pretty fighter," he said.

"Yes, he is, Eddie. Yes, he is." Matt Nathan led them along the mezzanine to a flight of stairs at the end. "Come on. We'll meet Frank Murphy."

They moved down the stairs to the gym floor below. The fighters had broken off sparring. The Black Avenger was leaning through the ropes talking to a tall, broad-shouldered, gray-haired man. Matt Nathan called the man over. "Frank, I want you to meet Eddie MacRae. He's going to be boxing for us."

Frank Murphy moved to them, nodding his head and grinning. He had a ready, pleasant smile; his broken nose, rather than marring his good looks, gave his face a certain patrician strength. "I remember Eddie," Frank Murphy said. "Fought preliminary at the Silver Slipper. I said to myself at that time, 'That boy looks real good.'"

"Yes, he did look good," Matt Nathan said.

"'If he has good morals, he could be a good fighter,' I remember saying."

"I think you'll find his morals are of the highest," Matt Nathan said. "Frank here does a lot of work with the Boys' Club and the church. Used to be a top-flight heavyweight."

"I was known as the Nevada Tornado," Frank Murphy said with a grin. "I was knocked out by Gus Lesnivich, Maxie Baer, and Billy Conn."

"He was knocked out by some of the best," Matt Nathan said. Angel Amato laughed softly.

"At one time I was rated by Nat Fleisher number six in the world."

131

"Now, Frank, I want you to do a good job with Eddie. I want him to go against Julio Martinez in two months. What do you think he needs?"

"I'd like to work on him on defense, Mr. Nathan."

"You're not going to neglect offense, are you?"

"No, sir. But defense is very important."

"Yes," Matt Nathan said, "defense is very important."

"Particularly with a heavyweight. Even a bum, if he hits you, can do damage."

"Anything else?"

"Legs. I want to put some power and endurance in those legs."

"Fine. I'll leave it up to you, Frank. I'm sure you'll do an excellent job."

Matt Nathan led the group over to ringside. "How are you, Joseph?"

"Fine, Mr. Nathan," the Black Avenger said.

"Keeping your nose clean?"

"That's the only way to go, Mr. Nathan."

"Say hello to Eddie MacRae."

The two fighters nodded at each other. "I know Eddie," the Black Avenger said.

"Give him some pointers, would you, Joe? He's going to be fighting with us."

"I certainly will, Mr. Nathan."

"You see that, Eddie? We're all going to take care of you."

"Thank you," Eddie MacRae said.

They left the gym and headed back through the casino. Matt Nathan instructed Angel to take Kitty and Eddie Mac-Rae to dinner in the Gourmet Room. "There's something I want to discuss with Don," he said. "You don't mind, do you?"

"No."

"I have an apartment in the penthouse. We'll talk there."

They took the private elevator upstairs. Inside the suite

132

Matt Nathan turned Princess loose. "Just don't piss on the rug," he admonished the dog.

He seated himself on the couch. Porter sat on a blue velvet chair. "I'd like to know a little bit about you, Don, if you don't mind."

"What do you want to know?"

"What's the girl to you, if I'm not being too personal? I mean is she your wife or a shack-up or what?"

"She's my girl friend."

"She live with you?"

"Yes."

"Don't get me wrong. I have no moral objections to it."

Porter said nothing. He studied Matt Nathan. Every hair on his head was perfectly in place; his nails were cleanly manicured. There was a heaviness, a sadness to him. His eyes darted nervously about the room; he had difficulty looking directly at Porter. He smiled a lot. "How did you meet Eddie?"

"Just ran into him by accident. We hit it off, the three of us."

"I like your girl friend. A country girl, if I'm not mistaken."

"She's from a small town."

"What kind of work do you do?"

Porter shrugged. "I get along."

"Gamble?"

"Some."

"How's it going?"

"Not bad."

Matt Nathan grew quiet. Princess leapt up onto his lap, and he stroked the dog absently while staring down at the rug. "My mother was a wonderful woman, Don," he said after a while. "I lost her when I was young, but she taught me the best lessons there are to learn in this life. She brought us up to believe in the Almighty, to do an honest day's work for an honest day's pay, to respect our elders. We had it tough in the old days. Well, I don't have to tell you. You look to me like a man who wasn't born with a silver spoon."

Porter said nothing.

"Where were you raised, if I'm not being too personal?"

"Pittsburgh."

"Pittsburgh? A good, raw town. We speak the same language, then, Don. We both got where we are by a clean, hard fight."

"Where we got was sure different places," Porter said.

"It's a matter of opinion. Material things don't bring you peace, believe me." Matt Nathan sighed. He continued to stroke Princess's ears. "I like you, Don, believe me," he said after a while. "And I hope you like me, too." Porter did not answer. "I didn't always live up to my mother's high standards, and I've suffered for it. It's not that we want to do the wrong thing. On the contrary we want to do the right thing, but the complexities of our lives create phantoms to deceive us." He grew silent again. The room was heavy with silence. Porter leaned forward and took a handful of peanuts from a silver dish on the cocktail table. He began to pop the peanuts into his mouth. "I had a kid brother. You remind me of him," Matt Nathan said.

"Yeah?"

"He was blond like you. Thin. A terrific athlete. Boxing. Baseball."

"Where is he now?"

"He died very young." There was a long pause, while Matt Nathan stroked Princess's ears. "Some people didn't like me, so they took it out on him. Can you imagine that? Can you imagine the terrible viciousness of people? He was a kid. . . ."

Matt Nathan was staring at Don now with wide, sad eyes. His face, despite the tan, appeared gray and slack with fatigue. "I love my wife very much, Don. I'm not here to preach or anything. What she does is her own business. That's our relationship. You may not realize it. I just want you to know. She's a fine woman."

134

"Yes, she is."

"I don't know what you know about me. I don't want you to judge her by me."

Porter had a strange sense that Matt Nathan was toying with him. There was something elusive in the conversation, something unsaid that snaked around in it, something that Porter could not grab hold of.

Matt Nathan stood up. "Let me introduce you to someone. A girl. You don't object to that, do you?"

"I have a girl downstairs."

"Please. It would give me a great deal of pleasure." He walked to the phone and made a call. Then he returned to Porter and shook his hand. His handshake had no firmness to it. It seemed to melt in Porter's grip.

"We got a relationship here, Don. Let's keep it on the level of mutual respect. How does that sit with you, Don?"

"That sits good with me."

"Fine. Believe me, Don, what I said before. I really like you."

Then he was gone. Porter rose and walked to the window. He stared down at Paradise Road below. It was early evening and the road was bathed in a soft, pinkish light, the unreal, dying flicker of day. Porter felt strangely calm. There was a flaccidness about Matt Nathan that was reassuring. He was burnt out, weak, he would not fight. That was Porter's emotional assessment; intellectually he knew better. But fear works through the gut, not the head. . . .

There was a light knock at the door, and Porter opened it. A bellhop was standing there with a short, dark-haired girl in her early twenties. She had a round, doll's face, very white skin, and large black eyes. She stood there smiling, a wide, very open, sweet smile. The bellhop moved off, and the girl entered the room. "I'm Adele," she said.

"I'm Don."

"Hi, Don." She strolled through the living room into the bedroom. She sat down on the edge of the bed. Porter sat in a chair opposite her. "You from out of town, Don?" she asked

135

pleasantly. She was a good actress playing a part she had played many times before.

Porter nodded. "What line of work are you in, Don?" Her eyes were wide with feigned interest.

"I'm an executive. Computers."

"Is that line of work interesting?"

"Is your line of work interesting?"

"I like it. You get to meet a lot of different people. Beats being a secretary, which is what I was."

"How's business?"

"Lately, not so hot. Too much competition from out of town whores." She kicked off her shoes and made herself comfortable on the bed. "They take a bus up for the weekend, rip guys off, then jet-plane back. They never seen this much money, and when they see it, they just got to take it, without giving proper service." She looked at him and smiled. She was wearing a dress of wide, white net. Porter could see flesh and the white of her bikini panties through the net. "A couple of weeks ago this black whore come up from Los Angeles, picks up a trick who had just won $5,600, and she hits him on the head with a whiskey bottle and kills him. Now, that's just plain tacky."

"What happened to her?"

"They took her out in the desert and buried her."

"Who?"

She shrugged. "Look, this is a no-nonsense town, and the people who run it have no sense of humor. When you're dealing with cash money, it's no joke, you know. That's why they all have very serious looks on their faces."

"Yeah."

"Take for instance your cocktail waitresses. You got your cocktail waitresses hustling on the side."

"It's all money."

"Definitely. And you got your bell captains. The bell captains cut themselves in for 40 percent. And your security guards—"

136

"Security guards?"

"They want to pimp you."

"Is that a fact?"

"No kidding. Then you got your vice squad. No one can touch them. They take you to a hotel room. They give you money. You strip down, they screw you, then they pull a badge and gun from under the mattress. Then they take your picture naked. It's very degrading."

"It's a hooker's life."

"I don't consider myself a hooker," Adele said, offended. "I'm a call girl. A call girl's got more class than a hooker and more finesse and a lot more smarts." Porter laughed. "I'm not bullshitting," she said, annoyed now, but masking it. She glanced at her watch, then began to undress. "Nothing moving but the clock," she said with a laugh.

"Leave your clothes on."

"Why?"

"I just want to look at you."

"You're too much. A little freaky, right?"

Porter said nothing.

She smiled. "You're too much, is what you are."

He just stared at her. He stared at her for a very long time. He was thinking about Caesar's Palace, about the big hit, about what he would do afterward. He might take Yolande Nathan away from her husband. It was worth thinking about.

They were just beginning dessert when Porter joined them. Matt Nathan was there, sipping a brandy. Angel Amato sat to one side, looking bored. Eddie MacRae seemed uncomfortable. Kitty was slightly drunk and enjoying herself. "Donny, we had the most fabulous meal! Fabulous! I had this duck dish and some little snails and you'd think they'd be icky, but they weren't, they were ever so good! Then I had a salad, and the waiter explained the lettuce was shipped in special from Connecticut—"

"Eddie had the filet mignon," said Matt Nathan. "Did

you ever have a filet mignon taste like that? Like butter, right?"

"It was a good steak," Eddie admitted.

Porter declined dinner and ordered a brandy. Matt Nathan raised his glass in a toast. "Here's to you, Don. And Eddie. And Kitty. Welcome to Paradise Road!" They all drank to that, except Angel Amato who sat there with his arms folded across his chest, looking infinitely bored.

After the toast Matt Nathan rose. "Move Eddie in tonight," he said. "Carlos at the front desk will take care of him."

At the top of the stairs leading from the restaurant, Matt Nathan paused to stare back at the table. His heavy-lidded gaze held on them. All humor was gone from his face. He stood for a short moment, the poodle cradled in his arms, peering down on them. There was something somber and chilling, dead, in his look. Then he moved quickly off, followed by the knife-blade form of Angel Amato.

Outside it had begun to rain. A desert storm was brewing. The rain fell in large, widely spaced drops, spattering the dust on the windshield and hood of the car. Porter put up the top on the convertible. Off in the distance flashes of lightning illuminated the hard, black edges of the mountains, flickered momentarily, then died out, followed by a low rumble of faraway thunder.

Eddie MacRae was tense. He did not speak. His blue eyes reflected fear. During the drive back to the motel he continued to squeeze his hand exerciser with an intensity that approached fury. His chin jerked forward in a ferocious twitch.

"That's some set-up there at the Paradise Hotel," Kitty said. "You can't help but realize all your ambitions."

Eddie MacRae remained silent. They pulled into the drive of the Excelsior Motel and got out of the car. A strong wind was blowing now, whipping through the mesquite and yucca surrounding the motel, carrying a fine dust along with it. The three hurried upstairs, their heads down against the wind, eyes squinted against the dust.

Eddie MacRae began to pack, and Kitty joined him in the room. Don went downstairs to the office to check Eddie out.

"I'm going to miss you all," Eddie said, as he stuffed his sweat suit and boxing shoes into a large, cracked leather bag.

"We're only around the corner," Kitty said.

"I don't like that place."

"Mr. Nathan seems very friendly-like. Everyone seems friendly."

"I guess so," Eddie MacRae said. "I'm sorry about that other night," he added quietly.

"You have nothing to be sorry for. It was my fault."

"No, it weren't. I had no business laying a finger on you."

"Eddie—"

His face was pale and tense. The knuckles on his large hands went white as he forced the lock shut on his equipment bag. His eyes contained a look of terrible pain and confusion, and Kitty grew quiet.

Porter returned, and they walked back down to the car. The wind and rain had increased. Great sheets of water whipped across the roadway. Desert debris, tumbleweed and dead cactus, rolled and hopped across the rocky open spaces between the hotels along Paradise Road.

The lights in the parking lot were out at the Paradise Hotel—a power line had been blown down by the wind—and the black forms of the parking valets in rain slickers shimmered behind a screen of water, caught in the beam of Porter's headlights as they hurried along the lanes of cars. He drove through the lot to the canopy at the hotel's entrance, where he gave the Eldorado over to one of the valets.

They checked Eddie MacRae in at the hotel desk, then walked with him down to his room.

They sat in his room for a long time. Eddie MacRae, tense and frightened in the vinyl impersonality of his new surroundings, didn't want them to leave. They talked about the System and Eddie's new life. The talk was rambling and forced. After about an hour Porter got up. "You'll be wanting to get to sleep—"

"No, that's all right—"

"Don't worry about nothing, Eddie. If you get lonely, you just call us," Kitty said.

"I'll be okay," he said, not really meaning it.

"Next week we make our big move," Don said. "Don't forget."

"You can count on me."

"Good luck, Eddie," Kitty said.

"Thanks," he said. He walked them to the door. He looked excruciatingly forlorn as he let them out.

During the ride back to the motel Kitty was upset. "I feel so sorry for him," she said.

"Why? He got a beautiful set-up there."

"He just seems so helpless-like—"

"Don't you worry about Eddie MacRae. He got dynamite in his fists. Don't nobody have to worry about Eddie Mac-Rae."

Porter was depressed. Eddie's mood had somehow infected him. He felt as though his life was void of all purpose, as though he were drifting. The pouring rain seemed to be washing all meaning away; he seemed to be drowning in his own aimlessness. Yolande Nathan's smile festered in his brain. The System was foundering. . . .

He made love to Kitty that night for the first time in a long time while a steady rain drummed on the roof of the motel. "Would you marry me?" Kitty asked in the dark. Porter did not answer.

Eddie MacRae couldn't sleep. He tossed on the bed, bathed in perspiration.

He felt somehow totally deserted. For years this had been a battle with him. Whenever he had traveled to a strange town to fight, that first night alone in his room had been hell.

He remembered as a kid being shipped off to a boys' camp for underprivileged kids. He was suffering the tail end of whooping cough. His parents had managed to get him past the physical examination, but once at the camp he began throwing up everywhere—in the dining hall, in the bunk, on the ball field. He tried to conceal it, but the counselors found him out and took him to the camp infirmary. His father had made him promise not to tell that he had been sick. The nurse kept him in the infirmary overnight, and he lay there in terror, isolated from the other children in the camp. The branches of a tree outside the infirmary window cast a shadow of monster fingers on the white wall opposite his bed, and he had whimpered softly all through the night and begged to be sent home when the nurse visited him the next morning. They shipped him home, and his father had been angry and screamed at him and accused him of being a coward.

He got up now out of his bed at the Paradise Hotel and stood in his shorts in front of the bureau mirror. He began to shadowbox. This had been his prescription against fear for a long time now. His whole boxing career, he dimly realized, had been one long fight against the terrors of the night.

He threw short, chopping punches, worked combinations, kept up a steady, driving pace against his own reflection. He drove himself until he was bathed in perspiration and his breath came in burning gasps; then he climbed into the shower and turned the water full on.

It was after two A.M. when he climbed back into bed. He fell into an uneasy sleep. He dreamed a rat was gnawing at his head. He was punching out at a shadowy opponent, and the rat had sunk its claws into the top of his head; its teeth were cutting into his head. A bell rang. He awoke in terror. Frank Murphy was on the phone.

"See you in the lobby in a half hour. We're gonna take you boys for a little run."

Joe Fletcher was there, and two other fighters, the large

141

Indian, who had been sparring with the Black Avenger the day before, and a lean, sandy-haired kid. The Indian was called Sam and the kid, Wendell Glory. Wendell Glory brimmed with energy. He kept a wad of gum in his mouth, and when he wasn't talking, he was chewing. He moved his weight from foot to foot, feinting at imaginary opponents with his shoulders, bobbing his head constantly, humming off-key to a melody of his own invention. Eddie was surprised to discover that although he looked to be no more than eighteen years old, he already had had thirty professional fights.

The sun was just coming up over the pink rims of the mountains as they drove out to the desert beyond Nellis Air Force base. It shone a huge, hard-edged blood-red, spilling shades of orange and salmon dawn light over the rocky foothills. The desert itself was still dark, a cold gray black that spread like a huge buzzard wing beneath the mountains.

Wendell Glory kept up a nonstop, staccato monologue. "Uh huh, I fought this guy over in Inglewood ten rounds, you know, and caught him a left hook, bam!, to the ear, uh huh, and the damn thing, pow!, just blew up like a balloon! Goddamn, hmmm, to this day he won't talk to me 'cause of that piece of cauliflower he's walking around with. . . . Hey, Sam, speaking of cauliflower, you beginning to get you a little salad up side your head. Uh huh, yessir, if it's a lie I told it. . . ."

The big Indian, black eyes shining morosely beneath tufted clumps of scar tissue, cast a sour glance in Wendell's direction, then shifted his gaze back to the barren landscape. They were driving by a cluster of low, cinder block houses. Set in the gray expanse of desert rock, the houses appeared sad and forlorn, abandoned, and the occasional sight of a dim lamp burning behind a crumpled window shade was a cause of minor wonderment to Eddie MacRae. He had seen similar houses all his life, and yet it constantly amazed him that people would choose such a harsh, isolated existence.

Eddie MacRae was trapped beside Wendell Glory in the

142

back seat of the car. The kid rambled on, and Eddie listened, dazed, having no idea whom or what he was talking about. The other people in the car, having suffered his stories for months without let-up, had withdrawn into themselves and stared wearily out the car window. "He's the same guy, goddamn, beat Emilio that time up in Oakland, hmmm, you remember Emilio, Sam, that Filipino guy?" Sam grunted, and Wendell continued right on. "Anyhow, ah, they wanted to rematch me with him out in Santa Monica. I told Mr. Nathan I didn't want no part of that fight, no sirree, 'cause sure as hell he was plotting something slick for me. But Mr. Nathan, he says—ah—that it would be a good move for my —ah—career. Hmmm, da, da, dee—"

They were now some miles out in the desert. Frank Murphy pulled the car to a stop, and the fighters climbed out. Wendell was still chattering on, though by this time even Eddie MacRae had stopped listening. "I was at the Union Plaza last night, just dripping around, you know, playing a little twenty-one. Peyton Plaza they ought to call that place with all them little chippy dealers. This one chick dealer, you know, she kept tipping it to me, when to hit and stick and the like—you know she give me a signal, like she *raises* an *eyebrow* and like that. I was on my way to Paradise Road, man, winning me a bundle, when the damn floor manager comes over and says for me to *split*. He spotted out the situation right away that that little chippy had eyes for me. Damn! You know a situation like that is money in the bank—"

The morning was cool and the air sweet. They began to run back toward town, while Frank Murphy followed them in the car.

Eddie MacRae felt fine. The fear that seized him in the night seemed dim and unreal. He felt close now to the other boxers, a member of their particular gladiatorial brotherhood. It was one of the things that had drawn him to the sport— this sense of belonging. In the ring the boxer is a man alone. But the training sessions, the hours in the gym, the locker-room horseplay, the hanging around on street corners and in diners—these were the times that a man belonged. A bond between men, professionals at their craft, was formed. It was a bond that Eddie MacRae had only occasionally and feebly known, and still it warmed him.

He ran easily, filling his lungs with the clean, dry desert air. The rush of blood quickening through his system caused his whole body to glow. He felt so damn good he wanted to scream up to the sky!

Joe Fletcher ran by his side, while Wendell and Sam followed behind. Wendell, even as he ran, kept up a steady stream of chatter: "Ah—I didn't want to hurt the man, Sam, you know, hmmm? I knew he was a family man. You'd do the same thing, right? Right? But still—ah—you want to win—"

"Let's get out of the bullshit, man, before we get buried in it," the Black Avenger said, quickening his pace. The two of them raced for a while until Wendell's voice was lost in the wind.

"He can fight almost as good as he can talk," Joe Fletcher said after a while.

"No kidding?"

"He's hot stuff, believe it! Could really make something of hisself only he's so damn goofy and centered on hisself. Sometime they schedule him with a bout, he don't even show up."

"Wow!"

"That's right! Happened in San Francisco last year, he just never showed up! Come by with some ding-bat story about how some old broad kept his ass prisoner in a hotel room, or some shit like that. Man, he got more bullshit than a horse got flies."

They ran on for a while in silence, the two of them hitting the same rhythm, moving together in easy, loping strides. "How's it feel to be rated?" Eddie asked at last.

"Don't feel like a damn thing. That's just some man put

144

something down on a piece of paper, and all peoples believe it, and it ain't nothing but a lot of chickenshit."

"I want to be rated some day."

"And you will be! You'll be rated. You listen to Frank, and let Mr. Nathan bring you along, and you'll be rated fine. You'll be a ten or a nine or an eight some day, and you'll wake up and you'll say, 'Damn, I feel just like I did when I didn't have no rating.' You'll see what I mean."

"I want to win a championship some day." Eddie MacRae said this softly and with difficulty. It was an ambition that seemed so foolish it embarrassed him.

"Champion? Now that's another thing—"

"You ever think about it?"

"Sure, I *think* about it. I think about a lot of things. I think about going to the moon, but it don't mean I'm ever going to get there."

"Don't you have that confidence about yourself? You know, that feeling you're something special?"

"Eddie, let me tell you something: champion is just like that rating. It's something man-made. It don't come from God. Man got to give it to you—"

"You gotta win it—"

"That's a crock o' duckshit. The right guy got to put you in the right place at the right time, and you got to have the right look and the right line of lip, and you got to be good, but you can't be *too* good or no fool's going to fight you. And you got to have the right connections, and all like that. And by the time you get your break, all the world knows you're a wasted dude, man, washed up, done and gone—"

Eddie MacRae had to pause for a moment at the side of the road and get his breath back. He had a stitch in his side and his lungs burned like fire. The Black Avenger danced around him, laughing. "You wasted now, Eddie! You done and gone now!" he called out.

Wendell Glory and Indian Sam caught up and jogged past them. Indian Sam was huffing like a wounded bull;

145

Wendell Glory was scarcely winded. He jumped up and down and shouted back at them: "Hey, old women, I'll whip both your asses, let's get to that gym, I want to whip ass royal!"

"You can lick my ass, that's what you can do," Joe Fletcher said softly, and he and Eddie started up once more. "Onliest way he's going to get to my ass is by using his tongue, which I admit he got plenty of," the Black Avenger added with a sly wink at Eddie MacRae.

They ran five miles at a good, brisk pace, then Frank Murphy drove them back to the hotel. They did some light calisthenics in the gym and afterward showered. Wendell began to snap at Joe Fletcher with his towel, and Joe went after him and they sparred around open-hand. "C'mon Black Avenger, let's see if you can get you some Glory!" Wendell shouted, cupping his hand over his crotch. Joe Fletcher laughed so hard he sank down on the floor. "Man, Wendell, you *crazy!*" he said. "Get me some Glory! Goddamn, that hunk of sausage you got there, that ain't no glory, that's a *disgrace!*"

"You never saw me use it, man, you never saw me use it."

"And I ain't never going to neither."

"Hey, what's the bravest kind of person in the world?" Wendell Glory called out.

"Anyone listen to your bullshit," the Black Avenger said.

"No, man. A faggot. He takes six inches of dong up the keister, man, and that's *brave!*"

"Damn, Wendell, you too much!" Joe Fletcher said, tears of laughter forming in his eyes.

Indian Sam grinned at Eddie through a wide, toothless mouth. "They're going to lock ol' Wendell away one of these days and throw away the key. I seen punchies, you know, but that's the first kid I seen punchy."

"Hey, Chief, if I was you, I wouldn't say nothing about punchies."

"Yeah?"

"You and Eddie there. I see you both catching a few invisible flies with your chin."

Eddie MacRae forced himself to smile, although inside he felt a sense of profound shame.

Afterward they had a huge breakfast in the hotel coffee shop. Frank Murphy told them they could have off until one o'clock. Wendell Glory tried to set up a date with the waitress, who was on the far side of fifty. "I'm old enough to be your mother," the waitress said.

"That's all right. I always wanted to do a little ring-a-ding-ding with my mammy."

The waitress, offended, flounced off. "Damn, Wendell," said Joe Fletcher. "You're just like a cabbage—all ass and no brain."

"Old enough to be my mother! She's old enough to be my *grandmother!*"

The Black Avenger grinned and winked at Eddie MacRae, and Eddie felt terrific.

He returned to his room after breakfast and lay down for a nap. His belly was full and his body tingled with the morning's exertion. He felt warm inside and relaxed. He had found a place for himself. He slept soundly and well.

In the afternoon he spent some time on the heavy bag, then the speed bag; after that Frank Murphy put him in the ring with Indian Sam. Sam, though a plodder and easy to hit, packed a punch. Weighing in well over two hundred and fifty pounds, he was hard to move and carried a lot of power behind his fists. Eddie, even with his size, knew he was up against something.

Murphy kept drilling him on defense. "Stick and run, stick and run," he would call out over and over again.

During a break Murphy said: "Eddie, I seen you fight, and I know you got terrific potential. You're a big guy, and you got quick hands, and you hit hard. But you got to learn to *protect* yourself. It's not enough just to *hit*, you got to avoid *being hit* yourself. You're going to be in with a tough boy in Julio Martinez. No six-round prelim fighter. You got to protect yourself, or you'll end up hearing bells twenty-four hours a day."

They sparred an easy four rounds. Eddie chopped in a couple of solid blows, but with the twelve-ounce gloves and head-guard they had very little effect. Indian Sam also got in some good ones. One, an overhand left, caught Eddie across the bridge of the nose, and he saw black for an instant, then a spray of red butterflies dancing in front of his eyes.

In the fifth round Frank Murphy gave Eddie the go-ahead to open up. "Move in on him, Eddie! Move in! Push him forward! Push him forward!" He shouted from the edge of the ring, pounding the canvas with the flat of his hand.

Eddie continued to back-pedal as he had done in the previous four rounds. Indian Sam lumbered after him, throwing an occasional lurching punch, which Eddie would catch on his forearm or shoulder.

Midway through the round Indian Sam threw an awkward haymaker. He went off balance and stumbled past Eddie. Eddie suddenly lashed out with a blizzard of punches. A terrific, electric energy surged through his body; the shock of his fists connecting with the bulk of the other man thrilled him; it shivered down his arms to the pit of his stomach.

And now an incredible fury took possession of him. He banged punch after punch into the helpless Indian. He lost all sense of the ring, of the man he was sparring with. Nothing existed except a terrible desire to devastate, to tear apart, to wreck.

Indian Sam backed up against the ropes and looked helplessly about him; his eyes were glazed and blood poured from his nose. Eddie continued ripping punches into him, batting his head from side to side with loud, sickening thuds that resounded through the training room. Frank Murphy was up on the apron of the ring screaming: "That's enough, Eddie! Leave him alone! Eddie!"

Joe Fletcher and Wendell Glory leaped through the ropes

and grabbed Eddie around the waist. They wrestled him across the ring. His eyes were bright and empty. He didn't recognize the two men holding him back in one corner of the ring.

Frank Murphy rushed forward, his face flushed with anger. Indian Sam was on his knees. Blood was dripping from his mouth and nose. "Are you crazy, Eddie? What the hell's the matter with you? Are you crazy?" he screamed.

Eddie MacRae stared straight ahead, dazed. He wasn't quite sure what had happened. He had just suddenly grown very wild and light inside. He looked helplessly around the training room, expecting someone to explain. . . .

On the mezzanine Matt Nathan gazed down on the ring.

VIII

Wayne Newton was at the Sands, Debbie at the Desert Inn, Andy Williams at Caesar's Palace. Elvis was due to open at the International. None of this was of any interest to Don Porter. He was weighing possibilities: how to make the push on a casino.

Dressed in a light blue sport jacket, white trousers, Stetson hat, and Tony Lama cowboy boots, he sat in the cocktail lounge area at Caesar's. He had on sunglasses and smoked a Marsh Wheeling stogie.

It was showtime and the casino was relatively empty. Most of the action at this hour centered around the baccarat table where a group of wealthy South Americans was busy tossing away a portion of the financial reserves of their various countries. The players—the men, fat and sleek with trim mustaches and diamond tiepins, their wives and girl friends dripping jewels, hefty, tanned, heavy bosomed—were irrepressibly gay. The table overflowed with shrieks of joy, groans of disappointment, giggly consultations, Spanish imprecations, whooping, hugging, familial kissing.

Porter, sipping a Bloody Mary and puffing slowly on his stogie, studied them sourly while Joe South's ever-present voice sang out on the loudspeaker: "Oh, the games people play now, every night and every day now, never meaning what they say now, never saying what they mean. . . ," occasionally interrupted by the nasal whine of the page girl: "Princess Fatima . . . Princess Fatima . . . Princess Fatima . . ."

Porter had come here to work out the final details of the big push. The plan itself was fairly simple: he would go head-to-head with the dealer on the hundred-dollar table, betting table limit. When the deck flamed hot with a heavy count for the player, Eddie MacRae and Kitty would enter the game on a signal from Porter and pick up the betting lead from him. They would cover all the hands at the table and hit it fast and hard.

He was here now to check out eventualities, appraise the dealers, spot the shills and casino detectives, size up the floor managers and pit bosses.

He had spent the evening strolling through the casino, studying the center table where the single-deck, hundred-dollar-a-hand-minimum game was played. He tried a few runs through the deck on the table and purposely lost. Then he switched to the four-deck shoe, twenty-five-dollar minimum. Gradually he was beginning to pick up on the four-deck game. But it would take time.

The casino was slowly beginning to fill up again. Three middle-aged racket boys, seated on a level below Porter, held a conference with a rat-faced bellman. One of the racket boys, with slicked-down hair, dyed black, swarthy, wart-studded complexion, cashmere sweater, silk sport shirt, alligator shoes, and diamond pinky ring, flashed a thick roll of money. Several bills were pressed into the hand of the bellman. Five minutes later he returned to the table with three stunningly endowed girls. One of the girls looked over at Porter and smiled. It was Adele, the girl Matt Nathan had procured for him several days earlier.

The show broke and suddenly the casino was flooded with people. They strolled the swath of red carpet that rimmed the gambling area. Porter watched them, musing on their diversity.

Each casino attracted its own crowd: businessmen with well-tailored wives in one, flashy, high-roller wheeler-dealers in another, country-style folk in yet another. Only Caesar's Palace seemed to drag them all in—the hicks, the hustlers, the squares, the cheats, the pros, the weirdos. They rotated through the casino, ambled along its perimeter: Cardin jackets and Dior gowns, Robert Hall wash-and-wear and Sweet-Orr overalls, dashikis and saris—tanned real-estate developers and platinum bleached hookers, pasty-faced accountants and weather-beaten cowhands, African princes and Indian begums.

They searched, gawked, flirted, conned along the promenade, calculating losses, scheming angles, parading their desires, rotating slowly toward the center, toward the gaming tables, irresistibly swept in by the churning maelstrom of chance.

Porter heard his name announced over the loudspeaker, and he moved to the house phone. The operator put Yolande Nathan through to him. "Are you winning?"

"I lost a little."

"Feel like taking a break?"

"Where are you?"

"Turn to your right."

She was ten feet from him at another house phone. She stuck her tongue out. They both laughed and he moved toward her.

She was dressed in white. Her laugh had faded to a sad smile. The expression in her eyes was sad and somehow knowing. Her cheeks held a faint blush. He wanted to swallow her with a kiss.

"How'd you know I'd be here?"

"I just knew."

"Pretty smart, aren't you?"

She nodded her head. "Pretty smart."

They moved through the lobby and out the front door. While they waited for the valet to bring Yolande's car, Porter became aware that he was being watched. He looked back through the glass doors into the hotel lobby. A man in baggy brown suit, frayed shirt, and steel-rimmed glasses was peering at him. His eyes were wide and forlorn, his fixed stare chilling in its intensity. The man's trembling lips moved without sound, as though he was praying. It was the man Porter had given the twenty-five-dollar chip to at the Paradise Hotel some days back.

The Strip was swollen with traffic, and they moved at a crawl. "I'm going to win us a lot of money," Porter said. "Then we're just going to disappear."

"I'd like that," Yolande said.

They found a breach in the traffic and turned onto Charleston. "Where are we going?" Porter asked.

"To my place."

"What for?"

"Why not?"

The front door to the house was open. Angel Amato, wearing white slacks, white tee shirt, and tennis shoes, was standing in an alcove, leading into the living room. He showed no surprise that Porter was there. "Where's my husband?" Yolande asked.

"Downstairs with some people."

She led Porter to the rear of the house, then down a flight of stairs. Angel Amato, footsteps delicate as a cat's, followed behind them.

A half dozen men were seated with Matt Nathan. They lounged in leather chairs beneath framed photographs of Nathan and his wife and his child, which lined the redwood-paneled walls. The men were dressed in casual western garb; their faces were tanned and leathery.

On the table in front of Matt Nathan was a large sheet of graph paper with rows of figures penned on it. The poodle,

Princess, was seated on his lap. Nathan seemed vaguely annoyed at the appearance of Yolande and Porter. She moved to him and kissed him lightly on the cheek. "How's the town tonight?" Matt Nathan asked.

"Quiet," she said.

"It's quiet all over," one of the men said in a deep western drawl.

Matt Nathan looked over at Porter. "Eddie's doing real well," he said. "He got something wild inside him. That's good."

"He's a good boy," Porter said.

"That new boxer of yours?" one of the men asked.

"Yes."

"Which one's that?"

"Big guy from Fresno. Fought at the Silver Slipper a couple weeks ago."

"White boy?"

"That's right."

"I remember him," said another of the men. "Punchy, though, isn't he, Matt?"

"He got a little twitch. I don't think it's anything."

"Twitched more than a mule shaking flies, as I recall it," the first man said. The other men laughed softly.

"He'll be all right," Matt Nathan said, returning his attention to the sheet of graph paper in front of him.

"We'll be on the tennis courts," Yolande said.

"Nice seeing you again, Don," Matt Nathan said with a soft smile. "Maybe I'll see you later."

Porter followed Yolande back up the stairs. At the top of the stairs Yolande stopped short and pressed back in against Porter. He kissed her in the ear. She took his hand and cupped it over her breast and squeezed.

They walked through the French doors out onto the patio. Porter glanced back into the house. Angel was now standing at the top of the stairs to the game room, leaning against the doorjamb. His thumbs were hooked through his belt, and

154

the bottom of his tee shirt was pulled awry; the handle of the .32 pistol was clearly visible protruding above the waistband.

They crossed the patio in the dark and followed a stone walk down to the tennis courts. They moved along a path outside the tennis court fence to a white stucco field house on the far side of the courts. Yolande inserted a key in the door, and they entered.

She flicked on a light in the field house, then opened a metal switch-box and threw a lever. "See if the tennis courts are lit, hon," she said.

He moved outside. The tennis courts were flooded in a bright, white light. He looked back at the house to see if he could spot Angel Amato. Through the palm and bougainvillaea surrounding it, he could see no one.

He returned to the field house. Yolande locked the door behind him. She moved to a small bar in the corner. "What will you have to drink?"

"Scotch."

The floor was covered with a blue shag rug, and there was a row of blue lockers along one wall. There were two white leather chairs and a white leather couch. At the far end of the room, beyond the bar, was a redwood door with frosted glass window, which led to a sauna and shower. Porter sat on the couch.

Yolande, at the bar, poured two Scotches. She handed him one, then sat down next to him on the couch. "Did you play football in high school?" she asked.

"I played sandlot."

"Were you any good?"

"Pretty good."

"Why didn't you go out for the high school team?"

"I was too busy hustling cards. I went out one time. They handed me a uniform and equipment and all that, and I was just signing out for it when they bring this guy I knew past me—they're carrying him on a canvas stretcher and I can

155

see his damn leg is bent at a crazy angle. I mean it's bent between the knee and the ankle where there *ain't* no bend. And I said no way, no how!"

"What did you do?"

"I just turned everything, uniform and all, back in."

Yolande smiled a private smile and stared down into her glass. "We used to have big parades, you know?" she said. "We'd be playing in some small town, and we'd parade from one end of the town to the other. I'd throw that baton so high, sometimes I'd just see it flashing up there, and I'd catch it purely by instinct because the sun would blind me to it!" She swallowed her drink in one long gulp and moved back to the bar and refilled her glass. "Did you mean that before?"

"What's that?"

"That we'd disappear together?"

"Would you do it?"

She thought for a long time, her glass pressed against her cheek, her legs tucked under her on the couch. "I don't know," she said at last. She drank deeply from her glass, draining it. "Whoa," Porter said. She looked at him and smiled.

She took his glass and walked a bit unsteadily to the bar again and poured out two more drinks. "I'd be worried about Matt," she said. "I'd be worried about what he'd do."

"We'd go far, far away. . . ."

"We could never go far enough."

"You're afraid of him?"

She shook her head slowly. "I know just how much to push him." Her face was flushed, her eyes watery. "Besides, I have a child." She laughed wryly.

"What?" Porter asked, expecting her to continue.

She just shook her head. She looked as though she were about to laugh and cry at the same time. "It's just that—"

"Yes?"

"I love you so damn much. Isn't that ridiculous?"

156

"What's ridiculous about it?"

"I don't even know you. I don't even know what you do, what your story is. What's your story, Don Porter?"

"I'm a bum."

"A bum. I knew it."

" 'Can that matchbox hold my clothes? I don't got so many, but I got so doggone far to go.' " He laughed to himself. "A guy told me that once."

"What guy?"

"A guy who wasn't going nowhere."

"That's sad."

"The law said he was through going places. He had gone too many places."

Yolande laughed, a bit drunk now. She stood up and started back to the bar. "What about the girl living with you?"

"What about her?"

"What are you going to do with her?"

"What are you going to do with your husband?"

She shrugged and he shrugged, and they both laughed. She began to unbutton her dress. It was one-piece, white knit. "Jesus, I was a terrific majorette," she said. She threw an invisible baton into the air. "Wheee!" she said.

Her dress slipped to the floor. She unhooked her brassiere. Her breasts seemed to flow out of the brassiere.

He sat watching her, sipping slowly at his Scotch. She was standing bare-breasted now in her slip and panties. She pulled them down, and then she was standing completely nude.

"You're not concerned about anybody popping in on us?" Porter said.

"I told you. I know just how far to push him."

"What about Angel?"

"Don't worry about him."

"I'm worried about that piece of iron he carries under his belt."

"I hate him," she said. "Jesus, I hate him. He's a rotten person, you know?"

"Aren't we all?"

"Are we?"

He did not answer. He grabbed her by the buttocks and pulled her to him. Her buttocks felt soft and cool. She reached forward and unbuckled his belt and zipped down his trousers. He brought her on top of him. She tilted her head back and gazed up at the ceiling. She saw blue sky and the propeller flashes of innumerable batons.

When they returned from the field house, Matt Nathan was seated on the patio. There were no people around. He was sipping a Tab. Princess was asleep at his feet. He was staring out over the tennis courts. "What did those men want?" Yolande asked.

"State Gaming Commission again."

"Bad?"

"They never leave you alone." His voice was heavy with fatigue. "You'd think every little mistake you made in this life was written in blood." He finished his soda and got up. "I'm going to turn in," he said. "You left the lights on on the tennis court."

"I forgot. We were going to play, then we started talking. I was telling Don about my days as a majorette."

Matt Nathan smiled. "What did Don tell you about?"

"I didn't tell her very much," Porter said.

"I didn't think you would," Matt Nathan said without malice. "Are you coming in now?"

"I'll drive Don back to his motel."

"Why don't you have Angel drive him?"

"No, that's all right."

"Good seeing you again, Don," Matt Nathan said, walking away. Princess yawned, shook herself, then staggered slowly after him into the house.

Porter was quiet on the drive back to the Excelsior. "What's wrong?" Yolande asked.

"Something's digging at your husband."

"Business problems. For years they've been trying to get him out of the Paradise Hotel."

"Why?"

"It's all big corporations now. He's a dinosaur in this town."

"It had nothing to do with me?"

"No."

"I can't figure him out."

"That's the way he is."

"His eyes. Something always spinning behind his eyes. Like a slot machine."

"He's a very secret person. His whole life is a series of plots within plots."

"How do I know I'm not part of one?"

"It's just not his style."

"What is his style?"

"Some years back an old friend of his crossed him in business. Matt never said a word about it. He accepted it and remained perfectly quiet. But he baited a trap. It took him three years. He set up a deal, and his old friend had the opportunity to cross him again. Only this time there was someone else involved. They all had dinner together. Everybody was in a good mood at the dinner. There was a lot of drinking and reminiscing about old times. Matt put his arms around the man and said if he ever had a friend in life it was this man. I was watching the other man, the man who had been crossed. His eyes were like ice. Matt and I left the old friend there with this other man."

"What happened?"

"The old friend was never seen again."

"The desert?"

She smiled and shrugged. "The point is Matt didn't do it. He just arranged the circumstances where the man did it to himself."

"Maybe he's doing that to me."

"Not over me. I've had lovers—I can't even count them. Some of them he's genuinely liked—long after I've finished with them." She glanced over at Porter. "Angel Amato used to be my lover. That's how Matt met him."

They were just below the Strip on Las Vegas Boulevard. They were driving through an area of cheap motels, discount liquor stores, garishly lit wedding chapels and drive-in hamburger joints. Porter grew silent again; he stared out the window. The boulevard was quiet now. Tawdry neon signs unreeled with the boulevard, flashing by Porter's vision: motels—the Golden West, the Yucca, Rancho Anita, Sun 'n Sand, Bagdad; Denny's Restaurant, Bob's Big Boy, Winchell Donut House; the Cupid Wedding Chapel, with its sign of infant archer, bow and arrow, punctured heart. At Sahara Avenue, an explosion of neon: HONEST JOHN'S CASINO, BIG WHEEL CASINO, LUCKY CASINO . . . "Win Gold And Silver Dollars Play Here Wild Slots Play Here Fun Arcade For The Kids Breakfast 24 Hours 48¢ Steak Dinner 98¢ Chicken Or Shrimp Dinner 79¢ Burger A Dog And Drinks 25¢ . . ." Then: The blue and white neon of the Sahara Hotel . . . the Congo Room . . . and before them the Strip itself, insane with spinning lights, a raw, electrical tear in the belly of the desert, magical, brutal, a desperate mirage . . .

Kitty was still awake when he arrived back at the motel. She was sitting in a chair in front of the television. The set was on, but the screen was blank. She had been crying, and her face was streaked with mascara.

"What's wrong?" he asked. He put his arm around her. She was trembling.

"I don't know. I'm just unhappy is all. I don't like it here. I don't like being alone all the time."

He said nothing. Inside he felt his life was a lie, that everything he touched was a lie. Kitty's tears were a lie. Yolande's smile was a lie. And he thought: only the System is truth.

He held her in his arms a long time. After a while her sobbing stopped. Her breathing deepened and she was asleep. He undressed her and put her to bed. Then he sat by the window smoking a Marsh Wheeling stogie and attempted to run through his plans for the big push. He had some difficulty. Angel Amato's face kept obtruding on his thoughts.

IX

There were three stacks of bills on the bureau top. Porter folded them and placed them in his pocket. He gazed in the mirror and winked at his image.

He felt fine. He had showered, shaved, put on a new shirt —yellow Dacron—a pair of white slacks, and his sky-blue knit jacket. He considered, then rejected, his Stetson and cowboy boots.

He stepped out of his motel room at the Excelsior, and the night seemed perfectly in tune with his mood: cool, a light breeze, the sky rich with stars. He walked with a bounce, singing softly: "La da da da da da, the games people play . . ." He carried in his pocket fifteen thousand dollars in hundred-dollar bills.

He climbed into the car and drove along Paradise Road with the top down; the fresh night air, the cool wind, the sense of open sky and distance carried his mood lilting along. He was not nervous at all; rather, he felt a powerful elation. There would be no trembling, perspiring hands tonight; he knew exactly what he must do, and he knew he would accomplish it.

The last few days he had gone out of his way to be nice to Kitty. He had given her money for clothes; he had praised her. And she, under the attention showered on her, had blossomed.

The night before he had taken her and Eddie MacRae to dinner at the Flame Restaurant on Desert Inn Road. She bought a new dress for the occasion—a red satin number—and had had her hair done.

Porter smiled when he saw her waiting for him on the balcony of the motel. The dress was slit up one side, Oriental style, and her hair, augmented by a wig, was stacked high in blond swirls; she was wearing ludicrously long false eyelashes and uplift pads in her brassiere to fake some cleavage. She appeared ridiculous and somehow touching.

"Do you like it?"

"Terrific."

"Do I *really* look snazzy?" she asked, and when he answered yes, she beamed with pride.

Over steak dinner Porter had outlined his plan. He embellished it, exaggerating the possibilities, inflating the future. He was conning them, and that knowledge deeply disturbed him. Yet, he felt he must give them something—hope, belief, *something.*

Guilt gnawed at him. He was using them. He would eventually cast them off. . . .

"I figure we can take the place for maybe a couple hundred thousand dollars."

"Geemaneezers!" Kitty said. "Geemaneezers!"

"I've been studying the center table at Caesar's. They deal right down to the bottom of the deck. If we work it right—"

"A couple *hundred thousand!"* Eddie's voice was hushed with awe.

"And I'll tell you something else—after we make our strike, we're going to take the money and cut out. Do a tour around the world—the Bahamas, London, the Riviera. We'll play a little wherever we go, but mostly we'll just eat good and wear nice clothes and live like millionaires."

Kitty clapped her hands together like a little girl. "Donny, that's just so fantastic, because you know this town was beginning to get me down. I mean I like it and all, but except for the gambling and shows it doesn't tell me too much, you know what I mean? And the way people look at you—the dealers and pit bosses and guards. I mean, they look at you like you were dirt. Like they know you're working to beat them out of money. Let's put it this way. Basically, it's a pretty scurvy town."

"Yeah," Eddie MacRae agreed.

"I mean it would be all right if we were just up here on a vacation and we could lose a few hundred dollars and like that and not get all those dirty looks and people watching us all the time."

"I'm telling you, we're going to make this score, and then we're going to blow this town and just jet-plane around the world."

"Count me out of that," Eddie MacRae said. "I got my career. I was talking to this here fighter, and he said if I work right, I'll be rated in no time. And when you're rated, you got a chance—"

"A chance? What kind of a chance?" Porter asked.

Eddie MacRae struggled to formulate his ideas. "You got a chance to realize what you want to realize. You can push for a title shot. They're very anxious to have a white man up there pushing for a title shot."

Dessert arrived and Porter outlined his plan: "I'm going to start alone at about midnight. I'll cover three hands. When the deck gets hot, I'll bet up to the house limit, five hundred dollars a hand. Fifteen hundred dollars for three hands, triple that with double downs and splits. Now get this: the signal. When I light a *cigarette*—not a cigar—"

"Cigarette, not a cigar," Eddie MacRae echoed.

"—that's when I want both of you to come in and cover the rest of the table."

"How do we do that?" Eddie asked.

"I'm coming to that—"

164

He had devised a ruse to mask their entrance into the game. He explained it to them now, talking rapidly, sketching out various ideas for them on the edge of the tablecloth with a felt-tipped marking pen. "The two of you get into the game arguing. Eddie wants to bet big, you don't want him to. You know, like a married couple. Eddie takes 'first base' and the place next to it. He throws down five hundred dollars on each spot. You grab the bills from him. He pulls out more and lays them down. So you throw down the money you have like you're spiting Eddie—"

"I see what you're getting at," Kitty said.

"Yeah," said Eddie MacRae.

"Now you got to establish you're betting just to spite Eddie 'cause you been arguing. When the dealer gets to the bottom of the deck, you get up and tell Eddie you're leaving. Walk back a ways near the crap tables and keep arguing, then, you know, make an angry face, like that, then make up and so forth. Keep your eye on me. When I light a second cigarette, you come back and we just keep going like that."

Eddie MacRae thought for a long moment. "Why don't we all just sit down and play the System straight off from the beginning?"

" 'Cause if we all start upping our bets at every end-deck situation, they're gonna get a notion of what's going on. This way I just bring the two of you in for the big ones."

They had sat in the Flame Restaurant drinking cup after cup of coffee, going over every detail of the plan. Porter had even outlined the dialogue of their arguments for them.

Eddie MacRae was not happy. When they dropped him off at the Paradise Hotel, he said, "I'm just doing this 'cause I promised. But I don't think it's honest—"

"Of course it's honest," Porter said.

"It's honest, Eddie," Kitty said.

"After this here I'm going to just concentrate on my punches, you know, getting variety into my attack and defense. I'm going to get rated, and I'm going to get a shot at the top."

Back in their motel room Kitty had said to Porter: "Did you really mean all that stuff?"

"What stuff?"

"About traveling around the world and all that?"

"We'll see. . . ."

She did not speak for a long time. "That's what I thought."

"I mean we'll just see. . . ."

Porter turned off Paradise onto Tropicana and headed for the Strip. He glanced at the clock on the dashboard. It was 11:45. Eddie MacRae and Kitty would have been at Caesar's Palace for more than an hour. He had instructed them to make their presence known, to sit in at the five- and twenty-five-dollar tables, chat with the dealers, throw around an occasional nice tip.

The Strip was jammed with cars, but Porter was in no particular rush, so he remained in the slow lane and did not fight the traffic. He turned up the car radio, and Fats Domino, singing "Ain't That a Shame," blasted the car with song, and the music surged with his mood and his whole body tingled with energy. Tonight he could do no wrong.

Alongside him two girls, a blonde and a redhead, in a Chevy Impala with Nevada plates, looked over and smiled. Probably cocktail waitresses or hookers, Porter thought. The redhead called over through the open window of her car: "Hey, I like your car. Can I come for a ride?"

"Some other time."

"Where are you going?"

"I got some business to take care of."

Their lane opened up, and the redhead waved and they pulled away from him. He cut out of his lane and moved off after them. The redhead turned and looked at him through the rear window. She blew him a kiss and he blew one back.

Opposite the Dunes at Flamingo Road he pulled up beside them. "What kind of business?" the redhead called out. "Blackjack."

"Take me along. I'm good luck." The blonde shook her head and laughed, and the redhead laughed.

"There's no such thing as luck," Porter called out.

"Really?" the redhead mouthed in mock disbelief.

"You got to have skill." The redhead cocked one eyebrow in feigned surprise. He gunned his car away from them at the change of the light, feeling himself both lucky and skillful. He crossed in front of the Impala and signaled for a left turn. The girls passed him on the right, blasting their horn as they went, and he turned into Caesar's Palace.

He drove up to the main entrance, moving past the great headless winged statue facing the Strip, then the long pool with its geysers of water spouting over drowning and tortured Roman statuary.

He turned the car over to the parking valet and climbed the steps to the glass doors leading into the hotel.

He crossed the wine-colored carpet, passed the blood-red lobby couches, until he was standing beneath the white archway at the periphery of the casino.

The casino was dazzling, bright as a jewel: crystal chandelier all aglimmer, sparkling phalanges of crystal spreading from the chandelier across the mirrored casino ceiling; circulating below, coiffured and diamond-drenched ladies, and tanned, barbered, meticulously tailored men. The whole place appeared to Porter radiant with flashes of silver light.

He did not see—or, rather, chose not to—the grimy, the dowdy, the haunted: the losers. The night to him was bright and elegant: it was going to be his night.

Looking around for Kitty and Eddie MacRae, he spotted them at one of the five-dollar tables. Eddie appeared tense and bored, but Kitty was having the time of her life, chattering away as she played, joking with the other players at the table, flirting with the dealer.

Eddie's eyes rested on him for an instant, then, with a

twitch of his head, shifted away. He whispered in Kitty's ear and Porter saw her throw a quick glance in his direction. He moved to the center table.

The dealer, a large, bald man with a sagging belly, stood arms folded across his chest, gazing out at the casino with heavy-lidded, bored eyes. His deck was spread face up on the green felt table. A small neat sign, white letters on black plastic, read: $100 minimum.

Ported eased into a chair at the left side of the table; he chose the far chair, "third base"; should other players join the table, he would be in a position to observe their cards and maintain a running count on the deck.

He removed a packet of money from his pocket and counted out twenty hundred-dollar bills. He slid the money over to the dealer. "Paper," the dealer called out. "Two thousand." He had a vague accent. The name on the tag pinned to his shirt front read "Kakrimanos." A Greek, Porter decided.

The floorman approached and watched while the dealer recounted the bills, then pushed them into the slot in the drop-box with a plastic, spatulalike plug, which fitted into the top of the drop-box.

The dealer arranged twenty black chips in piles of five, setting up one pile of five, then leveling the other three to match the first one, doing it all with a quick, precise, practiced hand, sliding the stacks over to Porter in the same flowing motion. The floorman stood by watching, his eyes shifting from the chips to Porter, then back to the chips.

Porter lined the stacks of chips in front of his right hand and checked to his left to make sure there were cigarettes in the clear plastic house box at the corner of the table.

The floorman moved around the edge of the table to Porter. "Can I get you a drink?" He spoke with that special note of deference reserved for the big-money players.

"Not right now."

"How about some cigars?"

"Fine."

The floorman moved to a mahogany table in the center of the pit, opened a drawer, and drew out a handful of cigars. "Shuffle up," the dealer said, and began cutting the cards together.

The floorman returned to Porter as the dealer was performing a last humming riffle of the deck. "Good luck," he said, handing the cigars to Porter.

The dealer squared the deck and set it in front of Porter. Porter cut the deck. The dealer placed ashtray and matches in front of him. Tearing the cellophane from one of the cigars, Porter lit up. Over his shoulder he noticed a small crowd gathering behind him.

The dealer palmed the top card and placed it face down in the plastic card receptacle on his right. Porter tried to catch a glimpse of it and gain a point on the count, but the duck of the card was too quick.

The play began and remained even for a while. The System had become second nature to Porter and he played with assurance, weighing the edge, performing precise, rapid calculations, adjusting his bets to the delicate ebb and flow of the percentages, handling it all with an ease that filled him with a sense of tremendous power. He felt a master not only of the cards, but of his own fate.

He began to win—not much but enough to keep him ahead. The P.C. shifted between player and house, and he manipulated his bets carefully, managing to pick up a couple of black chips every fifteen minutes or so.

The dealer, heavy, cool, impassive, dealt the cards with little apparent concern for their effect. He had small, pudgy hands, and Porter marveled at their dexterity. They never fumbled or missed, never quickened or slowed. The short, stubby fingers, the immaculate nails coated with a thin layer of clear polish, the small emerald on the pinky, all moved in a kind of incredible ballet, a soft shuffle of the deck, then the cards sliced into small packs, a graceful sliding of these packs one atop the other in an easy, shifting motion, then the purr of the riffle, slice and riffle again, riffle yet again, a quick sliding of the ducked card, then, with that same gliding motion, the deal: cards snapped out, flicked back, fingers turning and dancing, pinky ring grabbing stabs of light, nails reflecting dull gleams of light as aces, deuces, treys, the whole wild panoply of red and black royalty, clubs, spades, diamonds, and hearts skimmed the green felt of the table, impelled by the extraordinary elegance of those soft, pampered hands. It was beautiful to watch, and Porter took it in and enjoyed it and still maintained the count, still carried on the System, still won.

Then the deal changed. The pale, plump hands clapped in a soft, brushing motion and waved palm out at Porter in a parting gesture, as the dealer moved off with a final, "Good luck."

The next set of hands were coarser—thick, peasant hands that matched the new dealer's face—square, beetle-browed, swarthy, the eyes black and suspicious, a deep cleft in the chin, a full head of greasy, jet hair. The deal was more aggressive now, faster, the rhythm choppier. The emerald ring had been replaced by a diamond, the nails were cleaned and trimmed, but not polished. Porter continued to win.

The crowd behind him had increased. Out of the edge of his vision he could see Eddie MacRae and Kitty on the crowd's periphery.

He was able to hear snatches of conversation: "How's he doing?"

"Winning."

"Winning, huh?"

"Winning like a bastard."

"Yeah?"

"Long as I been here—"

He decided he did not like the house cigars. They were expensive, but he preferred his ten-cent stogie. For this night, though, at the hundred-dollar table, he would smoke the house brand.

The P.C. started to establish a pattern in the player's favor. The deck began to heat up for him. He upped his bet to the limit—five hundred dollars a hand—and now began to catch the edge. He hit a streak of nines, tens, and elevens, and he doubled down and he won every one of them. He pulled soft sixes and sevens, doubled down again, and again took the hand.

When it was time for another change of the deal, he glanced at the stack in front of him. He was ahead seven thousand dollars.

The Greek dealer, Kakrimanos, was back. He looked at the row of chips in front of Porter and nodded approvingly. "You doing good," he said.

"You win a few, you lose a few."

"Well, continued good luck," Kakrimanos said, offering Porter a fresh deck. Porter split the seal with his fingernail and handed it back to the dealer.

The floorman approached and furnished Porter with a wooden tray for his chips. "How about a drink?" he asked.

Porter, though he had no intention of drinking it, ordered a Bloody Mary.

The crowd shifted a bit and craned forward as he transferred his chips to the chip tray. The Bloody Mary arrived, and Porter tipped the silicone-breasted cocktail waitress five dollars. He took a small sip of the drink and set it to one side.

Porter expanded his strategy, covering two hands; he continued to win, and he took on a third hand. With doubling down and splitting, he now had at times as much as two or three thousand dollars in play. In a short while he was more than fifteen thousand dollars ahead.

The crowd had grown to a point where it was backed up to the dice tables, blocking the center aisle. A uniformed security guard stood at the head of the table, his hand on his holstered revolver. The floorman was joined by the pit boss.

171

Both men were unctuously solicitous of Porter, supplying him with clean ashtrays, offering to freshen his drink, replenishing his cigar supply, making sure he had sufficient chip trays.

At last the opening he had been waiting for presented itself.

The initial two hands had brought nothing but low and middle cards. There were twenty-nine cards left in the deck. The count was an astonishingly high plus eleven, which meant the deck contained almost nothing but pictures and tens. He prepared to bring Eddie MacRae and Kitty into the game.

For the first time that night he experienced an attack of nerves. A wave of excitement spread from the pit of his stomach through his body. His limbs tingled; he felt he couldn't breathe; when he reached for a cigarette, he noticed his fingers were trembling.

He took his time playing. He gazed at the hole card, lit the cigarette, inhaled, blew out the smoke. Then he glanced down at his chips, began to count a short stack of them. All the while he was stalling for time, waiting for Eddie MacRae and Kitty to pick up on the signal. The thought entered his mind that they had missed it, that this incredible opportunity would escape them. Minutes seemed to go by—in reality it was less than thirty seconds—before he heard them. It started as a commotion in the crowd behind him:

"But look at how good that guy's doing! I'm telling you the deck is hot—"

"You can't afford a game like that—"

"I want to get in there while the deck is hot!"

"Please!"

It was Eddie MacRae and Kitty involved in an argument—the argument Porter had coached them on at the Flame.

Porter set his chips on top of his cards to indicate he was sticking. The dealer drew a card to win the round. Eddie MacRae shouldered his way up to the table.

His face was flushed and perspiring, and his head twitched

in short, sharp jerks; his eyes burned determination, the same fierce determination Porter had seen him display in the boxing ring. Kitty was right beside him.

Both of them were scared. Porter could read it in their eyes, Eddie's flickering from side to side, Kitty staring glassily straight ahead.

"I'm not going to let you—"

"Oh, yes, you are!" Eddie MacRae put down ten hundred-dollar bills on the table.

The dealer, about to continue with the deal, paused. "You want to play that?"

"Right!"

The dealer looked over at the floorman. The pit boss behind him gave a curt nod. The dealer spread the hundred-dollar bills out on the green felt. "Five-hundred-dollar minimum," he said.

"Put it on two hands, then."

Kitty grabbed at the money. "Oh, no, you're not! That's my vacation money!"

"That's what this is! This is a vacation!" There was a quaver in Eddie MacRae's voice. He reached in his trouser pocket and had difficulty extricating his hand. When he at last brought it out, it contained a thick roll of bills; he peeled off ten more hundreds and slapped them down on the table.

"All right," Kitty said. She spread the thousand dollars she had grabbed out on the table. "If that's the way you want to be, then I'm playing too!"

They were acting beautifully, Porter thought. The ineptitude, the awkwardness and fumbling, the fear, gave their behavior a quality of extraordinary spontaneity, made the performance totally believable.

"Do what you want to do," Eddie MacRae said. Perspiration poured down his face. Kitty's lips were trembling. *We're going to make it, we're going to make it*, Porter found himself repeating over and over again to himself.

173

The dealer waited patiently for the squabble to be resolved. "All right everybody?" he asked.

Eddie MacRae nodded and hunched over the table. Porter rubbed his chin and tried to appear nonchalant. At the edge of his vision he could see the pit boss and the floorman staring impassively at the three players.

The deal continued. Eddie MacRae caught a pair of queens and split them. Porter pulled two tens and an eleven. He split the tens and doubled down on the eleven. The dealer showed a five. No one had hit a blackjack—miraculously, considering how rich the deck was.

Between Porter, Kitty, and Eddie MacRae five thousand dollars were riding on the hand. The crowd had grown very quiet. Porter lit a cigar. A curl of blue-gray smoke spiraled up in front of him. The air was heavy with smoke and silence.

The dealer turned up his hole card. It was an ace, giving him a soft sixteen. He hit and pulled a ten. Hard sixteen. Porter held his breath. *We're going to make it. . . .*

The deck, crammed as it was with tens and pictures, forced the P.C. overwhelmingly toward a bust-out for the dealer. Smoke hanging in the air. Silence hanging in the air. *We're going to make it. . . .*

The dealer flipped the next card over. Porter's heart leaped, its beat suspended in a limbo of lost pulsation: then the blood crashed heavily in his chest.

The System had collapsed. The dealer had drawn a five, the only remaining one in the deck. He had caught a twenty-one.

A quiet groan came from the crowd. The dealer shrugged, almost apologetically.

The blood continued to crash in Porter's chest. He felt as though everything were falling apart. The System had failed! Again it had failed! The enormous weight of the P.C. on their side, and still the balance of fortune had gone against them!

Eddie MacRae stared, stunned and uncomprehending,

174

down at the table. Kitty began to weep. She gazed around the table, her eyes wide and confused, tears streaming down her face.

The dealer gathered in the cards and prepared to shuffle up. Dazed and stricken, Eddie MacRae and Kitty drifted away from the table. Porter looked back and saw them moving into the lobby area.

Then he spotted the man: standing close by, not three feet from his left shoulder, the man who had begged a chip off him at the Paradise, who had stared after him in Caesar's a few nights ago. He was wearing the same baggy brown suit; he was unshaven and peered at Porter with watery eyes through the thick lenses of his glasses; he watched Porter with a steady, mournful look.

Porter turned quickly back to the table.

He fought to regain his poise. He tried to reassure himself: they were still ahead ten thousand dollars on the night; the System, until this point, had worked beautifully. It was a question of percentages. They would win the next one. He would continue to play. The count would heat up again.

He puffed slowly on his cigar as he pushed out his next bet.

But the whole thing had gone sour. The P.C. continued to favor him, but the cards fell to the dealer. He began to lose badly.

Within an hour his ten-thousand-dollar winnings were gone. His eyes burned. His head, his neck, the backs of his shoulders ached terribly. He couldn't stop his hands from trembling.

Eddie MacRae and Kitty, bewildered, lost, roamed the casino like two abandoned animals, avoiding the table where Porter played, but constantly looking toward it. Fate, chance, luck—*wound!* They *wreck*, they *destroy!* Their expressions reflected fear and desperation at this terrifying realization.

Porter reached into his pocket and took out twenty one-hundred-dollar bills. "Paper," the dealer called out, sliding four stacks of chips over to Porter.

He continued to lose. He blew two thousand dollars and went into his pocket again. The percentages shifted to the dealer; Porter cut back on his bets. The rate declined, but still he lost. Again he went into his pocket.

"Can I get some coffee?" Porter asked. It was nearly four in the morning. He was exhausted. He was down to five thousand dollars.

The crowds in the casino had thinned out. A half dozen blackjack tables continued in action, a single roulette wheel, two dice pits. Three people stood watching Porter—a young couple and the man in the steel-rimmed spectacles.

The man in spectacles had moved to Porter's right and was gazing blankly at the play. From time to time Porter would catch his look, pale, somber, the eyes dead.

The man's presence ate away at Porter. He seemed to Porter the personification of ill-fortune. Porter had a sense that somehow that empty look, that sagging, flaccid body was wrecking the System. The man radiated defeat and loss. Porter desperately wanted him away from the table.

The cocktail waitress arrived with Porter's coffee. The deal changed. As the new dealer, a tall, ruddy-faced young man, began to shuffle up, Porter motioned the man in spectacles to him.

He approached hesitantly, his puffy face now suddenly alive with nervous tics. He smelled of stale cigarette smoke and perspiration.

"Get away from me," Porter said.

"I don't understand—"

"You're wrecking my luck."

The man's voice, tinged with a southwestern accent, was barely audible. "There's no such thing as luck," he said.

"I've done nothing but lose since you come here." Porter grabbed up a black chip and pressed it on the man. The man opened his grimy hand and gathered in the chip.

"Thank you," the man said. "I'm sorry if I disturbed you." He moved off, casting quick, nervous glances back at Porter.

176

The departure of the man in the steel-rimmed glasses did not help. The P.C. continued hot for the dealer. Porter continued to lose.

He now had less than two thousand dollars. Kitty and Eddie MacRae would have another two thousand. The money represented their total winnings since they had arrived in Vegas.

Kitty and Eddie MacRae were now playing at a dollar table directly across from Porter. They continued to watch him for a sign. He played along, praying for the P.C. to shift back to him. At last it came.

They were twenty-seven cards into the deck when the point count suddenly soared for the player. The deck was lush with high cards, and it was the time to crack the deal and crack it hard. He lit a cigarette.

Eddie MacRae and Kitty, sunk in gloom and fatigue, at first did not respond. Porter puffed conspicuously on the cigarette, dawdled with his cards, recounted his chips. Kitty at last picked it up and nudged Eddie MacRae. The two of them moved from their table toward Porter.

"Bets up," the dealer said.

"Let me just count up here a minute." Porter recounted his chips for the third time.

Kitty and Eddie MacRae eased into the chairs to the right of him. Eddie covered two hands with five one-hundred-dollar bills; Kitty did the same. The dealer called out, "Paper!" and the pit boss returned to the table.

"Give them chips," he said. The dealer replaced the bills with black chips.

The dealer held the cards poised above the green felt of the table. Thirty-five hundred dollars rode on the table, and with the possibility of splits and double downs, the amount could skyrocket well beyond that. They might even strike a blackjack or two: the P.C. rated it a high probability. They could score nicely. They could regain their momentum. They could carry it all off. . . .

But the dealer had caught them out. With a hint of a smile he gathered up the cards in the plastic receptacle to his right. "Shuffle up," he said.

He cut and shuffled the cards. The rich lode of tens, pictures, and aces was destroyed. The big push was destroyed.

Porter stared at the deck on the table in front of him. The criss-cross lines of the cards' pattern held him like prison mesh, trapped him. He wanted to get up, but he couldn't move. He couldn't leave the table. He couldn't salvage what little they had left. He cut the cards.

Porter pulled a twenty on the first hand, Eddie an eleven, Kitty a seventeen. Nice cards, but none of it mattered. The dealer was turning up his hand. He had a blackjack.

They moved like sleepwalkers from the table, drained now of hope, dreams exploded, treading a nightmare path across the casino floor. Above them the sparkling crystal phalanges rained down cruel diamonds of light. The crash and scream of casino sound shrilled in their ears.

On the stairs leading to the lobby, the man in spectacles stood blocking Porter's path. "Get out of my way," Porter said.

"I want to talk to you."

"Get away from me!" Porter screamed. He attempted to push by, but the man in spectacles would not let him pass. "I can help you," the man said. "I can help you. . . ."

He extended a thin, trembling hand in an attempt at a handshake. "I'd like to introduce myself, sir. Billy Ray Walker. Texas born. Nacogdoches County, sir." His face performed a tense, ugly grin. "A pleasure to meet a man of your *tenacity!*"

The ceiling was mirrors, and for a moment Porter thought the walls were, too.

X

They sat in the Noshorium, the coffeehouse at Caesar's Palace. The place was almost deserted. A few deep-night gamblers, bust-outs, and insomniacs sat at the counter. In the rear area a handful of dealers between shifts chatted over cups of black coffee, dozed, worked on crossword puzzles, or just stared at the wall, reflecting that special weariness that comes to men who must toil while the rest of the world sleeps.

Billy Ray Walker was a man resurrected. He sat at the black Formica table with Porter, Kitty, and Eddie MacRae, chain-smoking cigarettes, drinking cup after cup of coffee, talking with great animation about many things, but particularly the System. Gone was the blasted look, the emptiness in the eyes, the aura of defeat that had dominated his being earlier. Leaning back against the red leather of the booth, he exuded success; he was hearty; he glowed. The force of his personality was such that it made it almost possible to ignore the immense, pervasive shabbiness of his appearance.

This meeting up at last with Billy Ray Walker—a Billy Ray Walker so very unlike that splendid fantasy he carried around in his head—coupled with his disastrous experience at the blackjack table, had plunged Porter into the depths of a raw and raging despair. Nothing was right with the universe. All the power of heaven had conspired to shatter his life. Sitting at the table now across from this husk of a man aggressively attempting to justify his hopeless situation, Porter had to fight to keep from screaming out at the top of his voice that it was all a lie—the System, Billy Ray Walker, Porter's very existence.

Eddie MacRae and Kitty, however, were swept up in the magic of Billy Ray Walker's rhetoric. Having lost all, they were prepared to believe all. They sat in rapt attention, elbows forward on the table, taking in every word.

"Monty was never clued in to the heart of the System because prison carried him off just as the most *cogent* properties of the System were being developed." Billy Ray Walker, displaying the merest trace of Texas drawl, spoke rapidly with a certain pedantic aggressiveness, like a college professor lecturing his class. He jabbed at the air with a black holder kept continually filled with cigarettes from several packs of Salem Menthols secured by Kitty from the cigarette girl. His thick spectacles were fogged by perspiration and stained with bits of food. His fingernails were black with dirt. He stank.

"You see, you can't win with one deck in this town anymore. They always have the option to shuffle up on you. When I first came out here, eleven years ago, would you believe I was taking the casinos for *two hundred thousand a year*, Don?" He had picked up Porter's first name and insisted on using it.

Porter did not answer. He sat staring down at his coffee cup. Billy Ray, ignoring the lack of response, continued right on. "That's just about the time Monty and I were tight. Oh, I had a good six, seven years. At one time I had more than a million dollars stashed away. That's a fact!"

"Why didn't you just take that money and leave?" Kitty said.

Billy Ray Walker smiled. His teeth were pitted and rotting. "Where would I go?" he said, his voice a whisper filled with surprise. "Oh, I did a lot of travel. I've played all the big casinos around the world. But there's no town as *vulgar* as this town, and I got a nice measure of vulgarity in my soul." He chuckled and smacked his lips. The waitress passed close by, and he ordered a hot danish. "Best danish in the U.S.A. in Vegas," he said.

"What happened to the million dollars?" Porter asked. He had not spoken in a long time.

"Would you believe it was eaten up in less than two years? That's a fact. You see, a lot of very bright young men—computer experts and the like—began to get the idea that the games could be beaten when you fully investigated the laws of mathematical probability—percentages and ratios and the like. Of course, Don, they were right. But they made the mistake of coming in and openly announcing what they were doing. Would you believe I've seen them sitting there at the tables holding slide rules and little minicalculators in their hands? Well, it didn't take the casinos long to remedy *that*. You see, Mr. Casino is here to make *money*. As soon as the rules he's playing by don't make *money*, he ups and changes the rules. So they put in the four decks, they began shuffling up with one deck. And if they couldn't beat you that way, they'd slip in a mechanic. Oh, mechanics took a fearful toll with me. In a one-deck game, dealing seconds is the easiest thing in the world. You know *that*, Don."

The waitress arrived with Billy Ray's danish. He buttered it, then nibbled gingerly at it. "I wouldn't be surprised but that was a mechanic working on you that last round, a freelancer. He's cheating the house and to keep the P.C. on the table up, he slips a few seconds in on you. It's all *lies* and *deception*, Don. However, if one is very shrewd, all that can be *circumvented*. Then those mothers do the worst thing possible to you. They bar you."

"Were you barred?" Kitty asked.

Billy Ray laughed soundlessly. He sipped at a cup of fresh coffee. "I was not only *barred*. I was *barred* and *tarred* and *feathered.* It got so bad with me that I couldn't even get into the games at the Nugget or the Four Queens. I tried Reno, then Puerto Rico, but it seems like they have some International Network. Wherever the hell I've played the past few years, they've been on to me." He adjusted his glasses and sighed. "Ah, well. Winners talk, losers walk. I figure if I'm going to starve, I might as well starve with this whore of a town."

He lit a fresh cigarette. No one spoke for a while. Eddie MacRae, his initial enthusiasm now spent, leaned back in the booth; his eyes fluttered shut and he began to doze. Porter stared down at the table top. Kitty scratched a bit of polish from her fingernail. Billy Ray Walker puffed slowly on his cigarette and absently rubbed the underside of his chin. "More coffee?" he said at last.

"No," said Porter, shifting his weight in the booth.

"But you see I have a way now to get it all back. That's right. I've worked it all out." No one said anything. Eddie MacRae snored softly. "I've beaten the four decks! And when you're winning with four decks, there's no way they can stop you."

Porter signaled for the check. "You're good on one deck, Don, damn good. I could train you on four. We could work as a team—all of us." Billy Ray stared at Porter for a long moment. "Remember one thing, Don. God hates a coward."

Porter paid the check. Kitty roused Eddie MacRae, and they moved out of the coffee shop. The casino was quiet, muffled, almost deserted. The dealers stood behind their tables, arms crossed in front of them, staring with heavy-lidded eyes out across the empty casino floor.

They walked around the edge of the casino, through the silent rows of slot machines, past the sign-in desk of the hotel. A bleached-blond woman in her fifties, with blotchy skin, dozed, mouth open, on one of the lobby sofas. Two hookers sat in the cocktail area, staring with pale, tired faces out over the casino floor.

182

Outside, the Strip was washed in gray dawn light. The blues and reds and oranges of the casino signs along the Strip appeared soft, fuzzy and undefined, like a delicate watercolor. The traffic marker at Tropicana Avenue glowed a muted red. The air was cool.

They entered the Eldorado and started down the Strip toward Billy Ray Walker's motel south of Sahara on Las Vegas Boulevard. "I'm telling you, Don, believe me, we can do it, the group of us, working with four decks."

Eddie MacRae shifted in the seat. He was gray with fatigue. "Count me out," he said. "I got a fight coming up."

"Well, you got to do what you got to do," Billy Ray Walker said.

At Desert Inn Road Eddie said: "I'll get off here—"

"Don't you want us to drive you to your hotel?" Kitty asked.

"I'll run it. I need to get the kinks out."

Eddie MacRae stood embarrassed for a short moment beside the car. "Well, I'll see you around—"

"Yes," Kitty said, wanting to say more, but unable to think of anything else.

"Good luck," Eddie MacRae said.

"There ain't no such animal," said Billy Ray Walker quite seriously.

Then Eddie was off, jogging easily away from the car, heading down the road between the Desert Inn and the Flame Restaurant, heading for Paradise Road.

Billy Ray Walker lived in the Sultan Motel, a place of chipped and cracked stucco, burnt-out neon, and a swimming pool long abandoned by water.

His room was on the ground floor. It had a very low ceiling and smelled of mold, dirty bedclothes, and cigarettes. The bed was unmade. Paperback books and out-of-date magazines were heaped in such abundance they almost buried the furniture. Dirty glasses, empty beer bottles, ashtrays filled with cigarette butts, seemed to cover every available space in the room. On a table next to the bed rested a wooden four-deck dealing shoe and a stack of playing cards.

Billy Ray Walker smoothed a place on the bed for Kitty and Porter to sit. "I'm sorry I'm out of refreshments at the moment," he said with a broken grin.

He rummaged in the rear of the room through dirty laundry, old newspapers, a cracked imitation leather suitcase, and cardboard cartons filled with spiral notebooks. Porter sat glumly on the edge of the bed, while Kitty fiddled with the dial on the television set. It did not work.

What was he doing here with Billy Ray Walker? Porter asked himself. He had lost this night, lost disastrously. That was it. The System had built him up, and now it had brought him down. The only thing to do now was walk away. As Billy Ray said, *winners talk, losers walk.* . . .

But where? The System was his life. Where would he walk to? What would he do? How would he exist? Yolande Nathan lived in the back of his mind like a dream, but the System was his reality. The idea of abandoning it filled him with a sense of utter desolation, of overwhelming despair. If there were no System, there was nothing.

That's why he had accompanied Billy Ray Walker to his motel. The hero of the System, Billy Ray Walker, Monty's friend! No matter that he had fallen on bad days, that he was broken down, stumbling, groping. He was the guardian of the secret heart of the System, protector of its most arcane mysteries. He would share his knowledge with Porter and all would be right with his life.

Billy Ray Walker returned to the bed with a large sheet of poster board. On it, neatly inked in black, were percentages, ratios, odds. Billy Ray held the poster board in front of Kitty and Porter as though it were lettered in pure gold; he caressed its edges and he smiled, a slow, soft smile, a lost smile. Behind his stained spectacles his eyes shone brightly. He spoke in a hoarse whisper. "Six years it took me to devise this. I

184

worked with mathematicians from Berkeley and Stanford—
Julius Rhine and Herbert Futtermans and Wilson Oakley,
the best in their field, you may know their names. We em-
ployed the most advanced computer knowledge. It cost me
nearly fifty thousand dollars. But this is it. . . ." He stood
before Kitty and Porter, rocking back and forth on his heels.
His smile broadened to a wide, cracked-tooth grin. "The
Complete Billy Ray Walker Four-Deck System!"

He laughed stupidly. Porter leaned forward and studied the
poster board. The figures stood boldly out against the
smudged gray of the poster board. Porter looked at them for
a very long time. It was impossible at a glance to fully com-
prehend the Four-Deck System, but what he did understand
seemed good, very good, better than good—great. "You see
here," Billy Ray was saying, a grimy finger tracing a line along
a column of figures, "this here is your soft double-downs, this
here your splits. Notice the *puissance*, the *efficacy* of these
ideas!"

And now suddenly the System was alive for Porter again.
It glowed before him, crystalline, pure, extraordinary—the
Word, the Answer, the Reality beyond all good and evil. The
Complete Billy Ray Walker Four-Deck System. . . .

In the next few weeks Porter spent almost all his waking
hours with Billy Ray Walker.

He did not see Yolande Nathan, but he talked with her on
the phone: "Things didn't work out the way I had them
planned. I blew my stake and I'm scheming a way to come
back."

"Oh, Don." Her voice suddenly took on a note of panic.
"What does that mean?" He did not answer. "You don't
want to see me, is that it?"

"It's not that I don't want to see you. I just think—"
"What?"
"That for a while, until I build up my stake again—"
"It's something more than that—"

"No—"

"You want to break off. Is that what you're saying?"

"No, I'm not saying that at all. It means we just got to take it easy until I get my stake built back up."

There was a long silence on the other end of the line. Then he heard a soft sobbing sound, and he realized she was crying. "Look, I'm not going to throw you over," he said with some desperation in his voice. "I just got to get set up again."

He felt ugly and uncomfortable. How to get through to her? How to explain that nothing mattered to him now but Billy Ray Walker's Four-Deck System? "I like you, you know—"

She did not answer.

"I love you," he forced himself to say.

"Do you?"

"Yes."

He and Billy Ray would sit in the oppressive stench of the room in the Sultan Motel, sipping beer and eating pretzels, while they ran through the Four-Deck System together.

Sometimes Kitty would accompany him, more often he would be alone. The ancient air conditioner would groan laboriously beneath the lone window in the room, throwing off more warm air than cool. The room was like an oven, but once there for a half hour, lost in the frozen purity of the System, Porter would be oblivious to the heat.

Explaining the System, Billy Ray would become a changed man. The pomposity, the aura of defeat, and fuzzy eccentricity would fade, and suddenly he was all business, lucid, serious, preeminently capable. Face somber, brow furrowed in concentration, he would lead Porter through the complexities of the System, its maze of pinpoint percentages and ratios, the delicate interplay between probability and certainty.

He would deal from the shoe, cards face up, and Porter and he would consult the chart, evaluate, test, discuss, adjust, hone each advantage to its sharpest edge. On these work sessions Billy Ray would abandon his black holder and take his cigarettes unfiltered, burning them down to the smallest possible stub-end. The butts would dangle from his lip or rest forgotten between nicotine-stained fingers, a thin, gray ash held in precarious suspension by some delicate cohesiveness. Eventually the ash would fall, dusting the bed cover with gray and spotting it with burns.

They would work for hours on end, their talk limited to dry technical comment punctuated by toneless grunts and ahs, the only other sound the soft slap and riffle of the cards and the incessant rattle of the air conditioner.

The Four-Deck System in action was even more impressive than Porter had imagined in viewing the chart. It was delicate, it was complex, yet its basic thrust was simple; it posited the game of blackjack as war. The green felt table was a battleground between player and house, with gains measured in grabbing and holding hair-thin advantages. "It don't seem no bigger than a gnat's ass now," Billy Ray would say of a small percentage edge, "but when it comes to a showdown, when them ol' four decks are richer than a tree full of owls, you'll see the *effect!*"

It waged constant guerrilla war with chance; if one could master its basic weapons—a memory able to encompass two hundred and eight cards, a grasp of mathematics capable of translating the System's myriad laws into precise ratios—it appeared unbeatable. Concentration, training, faith—these seemed to be the requisites for attaining total mastery of its cabalistic intricacies.

Gradually, over the weeks, the System began to take hold in Porter's mind. As each training session came to an end, Billy Ray Walker would loosen up, grow expansive, puff out, glow. Popping the aluminum top of a beer container, tilting his head back and guzzling straight from the can, froth dribbling from the corners of his mouth and spilling down on his stained shirt front, he would prepare to launch into one of his rhetorical torrents of bombast and platitude. He would gasp, laugh, and belch, fish in his pockets and among the bed-

clothes for his cigarette holder, secure it, plug it with a cigarette, light up, and start in. "Don, I don't want a *gambler*
for my system. A gambler is a loser. I mean, any man that
bets on anything where he knows the percentage is loaded
against him is a loser. He must *lose*. I want a man who's like
a machine, who feels with his *mind*. That sort of man is a
winner."

Porter loved these long, rambling sessions. True, he had
been prepared by Monty to offer all homage to Billy Ray and,
when he had first come to him, had been bitterly disappointed. But now, delving with him into the heart of the
Four-Deck System, he once again discovered the awe and
respect he had felt before knowing the man. For him, no
philosophy, no religion contained the grace and purity and
power of The Complete Billy Ray Walker Four-Deck System. And it would not be long before they were once more
in action with it. It would not be long before Porter would
triumph once again. . . .

"Monty's a good ol' boy, Don, but he was infected by
daring and *bravado*. They'll carry you a certain distance,
that's for sure, but in the end they'll destroy you—*unless* they
are reined in by the most powerful strength of mind and emotion. Always temper *daring* with *logic*. Monty could never do
that. That's what turned him from a pretty fair man with a
deck of cards into an out-and-out desperado. One day he just
woke up and decided, what the hell am I doing nursing these
damn pasteboards? Let me just get hold on a .38 Special and
break the bank—and I don't mean any old casino, but the
First National or something like that. Do you get my meaning?"

Porter would nod, fascinated. "Have a Cheez Whiz," Billy
Ray would say, ripping the cellophane from a package of yellow crackers. "When I started to lose, Don, I knew what was
happening. I couldn't avoid it. But I had to follow through
on the logic of the System. Perhaps that was a mistake, because they had shuffled up the rules of the game on me, and

the System no longer held up. But all the while I was work-ing, carving away at this new edifice they were constructing. I blew everything I owned, but a dedication to the mind, to logic, led me, bless heaven, to the Four-Deck System. And there's nothing on this earth can defeat Billy Ray Walker's Complete Four-Deck System."

The summer was slipping inexorably toward September, and the days were growing cooler now. The temperature dur-ing the day began to dip below the hundred-degree mark, and Vegas grew quite pleasant. Billy Ray Walker and Porter continued to work on the System; Kitty would occasionally work with them, but more often she stayed at the Excelsior, stretched out beside the pool or watching television in the room.

They had almost no money now, but Porter was as sure as anything in his life that they would bounce back. They would get back all they had lost, and five times as much.

Yolande Nathan drank a lot and grew thin and cried her-self to sleep and yearned for Porter. She left messages for him at his motel, and he would call her and they would talk for long, long periods, and he would explain to her that every-thing was going to be fine, that he couldn't see her, that he was working on something very important.

Eddie MacRae continued to train. Frank Murphy was happy with his progress. One afternoon Matt Nathan ap-peared in the gym to announce to the two of them that a ten-round match with Julio Martinez had been arranged for the Silver Slipper in the middle of September.

Billy Ray Walker and Porter had been at work together on the System for almost three weeks when Billy Ray decided it was time they ventured onto the Strip for a trial run. He started out by shaving for the occasion.

As he lathered up his face with an old raggedy brush and plain soap, Porter, leaning against the doorjamb to the bath-room, brought up something that had been gnawing at him. "Why is it you never put the Four-Deck System into play? I mean, why is it just now that you're getting ready to use it?"

Billy Ray Walker guided the razor over his face with great care. He didn't shave often, but when he did, he performed the task with extraordinary attention to detail; he didn't miss a hair. "One reason is psychological, the other practical. When I blew all my accumulated winnings of ten years, it took the heart out of me. I admit it. I became a psychological defeatist. The practical side concerns financing. I was so flat it looked like an elephant stomped on my stake. You need *capital* to play the Four-Deck System."

And it was true. It had become readily apparent to Porter that the Four-Deck System required a solid reserve of money. In playing four decks, the arid stretches when the P.C. was running against the player went on and on. It wasn't like one deck where you got a new shuffle every fifty-two cards; no, with four decks a cold deal carried over two hundred and eight cards. "Sometimes days will go by before you hit a rich run of the deck, and you got to play it tighter than the bark on a tree, but when you hit it, Don, those tens and aces and queens and kings and jacks come falling faster than shit from a donkey. You might be working with a point count of plus twenty, and you got to bet that son-of-a-bitch to the limit, 'cause one thing sure as I'm standing here—God hates a coward!"

Billy Ray Walker finished shaving. He removed a green metal fishing-tackle box from the bureau drawer. Out of the fishing-tackle box he withdrew an array of strange items that he proceeded to spread out on the bed coverlet: bottles of lotion and jars of cream, sprays, pencils, small brushes, toothpicks, sponges. On the inside of the lid to the tackle box was affixed a mirror. Billy Ray Walker began to make himself up in the mirror. "Every damn casino manager in this town knows my kisser. But I've got my ways to outfox them!"

He painted his upper lip with a harsh smelling liquid, then attached a thick brush mustache. The mustache was a realistic piece—custom-made, Billy Ray explained—with even a sprinkling of gray hairs subtly woven into it. Next he went to work on his own hair. It was a dirty gray, limp and thin and receding far back from the top of his forehead. He applied a spray to it and transformed it into a deep brown. He then combed streaks of silver gray into it. Next he fixed a forelock toupee at the edge of the hairline and combed it back so that it blended with his own hair and provided a rich, gray-streaked pompadour.

He removed his spectacles. It was the first time Porter had seen his naked eyes. They were small and black with bizarre, dilated irises. From a small plastic box he removed a set of contacts, rolled his eyes back, and inserted them. When he lowered his gaze on Porter, his eyes were blue.

From his closet he removed a dark blue blazer and a pair of gray trousers. He donned a striped silk shirt and a wide red cravat. On his little finger he slipped a ring with a huge, many-faceted stone. He held his hand out for Porter's inspection. "Looks like a biggie, doesn't it? She's a fake, but a beauty nonetheless."

He stood now in the center of the room amid the beer cans and paperback books, the dirty laundry and cigarette butts, and appeared every bit the posh custodian of great, probably inherited, wealth. "Let's go, Don," he called out gleefully after inspecting himself in the large bureau mirror. "We're going to make us some *stake!*"

Billy Ray Walker still had the hundred-dollar chip Porter had pressed on him weeks before at Caesar's Palace; Porter had scraped together another two hundred dollars. It was a small beginning, but with a good run on the four-deck shoe, it could pyramid dramatically for them.

They chose the Desert Inn to initiate the Four-Deck System. Because of their limited stake, they were forced to start out at the dollar-minimum table.

Billy Ray Walker left Porter at the door and selected an empty table. Porter, as planned, hung back a bit to keep people from suspecting they were working in concert.

Billy Ray greeted the dealer with a thick, hearty Texas accent. "Howdy, sir, how's the cards falling?"

"Sixteen aces to the deck," replied the dealer, a short, bald-headed man with a dour expression. "Shuffle up," he said to the pit boss.

The dealer, his face grim and tired, laboriously cut the four decks together, then split them into sections, shuffled each section, then cut them back together again. He performed the task without joy, annoyed. Why should he be forced to work when there were other tables already in action?

Porter sauntered through the casino until he was standing behind Billy Ray's table. He watched the play. The percentages ran a fairly even balance. Billy Ray varied his bet between one and three chips depending on the shift in odds, keeping up a steady stream of chatter all the while, a feat Porter found incredible considering the amount of complex calculating he was forced to perform in his head. "Sometimes lady luck is all for you, sometimes she goes against you. It's like the tides of the sea. I know there's some reason to it, but it's not up to a man to discern it. . . ." Peeking at his hole card, then performing a short, whisking motion with his cards, he chattered right on: "I'll take a five if you have one in the deck, sir. No five? All right, I'll settle for that there four. Lovely. Yes, sir, all my life I've been trying to figure out that movement, that wave of good luck that sweeps in and sweeps out. Twenty? I guess that beats nineteen every time. Could you summon that ample-chested girl over here so I can weasel a Jack Daniels and water out of her? Thank you, sir!"

The performance was enormously impressive. Not only his appearance, but his whole physicality had changed, the timbre of his voice, the thrust of his personality. Gone was the shabby, vaguely pompous, professorial man; in his place was a take-charge guy, oil- or cattle-rich, a man one could picture riding the range, hunting for bear, flying his own airplane, rolling in the sack with two prostitutes at the same time.

192

Porter moved into the seat next to him. Billy Ray lit up a house cigar and sipped at his bourbon. He kept talking—to Porter, to the dealer, to no one in particular, his small hands performing rapid, fluttery motions as they fingered the chips, setting his bets out like a chess player pushing pawns, with a movement both delicate and precise. "Take it easy on us now, dealer. Remember, you can shear a sheep a many-a-time. You can only skin him once." He laughed and winked. The dealer did not smile. "There's only two vices worth having in this world—gambling and humping. The first 'cause it makes you rich, the second 'cause it makes you feel good."

"No one ever got rich gambling," Porter said, attempting to enter into the spirit of the thing.

"No one ever got rich gambling? Did you hear that, dealer? You can tell this young fellow's never been around. I'll bet you could tell him a few stories! A ten, sir. A ten. I'd be deeply grateful to you if you'd drop me a ten. That three will never do, I'll just have to ask you for a seven. A four? We'll have to rest and recuperate with that."

"I never seen anyone get rich," the dealer said glumly.

"Perhaps not when *you're* dealing. That's understandable. You're an old shark cruising placid waters. But in other places and at other times—"

They were halfway through the shoe when the percentage suddenly soared for the player. Billy Ray pushed ten chips out in front of him. "I feel a wave of *good luck* coming in, my friend. Bet this mother to the hilt." Porter followed with ten chips, and they both won. The P.C. remained high for the player. "Let it ride. You see the important thing, if you want to get rich gambling, is sensing the ebb and flow of the cards, just like the tides of the sea. When that tide is coming in, swim with it, my friend. Blackjack! Very nice. And what do you have? A twenty? You'll settle for that, won't you?"

They won seven times in a row, escalating their bets each time. Then the advantage to the player began to run down. "And now, sir, I feel the tide flowing out. It's going out to

193

sea, and if you were smart, my friend, you'd follow me out of the ocean and up onto dry land."

Billy Ray changed his dollar chips into fives, tipped the dealer a single five and departed from the table. He left with three hundred dollars. "That's some character," said Porter, hanging around the table for a few more desultory hands. The dealer was unimpressed. "I've never met a loudmouth that was a winner. In seventeen years not one."

Porter lost a string of one-dollar hands, and when the shoe was empty, rose to leave. "The deal's gone cold," he said.

"It's always cold," said the dealer, without looking up or smiling.

At the five-dollar table Billy Ray Walker continued his winning ways. As Porter slipped into the seat next to him, he was declaiming: "Catch the brass ring when you can, that's the important thing in this game. God hates a coward. Saw a man in Reno once sit down with a single five-dollar chip, run it up to ten thousand dollars in an hour. Something told him his ship was coming in, and goddamn it, he bet it and sure enough it did come in! Hello, young fellow, how's lady luck treating you? I feel she's got a nice smile on her face right now, that's why I'm betting—how much? Twenty-five dollars a hand! I might even go up to fifty! Blackjack! Look at that! I had a feeling!"

The deck stayed hot for a time, and soon Porter and Billy Ray were riding winners on more than a thousand dollars each. They had cashed in their red five-dollar chips and were now playing with the twenty-five-dollar greens. Billy Ray Walker was irrepressible. "Did you see that, my friend? I hit with a seventeen, and damn if it didn't come up! Do you know why? I had a *hunch*. That's the kind of player I am. Follow lady luck wherever she leads and always follow your hunches! What's the table limit?"

The dealer, florid-faced with solid white hair and a thin mouth said: "Five hundred dollars."

194

"Too rich for my blood, but—" Billy Ray gently fingered eight twenty-five-dollar chips—"I'll venture *that*, because I have a *hunch, premonition* you might say." Turning to Don: "Don't be timid, my friend. Daring and luck, that's what you need for this game!"

Of a sudden, things began to go bad. The point count stayed high for the player; Porter and Billy Ray continued to bet heavily, but the cards now defied the P.C. and began to fall for the dealer. Both began to lose.

Billy Ray kept up his stream of chatter, but signs of nervousness began to appear: his face grew pale, perspiration formed on his brow, his smile became frozen and awkward. He clenched and unclenched his hands over the cards. "Yes, sir. You can't win 'em all. If you could, you wouldn't be a gambler, but a banker. Damn a six! I could have sworn you had a ten in there for me!"

The dealer caught three blackjacks and two twenty-ones in a ten-hand stretch. Billy Ray Walker's fingers began to tremble. "Yes, sir, it's just like the tides of the ocean, it comes and goes in waves—" he said weakly.

Porter's fortunes collapsed along with Billy Ray's. Nothing fell right for him. In a half hour both were back where they had started.

They returned to the one-dollar table. Billy Ray Walker said under his breath: "Tenacity, Don, tenacity."

To the dealer, he presented a hearty façade, though Porter could see he was coming apart. "Thought we'd return to pay you another visit—" He laughed. The dealer just stared at him. "Those other guys might as well use a gun to take it off you, the way they deal those cards. . . ."

He was breathing heavily now and his face was ghostly pale. He took a small plastic bottle out of his pocket and swallowed a pill. "I have a minor cardiac problem," he said to Porter. "Nothing serious, you understand, just a damn nuisance."

Another hour of continuous losing and they were each

down to their last twenty dollars. "Some days you can't piss a drop," Billy Ray said glumly.

The pit boss had been watching them; he now moved to a telephone on a wooden stand between the blackjack tables and placed a call. A moment later a heavy-set, pleasant-looking man approached the table. He leaned close to Billy Ray Walker. "All right, Billy Ray," he said politely, "you and your friend will have to be moving off now."

"I beg your pardon?"

"Move off, Billy Ray."

"Name is Ogden Semple of Fort Worth, Texas—" Billy Ray began to fumble in his pockets for identification. To Porter's surprise, he was able to produce a raft of credit cards made out to Ogden Semple.

The casino manager was unimpressed. "I know, I know. Ogden Semple and Reverend P. Dickson and Luigi Fortunato and all those names and faces you been trying to pawn off on us for years. You're beginning to repeat yourself, Billy Ray."

"This is outrageous!" Billy Ray exclaimed loudly. "I fly up here from Fort Worth, lose damn near ten thousand dollars, and you kick me out like a dog?" He was shouting now, but Porter could see small tics of insecurity dancing in the flab of his face.

The casino manager reached forward and grabbed Billy Ray's mustache. He ripped it clean from his face. Billy Ray bolted from the table. He ranted all the way to the door. "Lower than a goddamn rattlesnake! Bunch of goddamn cheats, skin you of all your money, then insult you to boot! I'm taking my business off to Caesar's Palace or the Sahara where they know how to treat a gambling man!"

He stormed from the Desert Inn, Porter following fast after him.

In the car all energy seemed to drain from him. He sat, drenched with perspiration, slumped in the seat. He popped another pill in his mouth.

He was silent for a while on the drive back to the Sultan Motel. Then: "That damn mustache cost me seventy-five dollars. Custom-made." He attempted to revive his enthusiasm but did a poor job of it. "You see, Don, you have to keep betting right into *them*—don't back off when the P.C. is going your way. You're not going to win them all, but you're going to get your share. . . ." His voice trailed off, and he lapsed into private muttering. "Where the hell am I going to get another mustache like that? I should have taken my remaining chips and shoved them up his ass!"

Back at the Sultan Motel Porter declined Billy Ray's invitation to join him for a beer. Billy Ray stood outside the car, a whipped man. "Don't lose faith, Don. The Four-Deck System's good as gold. You saw that, didn't you? Just some days you can't piss a drop."

Porter had not lost faith. He was just tired. Despite the way the evening had turned out, the Four-Deck System had shown him limitless possibilities. It was as near to perfection as you could get in the gambler's life.

"Billy Ray—" Porter said.

"Yes?"

"The Reverend P. Dickson? Were you broadcasting on the radio awhile back?"

"I gave it a try there at a low point in my life," Billy Ray said very quietly, staring down at the ground.

"Damn if Kitty and I didn't hear you on our way into this damn town!"

As tired as he was, he managed to laugh.

XI

Kitty stood at the nickel slots in Caesar's Palace trying to figure out what to do. She had been playing the slots for hours this night.

She would drop the nickels in the slot from a paper cup in her hand, pull the lever on the machine, and stand hypnotized by the flash and whirr of the cylinders, the rapid clickety-click as cherries, oranges, bars, and sevens fell into place.

It didn't matter to her whether she won or lost. It was the feel of the lever, then the soft humming sound as the cylinders spun, followed by the clicking in place of each symbol that somehow relaxed her.

Kitty had discovered that Porter and Yolande were having an affair. She had suspected something, but now she knew for sure. She had intercepted a note Yolande had left for him.

It was a small envelope left at the desk at the Excelsior. It was addressed to Porter, but Kitty had opened it. It read: "Darling, my life does not exist without you. Every night I dream about you and pray for the time when we will be together again, when you will hold me again. Do you know how barren my life was until you came into it? Can you imagine it? I don't think you can. How I love you, my darling! How interminable the days without you are! How I

198

yearn for you! Please Don, we must go away. Please. Far away. An eternity away . . ."

Kitty burned with shame and despair. The words were knives cutting into her heart. She felt small and stupid and overwhelmed by her own inadequacy. Never, never, never could she have written a note phrased like that. "Interminable days . . . how I yearn for you . . ." Did Yolande Nathan love more deeply than she? Or was it some basic ignorance that prevented her from even *thinking* such exalted thoughts? She felt trapped, trapped by her background, her limited intellectual capacity, the poverty of her education. She was a prisoner *forever* to her own ignorance; and that certainty ravaged the image she held of herself.

She had grown to despise her life. She hated the motel room, the absence of Porter, the idea that he might be with that woman.

He had lately taken to sleeping at Billy Ray's. At least that's what he had told her: they were working around the clock on the System. She didn't believe him and would call there at odd hours, expecting to catch him out. He was always there.

"What is it?"

"I just wanted to talk to you. I'm lonely."

"Why don't you come over here?"

"No, that's all right."

She had grown to dislike Billy Ray Walker. At first she had been fascinated by his Four-Deck System, but then an oppressive boredom set in. Boredom and anger. She had decided the Four-Deck System was no more effective than the One-Deck System. It was all an illusion, a fraud, and they were wasting their lives.

She resented the hold Billy Ray had on Porter; she somehow even blamed Yolande Nathan on him. His grubby appearance revolted her, the smell of his room, his condescending manner, the way in which he presented the Four-Deck System as the key to all existence.

199

She could feel the trap that was Vegas tightening about her. Billy Ray Walker, Yolande Nathan, the casinos, the System, the neon and automobiles and harsh narrow eyes and desert—such wide gray emptiness!—were strangling her. She was suffocating and she feared not only for herself, but Porter and Eddie MacRae as well. Whatever bond had once been between them was being destroyed.

For a time in the evenings she had taken to visiting Eddie MacRae at the Paradise Hotel. They would sit around the coffee shop or relax next to the pool. It was pleasant enough, but even Eddie had somehow become dead for her. He was obsessed by his training, by the impending fight, and she sensed whenever they were together that he begrudged the time spent with her. His eyes increasingly had a faraway look, as though he were trying to piece together some enormously complex puzzle.

Then she discovered the slot machines. She began visiting a different casino every night. She would walk to the places nearby the motel—the Paradise or the International or the Landmark. To get to the Strip casinos, she would take the bus up Las Vegas Boulevard.

For ten or fifteen dollars she could play the nickel slots all evening. When she grew weary of the slots or if she hit a nice jackpot, she would treat herself to a drink or two.

Every evening, though, the power of the slots to divert her grew less and less. A terrible awareness came over her that her life was trickling down the drain. She no longer owned her existence. She must do something to salvage herself. . . .

Two sevens came up, and the third cylinder flashed a seven, then clicked in place with a bar. Kitty took no notice. She was banging the nickels into the slot machine now without seeing or caring. She hit or missed and it was all the same.

She realized she was out of nickels. She stared down at the empty paper cup and tried to decide what next to do. She stood in front of the slot machine for a long time.

Around her, little old ladies in flowered hats, retired men in baggy gray suits, lonesome wives weary of keno, young newlyweds on their honeymoon visit to Vegas, poured nickels, dimes, and quarters into the slots; a jackpot bell rang, and a woman squealed. Kitty was indifferent to it all.

A heavily rouged woman with flabby arms and dressed in a faded cotton dress appeared next to her. "How's that machine, hon?" she asked.

"It's all right, I guess," Kitty said.

"Mind if I play it? I've tried this whole line and not a winner amongst them. I just know I'm due."

Kitty stood to one side and watched the woman play for a while. Then she drifted off. She arrived at the cocktail area still holding her paper cup. She felt empty and stupid and lost. She felt as though she might cry, and she really couldn't understand why. She just knew that she was, as she had been so often in her life, utterly alone.

She ordered a stinger and sat there slowly sipping it. People moved along the red-carpeted promenade in front of her; she did not really see them. She was thinking about another sort of life.

She and Don would get married and have children. They would move to some place different, a place they had never before been—perhaps Denver or San Francisco. He would get a job in a gas station or a supermarket. She would work as a waitress. They would have a not-too-expensive car—a Chevy or Ford would be fine. They would drive out into the country on weekends. They would go to the movies a lot. They would buy a small house. . . .

She was conscious that a man had joined her at the table. He was short and balding and smelled of a sweetish cologne. He was perspiring. "You don't mind me sitting here, do you?" he asked.

"No, that's all right."

"My feet are killing me," he said. "This town is nothing but action."

"I guess so."

"First the dice are hot, then they're cold, then they're hot again. Makes your head spin, you know?"

She smiled. "A man got to take a little break, you know? How about I buy you a drink?" he said.

"No, this is fine. . . ."

"I'm looking for a little bit of the right kind of action, you know. I'm from Chicago. Ladies' underwear. We make those ones with little red hearts on them. You may have seen them?"

"I think I have. . . ."

"Very chic." He pronounced the word "chick." "Even the most elegant women are buying them, you know? I got boxes and boxes of them up in my room."

She smiled again. He seemed like a nice old gentleman. He had very pink skin and large, watery eyes. He seemed sad and eager to be friendly. "You'd look good in that sort of thing," he said.

"I don't know—"

"Why don't you try on a couple of pair? For free, you know. Just see what you look like?"

"That's very nice of you, but . . ."

"They sell, you know, retail $6.95."

"I couldn't."

The man looked crushed. He peered about him in some desperation. "I'll tell you what. How about if I give you fifty dollars and half dozen boxes of underwear?" She looked at him, uncomprehending. "I'm dying to have a woman. I'm getting an ache in my prostate I'm dying to have a woman so bad—"

It now dawned on her what he was proposing. She laughed at her stupidity. "Are you looking for a girl who does that sort of thing for money?" she asked.

"To be honest, that's what I had in mind."

"No, thank you. I don't do that sort of thing."

The man became flustered. "I'm sorry, miss. I just thought . . . Oh, I'm very sorry . . ."

He excused himself from the table. He moved a few feet away and, jiggling several casino chips in his hand, gazed desperately around. He spotted a buxom redhead strolling along the promenade. He hesitated a moment then hurried after her.

Kitty finished her drink, feeling as naked and stupid as she ever had in her life. She took a mirror out of her beaded bag and stared at her face. She stared for a long while, aware for the first time how silly and cheap she looked, yearning for some magical cream that could wipe her face away. Then she left the casino.

Porter was back at the motel when she arrived there. It was the first time she had seen him in several days. He needed a shave, and his clothes looked as though he had slept in them. He was sitting in front of the television set watching a movie. He did not speak when she entered the room. She kicked off her shoes and sat on the bed. She massaged her feet and stared at television. Porter didn't even look at her.

An old movie with Dick Powell, Evelyn Keyes, and Thomas Gomez was playing. It was *Johnny O'Clock,* and she thought "O'Clock" was a funny name for a man. She tried to remember if she had ever known anybody named "O'Clock" and was certain that she hadn't.

"Aren't we talking tonight?" she said after a while.

"I'm just disgusted is all," he said.

"What about?"

His face had never looked so thin and pale. "Billy Ray's Four-Deck System is unbeatable, and we don't have the god-damn stake to pull it off—"

"Sell the car—"

"It's four decks. Even ten thousand dollars isn't enough. I mean four decks just gobbles that up and you got to have enough to last."

"I think Billy Ray Walker's Four-Deck System is a farce!

It's the biggest farce I ever did see!" She was lashing out at Porter, and she didn't know why. It was anger at her isolation, anger at Yolande Nathan, but she wouldn't admit that to herself. All she knew was that she was acting ugly, and that would only drive him further away, increase the gap between them. . . .

He did not say anything. He went into the bathroom and began to wash up. Kitty could hear him brushing his teeth. He came out of the bathroom and changed his clothes. He stood in front of the bureau mirror combing his hair.

"Where are you going?" she asked. He did not answer. "Please, Donny, don't leave me alone no more—"

He turned on her. His face was fierce, contorted with anger. "You don't believe in the System! What the hell do you believe in?"

"I don't know—"

"Well, that's the way it is. The System is my life—"

She began to cry uncontrollably. The tears just choked from her. "I don't know what I'm supposed to do. I don't know. I just want you to be with me. I don't want to lose you, Donny. Please, Donny, please!"

But he was gone. She cried and cried and cried. She had never wept so hard in her life. The pillow was soaked with her tears. Her body was utterly drained. She had no idea life could be so ugly.

Matt Nathan sat in a purple silk robe on the patio to his home. He was smoking a long, black Havana, the real thing brought from Cuba by way of Canada. His poodle, Princess, lay sleeping on the glass-top table in front of him. It was late night and the house was quiet. Angel Amato was in his room at the front of the house, asleep. Yolande was out with Porter.

There were few things that depressed Matt Nathan. His son Stephen's fragile health was one. The boy was always ill. It seemed his childhood was a passage from one debilitating virus to the next. Matt Nathan was never ill and could not understand it.

This night Nathan had been awakened by the nurse. Stephen had had a nightmare and was hysterical, and the nurse could not quiet him. Nathan had sat by his bedside for a half hour stroking the boy's head and telling him a story.

He told him a long story about a pirate who had rescued a princess. He hid the princess away in a castle and kept her there for many, many years. A young sailor was shipwrecked and landed on the rocky island where the princess was held captive.

"Does she ever get out?" Stephen asked.

"I'll tell you tomorrow—"

The boy's eyes were wide and sad, and his pinched face was the color of chalk. Matt Nathan put his arms around his shoulders and pulled him to him. The boy's back was soaked with perspiration. Matt Nathan held his son to him for a long while.

At last the boy had fallen asleep. Matt Nathan poured himself a diet cola and then came out on the patio.

The night was cool, and it relaxed Nathan. He loved Vegas when the summer began to slacken off. The days were sunny and warm, but the heat lacked the scorching oppressiveness of July and early August; the nights were clear and crisp.

He puffed at his cigar and turned his life over in his mind, examining it as though it were something separate from himself. He admired that quality in himself more than any other: that ability to objectify his existence. Things touched him but never so deeply that he couldn't distinguish his essential interests.

He looked with some amusement on people: their dependencies, their fears, their need to love and be loved, their compulsion to compete. He never competed. He only won.

He had been alone ever since he could remember, and he liked it that way. He had never known his parents. Oh, he recalled them vaguely—two stooped, shabby people, who existed like a dream at some dim beginning of his memory and then were gone, whisked off by flu or pneumonia or cancer: there had been no one around to impress on him which.

He had invented a mother for himself, or perhaps she was based on fact—a woman who was wise and stern and infinitely loving, a woman who taught him good from evil, who always showed him the right path. She pointed it out for him, but somehow the way was inevitably swallowed up in a hopelessly tangled maze. The way was a phantasm.

His earliest clear memories were of foster homes, of running away, of living in the streets. He had a younger brother and sister and had taken care of them as best he could. Some years later, because of him, his brother had been killed. After that, his sister stopped talking to him. Alone.

At school, children were constantly taunting him. It had to do with the fact that he had no parents. He took to carrying a small length of steel pipe in his back pocket. When the other kids began to harass him, he would strike out with the pipe. The harassment stopped. He became a leader. He must have been eight years old then. He remained a leader the rest of his life.

He cared for only three things: his son, his dog, and his casino.

He had cared for his wife for a time, then lost interest in her. Now she was a possession. It did not matter to him what she did as long as she belonged to him.

The most important thing was the casino. He had invested in the casino all the energy and passion and belief he had. It was his soul.

Sitting now on the patio, he was aware of an immense heaviness inside. He was desperately tired and he could not tell why. He could never understand that terrible fatigue that constantly assailed him.

He thought about that now as he stared into the dark surrounding his house. Something was weighing on him and nothing—not even the Paradise Hotel—could ease it.

And now he thought of Porter. Porter somehow weighed on him. Why?

He sipped at the cola. He realized his cigar had gone out and relit it. The ash glowed red in the dark night.

He didn't know who Porter was, and that disturbed him. No one seemed to be able to discover anything about him. Red Polikoff had tried and drawn only blanks. Angel Amato had theories, but one was as good as the next. Even Caputo, the head of the Paradise Hotel detective force, an ex-cop with contacts all over Vegas, contacts that extended across the country—even he was stumped. All he could come up with was that Porter gambled a good deal and was friendly with Billy Ray Walker.

Walker. He thought of the man and was seized with an enormous sense of anger and disgust. There were people and there were cockroaches. Walker was a cockroach, a leech, insidiously sucking away at Nathan's lifeblood: the Paradise Hotel. He had taken the casino for more than a hundred thousand dollars—not taken it by chance, by good fortune, but by cunning and deceit, by beating Nathan's own edge, by, in a sense, cutting himself in as a partner.

Well, Matt Nathan needed no partners. If the man hadn't been essentially so insignificant, Nathan would have handled him in the only way that kind of audacity could be handled: he would have had someone put a bullet in the back of his skull. In the old days that's what he would have had done.

In the old days, when a dealer or a pit boss or anyone cut themselves in unannounced on the house's edge, they only did it once. We all only have one life, Nathan was fond of reminding himself. . . .

But it was a different world then. There were men of a different stripe in the casino business then. Now it was all corporations, conglomerates, computers, boards of directors, big business. Things were done differently now. Things were done in a businesslike way. Walker had been cut off, barred, that was all. It galled Matt Nathan. The man should be part of the desert: cactus should be sprouting from his eyes.

Porter was friendly with Walker. So that was the sort his wife had become involved with now! Still, Porter was not Walker. Porter had some sort of innate refinement, an indefinable quality that separated him in Matt Nathan's eyes from the creeps and cockroaches. It was like that with boxers. Two boys in the ring: both are fast, knowledgeable, can take and give a punch, yet one is class, the other a bum. It had to do with character, with a certain essential toughness. For Matt Nathan, character *was* toughness—not a superficial swagger, but the steel at the core of a man.

Matt Nathan realized, now, in a peculiar way he liked Porter. He liked the way Porter's eyes scanned everything. He liked a man who was watchful.

What gnawed at him was not knowing who he was.

Nathan found himself visualizing his wife in Porter's arms; the idea moved him. In reality she had long ago ceased to hold any attraction for him. Her body seemed dead, grotesque, with flabby breasts and vein-marked thighs and a chalky whiteness that was almost revolting. In his mind's eye, though, coupled with another man, she regained for him that exquisite and aching beauty that had so stirred him at the beginning of their relationship. Her expression in his imagination was tender, sorrowful, unsullied by time, pure. . . .

He had considered having her make love to another man in front of him. He had thought of her and Angel Amato. He rejected the idea, sensing how delicate his fantasy was, how the rawness of reality was bound to violate it. No, he would keep that fantasy buried in that special part of himself where the whitened bones of other secrets lay.

In some profound way Matt Nathan felt himself very different from the rest of humanity. At times he felt scarcely a member of the race. And, though never consciously admitted, this sense of separation, of distance from the race of men, while a source of pride, was also a source of dissatisfaction. His marriage, his home, his wife, his child, were necessary to reassure himself that he was, indeed, human.

He got up now, still feeling vaguely depressed. He returned to his room and picked up the phone. He pressed a red button at the side of the phone. Angel Amato, his voice heavy with sleep, answered.

"Come to my room."

Angel Amato, dressed in a short white terrycloth robe, appeared a moment later, looking surprisingly fresh for having just been awakened. He sat, hands folded in his lap, opposite Matt Nathan's bed. "I have something on my mind. I can't seem to nail it down." Matt Nathan sat on the bed puffing on a fresh cigar.

"What's it about?"

"Yolande's relationship with this guy—what do you think?"

Angel Amato shrugged. "He has no past. Nothing."

"Yes?"

"I never liked a person without a past."

Matt Nathan smiled. "Oh, he has one all right. We just haven't found it yet."

"I spoke to the boxer about him. The boxer come up with snake-eyes as far as I'm concerned. But then you know boxers—"

"What about that girl of his? She must know something." Matt Nathan removed his silk robe and placed it over the back of the chair. He was wearing a pair of pajamas with a Chinese dragon print on them. "I want you to move in on that girl. I want you to find out everything she knows about him."

"I understand."

"Now bring me a sleeping pill."

Angel Amato moved into the bathroom, took a green bottle down off the shelf in the medicine cabinet, removed a tablet, then poured a glass of water. When he returned to the bedroom, Matt Nathan was standing by the window. He downed the pill and returned to the bed.

Occasionally, in the middle of the night, Matt Nathan was seized by a nameless dread. He would do anything to protect himself from that dread. He did not feel it now, but he could sense its presence, like a ghost hovering on the edge of his consciousness.

He crawled under the sheet. "Wait until I'm asleep," he said to Angel.

Angel Amato sat in the chair opposite the bed. A dim lamp burned next to him. He removed his .32 from the pocket of his bathrobe and let it rest in his lap.

Matt Nathan saw the gun and was reassured. He closed his eyes and slept.

Yolande Nathan looked tired and old. Her pale face was puffy and there were dark circles under her eyes.

She and Porter had driven to a motel on the Strip. Inside the room neither one was in the mood to make love. Porter sat on the bed, while Yolande sat in a chair opposite him. They had spoken almost not at all. "What's wrong?" she asked.

Porter shrugged. His heart felt completely empty. Everything felt old and tired. "I told you. I blew my stake, and it doesn't look as though I'm ever going to get it back."

"How much do you need?"

"Twenty thousand dollars."

There was a bottle of Scotch on the dresser, and Yolande poured herself a drink. She had been drinking since they arrived at the motel. She offered the bottle to Porter, and he shook his head no. She held the glass in front of her and stared at the drink. The lamp on the dresser imparted a fine, clear, golden color to the Scotch. "I've missed you terribly," she said.

"I've missed you, too."

"I don't believe you."

"What can I do to prove it?"

She shrugged and smiled grimly. She returned to the bed and drained the glass of Scotch. "I hate it when I feel like wood," she said.

"Yes," he said.

"Do you feel that way, too?"

"Sometimes."

"It's terrible, isn't it?"

"Yes."

"I don't want that feeling with you," she said. "Do you think—"

"What?"

"I was just imagining. If we could run away someplace—"

She shook her head, smiling. Her hair fell across her face. "He would have us killed. I just know that's what he would do."

"If I had the money—"

"Twenty thousand? There'd be no problem—"

"I could build it real good. I know it."

"If I gave you the twenty thousand, could we run off together?"

"Yes."

"Could we go someplace where no one would ever find us?"

"Yes."

She stared up at the ceiling. The room was beginning to move gently around. "I'm drunk," she said.

"I know."

"Do you like to make love to drunk women?"

He leaned down and kissed her. He felt as though he were being carried along by a force ineluctable as time or chance. He felt as though he were being carried along into oblivion. He couldn't be sure she was serious about their going off together, but he realized that if she were, he would accede to it. And he didn't know why.

XII

Eddie MacRae was scared. Lately he had been having nightmares. He walked around in a state of perpetual anxiety. The fight with Julio Martinez was less than two weeks away, and the reality of it was just beginning to register. During his training sessions he fought well, but inside he was cold with fear. He was going in over his head, and he knew it.

Julio Martinez had been a ranking heavyweight for as long as Eddie MacRae could remember. True, he was old and slow and had looked ineffectual in his last couple of fights, but there were few fighters around with his experience or power. Even the Black Avenger, Joe Fletcher, had been impressed when he heard who Eddie's opponent was to be. Eddie had seen the concern in his eyes. "Ol' Julio capable of causing some *misery*, man. They's fighters just got a plain mean streak in 'em, you know? Ol' Julio, he's one of them cats would rather fight than hump, man, and you know there got to be something wrong with a cat like that!"

Frank Murphy, who had overheard the conversation, jumped in quickly to reassure Eddie. "He's a limp dick, Eddie, believe me. Last spring in San Diego he couldn't go six rounds. He has no wind, he has no legs. He still got the punch, but what's the punch without the wind and the legs? So, let's just keep working on that defense. Stick and run, stick and run."

Frank Murphy's strategy for the fight was to have Eddie stay back for the first four or five rounds. Jab and run. If Martinez got in close, go to the belly, then tie him up. Lean on him. Make him sweat. The older fighter would tire. That would be the time for Eddie to open up.

Every day Eddie MacRae improved. He was strong and fast and gaining in polish. He had little trouble handling Indian Sam, his sparring partner. But he was afraid.

When his own sparring session was over, the Black Avenger, who felt a genuine warmth for Eddie, would study his workout from the side of the ring and later, in the locker room, give Eddie some pointers. "Don't try to trade with ol' Julio, Eddie. Bless you, if you think you can get away with it. Clinch with him, Eddie, and work on his kidneys. You know them old guys, they got weak kidneys. Get him pissing some blood! That'll take the steam out of him." He smiled broadly, wrinkling the thick clumps of scar tissue above his eyes. "Yes, sir, that's one of my main weapons. Get a man pissing blood—"

Eddie's nightmares had him killing Martinez. His face would float about Eddie, bobbing, disembodied, much like a small speed bag, while Eddie lashed it with punches until it broke from some invisible anchor and flew across the ring.

He would charge forward only to be stopped by the referee, a man he knew to be Matt Nathan, but who didn't look anything like him. "He's dead," the referee would proclaim, and Eddie MacRae would jolt awake, bathed in sweat.

"Back pedal, Eddie! Back pedal! Now, counter! *Counter!*" Eddie MacRae glided gracefully around the ring, while Indian Sam plodded after him. Frank Murphy leaned on the apron of the ring and barked out instructions. "To the *gut!* Get him in the gut!"

Eddie suddenly shifted his weight and caught Indian Sam

213

with a right hook to the midsection. The slap of the glove resounded through the gym. Sam grunted and slowed in his pursuit. Perspiration flowed down his face; his open mouth sucked in air. "Now to the head! To the head!" Frank Murphy screamed.

Eddie chopped a glancing right off Sam's skull, then banged in two more punches to the belly. The big Indian slipped and grabbed hold on the top strand of rope enclosing the ring. Breathing laboriously, he leaned over the rope, his face contorted with pain and fatigue. "All right, enough!" Frank Murphy called out.

Eddie MacRae stood behind Indian Sam, his eyes cold, narrow, flashing anxiety, his head twitching sharply, his gloves still at the ready. "Enough," Frank Murphy repeated, climbing into the ring with a towel. He began to mop Eddie MacRae's torso with the towel. "That's the way to do it, Eddie. That's the way."

Indian Sam remained leaning on the ropes, gasping for breath. Frank Murphy followed Eddie into the locker room, his right hand massaging the muscles at the back of his neck. "Believe me, Eddie, you got him, you got him. Just like a tree. You chop away at the trunk, and the tree has to fall."

Eddie MacRae did not believe him. He sat on a bench in the locker room and brooded. Indian Sam was a pushover. He had seen Julio Martinez fight, and Martinez would never succumb that easily. There was something mean and scarred and ugly about Julio Martinez. To beat him, you'd have to obliterate him.

Wendell Glory adjusted his athletic cup and, nude save for it, sparred with himself in the mirror. He chewed rapidly on a wad of gum, while dancing around for Eddie MacRae. "Eddie, when you counter out there, you got to snap those punches in. Snap 'em. See?"

"Uh huh."

"When I work a guy over, I snap 'em in, crack 'em right in. Whap! Whap! In with the left, in with the left! Now

counter with the right. Whap! You get the power in the
punch not when it's going in, but it's coming back. A dago
taught me that once, and he was a good dago, knew what
he was talking about—"

Eddie nodded morosely. "Yeah, yeah—"

"You know Bert Julius, you ever heard of Bert Julius? I
snapped his head so damn hard, he broke one of them bones
in the back there, one of them vertebrate, retired him for
eight months."

The Black Avenger, attired in a pink jump-suit and plum-
colored beret, had just entered the locker room. *"Say what?"*

"What's that?"

"You did *what* to Bert Julius?"

"Cracked one of them vertebrate in the neck."

"Where was that?"

"Olympic Auditorium, two or three years ago."

"Bert Julius flattened your ass at the Olympic."

"He lucky-punched me, man. You know that. But he was
the one ended up in the hospital."

The Black Avenger doubled up over his leather gear bag
and laughed and laughed. "Bert Julius cut your ass every way
but loose. He hit you so hard if he done broke any vertebrate he done it from punching!" The Black Avenger winked
at Eddie MacRae.

"Ah, c'mon man—"

"If I'm lying, I'm dying."

"How about Freddie Max?"

"How about him?"

"I broke his jaw."

"Sheeet."

"Now I'm mad as a hog shitting razor blades, man. Black
Avenger, my dong! I'm about ready to tangle ass-holes with
you!"

He began to playfully push at Joe Fletcher, the Black
Avenger. Fletcher danced back, laughing. "Hey, man, don't
get your greasy paws on my new duds—"

215

"You'll see a week from Wednesday. I'm coming into that ring to eat me some *bear*."

"Bear *shit*, that's all you'll eat, and you'll like it, too!"

Eddie MacRae entered the shower stall and turned the water full on and hot. The muscles around his neck were tight, and the steaming water felt good stinging down on him. He stood in the shower for a long time and just let the water rain down on him.

Julio Martinez. In his mind's eye he saw Martinez dancing and stabbing and shifting. He had seen Martinez fight once on television, and the image of the boxer came to him now as he stood in the shower, an image of a large man with thick, rippling muscles, pushing out fast, bulling his opponent about the ring, putting together lightning combinations, devastating his opponent.

Eddie MacRae leaned forward now in the shower and began to throw punches. In his mind Julio Martinez danced in front of him, and he struck out at him. Jab, hook, hook, uppercut, hook . . .

"Hey, Eddie! Eddie!" It was the Black Avenger calling. "You're splashing damn water all over the floor."

Eddie MacRae leaned against the metal side of the shower stall, and his heart felt as though it would crack. He would never, in a million years, beat Julio Martinez. . . .

Later, he sat in the Paradise Hotel coffee shop eating a piece of melon. The sports page of the Las Vegas *Sun* was before him on the counter, but he found it impossible to concentrate on the paper. He felt a sense of desolation that he had only experienced before in the dark middle of the night.

He toyed with the melon and stared down at the newspaper and tried to imagine what would happen if he walked out on the fight. He pictured himself gathering up his gear and stealing away after dark. But where would he go?

He would hitchhike, but where? Fresno? L.A.? What would he do?

216

He sensed someone staring at him and turned to his right. Kitty was sitting there, smiling. "Wow, were you ever off somewheres!" She was wearing no makeup. She looked pale and drawn.

"I was thinking."

"You look like you lost your best friend."

"I'm getting nerves about the fight, that's all."

Kitty ordered coffee and a bacon, lettuce, and tomato sandwich. "How's Don?" Eddie MacRae asked.

She shrugged. "I don't hardly see him no more." The sandwich arrived. The toast was underdone and soggy. Kitty ate it without enthusiasm. "I'm thinking about moving out of there, you know—"

"What do you want to do that for?"

"He's working on that System, you know, which is nothing but a big bore for me. I don't see him, and when I do, it's nothing but a big hey rube about nothing—"

"Yeah."

"He don't care about me." They lapsed into silence. "That was a lousy sandwich," Kitty said after a while.

"Uh huh." They sipped at their coffee. Kitty lit a cigarette. Eddie MacRae noticed Kitty's lower lip was trembling.

"Kitty—" he said.

"I don't know why he brought me out here. I don't know what he expects me to do—" She was fighting tears.

"Don't you worry. I'll look after you," Eddie MacRae said. "I swear to you. I got this fight in the bag, you know? And after I get past this one, I'll be ready for the real big ones."

"I don't have anything to believe in, Eddie. You believe in your fighting and Don believes in his System. What do I have?"

"You got yourself," Eddie MacRae stammered.

"That's less than nothing, Eddie, and that's the truth." She finished her cigarette and rose to leave.

"Where are you going?"

"I don't know," she said.

"Why don't you stick around?"

She just shook her head, then turned and walked off. Eddie MacRae stared after her, feeling immeasurably sad and awkward, feeling he had nothing if he did not beat Julio Martinez, feeling in a bizarre and totally inexplicable way that he must beat him for Kitty, realizing he cared for her more than any other person in the world. . . .

He returned to his room and lay out on the bed. He closed his eyes and tried to think about the fight, but Kitty's face stayed with him. In his mind he stroked her hair and whispered in her ear. He strained in his mind to hear what he was saying. Nothing. He was saying nothing. A hoarse babble, inarticulate grunts. No wonder she had walked away from him.

Kitty wandered around the Paradise Hotel. She played dollar keno and the slots and even sat in at the roulette wheel. She was bored and edgy and desperately unhappy.

She had not seen Porter since the night he walked out. She tried calling him at Billy Ray's, but he wasn't there. Billy Ray was upset. "Where the hell can he be? We got the System down smooth as silk now. We just get our stake together and we're on our way! Do you think he might have been in an accident or something?"

"He's with that woman—"

"What woman?"

"Never mind."

She sat at the bar now, consumed inside by humiliation. He was with that woman, he was with that woman. . . . What could she do? How could she get to him? She realized, with a desperately sinking feeling, that Porter was on a level now high above her, operating on a plane that frightened and intimidated her. There was no way on earth she could compete with the wealth and style of Yolande Nathan.

She sipped at a stinger, growing ever more morose. She had a second and a third. The bar area became in her eyes dim and muted. People huddled together, whispered, engaged in veiled, conspiratorial assignations: women with sagging, demiexposed breasts, faces pale and slashed with red, men, dark and vaguely sinister, hair greased down, pale, pudgy hands. In the smoky light her reflection pulsated stupidly. Her eyes seemed unreal, two tiny blue lights. She stuck out her tongue at herself.

Suddenly Angel Amato was sitting next to her. She had no idea where he had come from. The bartender placed another drink in front of her. It was a very tall stinger. She realized she was drunk. "Here's to lady luck," Angel Amato said.

"Screw her," Kitty said.

"Better to do it to her than she do it to you." He swished the ice around in his glass and took a short swallow. "Where's your boyfriend?"

Kitty didn't say anything. She took a long swallow of her drink, wondering what he was doing next to her, where he had come from. She realized she did not like him very much. She sensed he was mocking her. Greasy Mex mocking her.

"He gambling or what?"

She shook her head. "He only plays sure things," she said.

Angel smiled thinly, revealing his two gold teeth. "A sure thing is the best thing."

Kitty finished her drink, and another one was immediately in front of her. She was getting very drunk. The air was thick with laughter all about her. Angel Amato pressed in close next to her. He smelled of a sickeningly sweet cologne. It reminded her of something. Then she remembered: it was the same cologne Matt Nathan wore.

"But where's he from?"

She had no idea what he was talking about. "Who?"

"Your friend."

"What friend? I don't have any friend."

"Ahhh," he said with phony compassion. "I'm your friend."

"I don't believe that."

"I think you're a very beautiful thing."

"Just a hick."

"I'd never take you for a hick."

"I'm from a town so small you never heard of it."

"Where's that?"

"South of Harrisburg. You ever hear of Harrisburg?"

"Sure I heard of Harrisburg. You mean in Pennsylvania."

"Well, I'm from near there." She drained her drink. She nibbled at some peanuts from a dish on the bar. The babble of voices in the casino seemed to her now a very happy sound. Angel Amato had a cute smile. The gold of his teeth flashed brilliantly and his eyes twinkled, and suddenly Kitty realized she liked him. "I'm glad you sat with me," she said.

"It's my pleasure." He signaled for another drink.

"I'm getting bombed," she said.

"You couldn't be in better hands."

"I believe that. I really do." When the drink arrived, she raised it in a toast. "To your gold teeth," she said.

Angel forced a laugh. "To your beautiful face and body."

"Yolande Nathan has a beautiful face and body."

"She's all right, but you're better."

"No, I'm not. She's beautiful, really beautiful."

"I've seen her body. It's not so nice."

"Have you really?"

Angel smiled and nodded. "You got a better body."

"How do you know? You've never seen my body. I'm very flat-chested." She patted her breasts. "These are falsies."

"I like flat-chested girls."

"Really?"

"Girls with a big chest are sloppy."

"Is Mrs. Nathan sloppy?"

"Yes, she is."

"How did you see her body? Did you peek while she was taking a bath?"

Angel laughed again. "Something like that."

Kitty leaned her hands on the bar and held on. "Whoooo," she said. "I'm beyond my limit."

Angel put his arm around her and helped her to her feet. "C'mon, we'll get you some air."

She looked into his face. He winked at her. He seemed to her now very kind and very good looking. "Why not?" she said.

Then she was walking through the casino, but she hardly felt the floor beneath her feet. It was as though she were floating. She was conscious of people staring at her, and they all seemed to be smiling. She smiled back and felt very good.

Outside the hotel the air seemed extraordinary to her, balmy like spring, cool and caressing. "This is terrific," she said.

Angel helped her into the car, a blue Jaguar. They sped off down Paradise Road. It felt as though they were flying. "Where are we going?"

"Someplace where you can show me your body."

Kitty laughed. "I'm not going to show you my body."

"Why not?"

She shrugged. "I don't know."

He pulled into a motel on Desert Inn Road. The sign on the motel had a green neon palm tree. It was called the South Seas. "We're going to the South Seas," Kitty said.

"That's right."

"I've never been to the South Seas."

In the room Angel Amato sat next to her on the bed. He put his arm around her and attempted to kiss her, but she pulled away. He took a deck of cards from his pocket. He shuffled the cards. "I'm going to show you a little trick."

"I like tricks."

"High-low," he said.

"What does that mean?"

"Low card takes off a piece of clothing." The room was moving gently around her. Everything smelled sweet. The bed felt unimaginably soft. The walls were patterned with palms and sand and water. "We're in the South Seas," Kitty said amazed.

Angel Amato shuffled the cards rapidly. His hands seemed to fly. He flipped over several cards. She had difficulty making out what the cards were but realized he was getting the picture cards. She kicked off her shoes, then took off her bracelet and wristwatch. "I'm losing," she said with a shrug.

"Your luck'll turn."

She lost every time. He zipped down her dress in back and kissed her shoulders. She pulled away. "No fair," she said.

Then her dress was off, then her bra and panties. She was completely nude. "I'm a loser," she said. "Goddamn, I always knew it."

He leaned forward and kissed her breast. She did not resist. "You got fine breasts," he breathed.

"I didn't win once."

He spread the cards out on the bed. They were stacked high-low, high-low. "I cheated," he said.

He stood up. Kitty gazed up at him, feeling suddenly rotten and used. "No," she said.

He ignored her and began to undress. He opened his jacket and removed a small pistol from beneath his waistband. He stripped down. His body was lean and tanned and finely muscled. He had a tattoo of a dagger on his left shoulder and a jagged scar across his midsection. He sat down next to her on the bed.

"I don't want to do anything," she said.

He nodded, gazing on her with almost no interest. His black eyes seemed terrible and cold. "You don't really like me," she said.

"Of course, I do."

She ran her finger over his scar. "How'd you get that?"

"A man tried to open me up."

"God," she said.

Suddenly he grabbed her by the shoulders and pushed her

back. She could not resist. He forced himself on top of her. He entered her, and she was dry. She could see the pained expression on his face, a look of disgust, and she felt stupid and ridiculous.

He rode in her for a while, then rolled off. He did not come.

She began to sober up. She felt filthy. "That wasn't much fun," he said.

"I can't help it."

He stood up and pulled his trousers on. His face was tight and angry. "What's your boyfriend's story?"

"What do you mean?"

"Where does he come from? What does he do?"

"Why?"

Angel Amato suddenly swung out at her, catching her face with the flat of his hand. She stared at him, stunned. Tears filled her eyes, but she did not cry. Her lip began to tremble. "Hey, wait a minute—"

She didn't finish the sentence. He hit her again. Her head jerked back against the wall. Her nose ached, and she could feel something warm spouting from it. It was blood. "I want to know all about him," Angel said.

He grabbed her by the throat and pressed her against the wall. "You slimy whore, you're disgusting. I'll break you into so many pieces they'll put you together with Scotch tape—"

She attempted to speak, but no sound would come out. She gasped for breath. "Where's he from?" Angel Amato demanded. "Where's he from?"

"All right!" she screamed.

She told him what she knew, how she and Porter had met, the fact he had been in prison; she told him about the System. It poured out of her, a long, sobbing, hysterical tirade. The blood continued to flow from her nose, soaking the bed under her.

Angel Amato seemed satisfied. He rose and finished dressing, tucking the pistol back into his waistband.

"Why did you do that?" Kitty asked in a small, pathetic, confused voice.

"I don't like whores," Angel Amato said. He reached into his pocket and pulled out a roll of bills. He peeled off two hundred-dollar bills and threw them at her. "I don't want your money!" Kitty screamed at him. She jumped at him, shrieking and clawing wildly at him. She got her nails into his face and tore at his skin.

He slammed her against the wall. She caught sight of her face in the bureau mirror. It was smeared with blood. He punched her in the ribs and knocked her to the bed. "Whore, rotten, filthy whore," he yelled.

He stood above her, dabbing at the gash in his cheek with a handkerchief. "I ought to kill you, you whore."

He entered the bathroom and washed his face and the knuckles of his hand. He came out of the bathroom and went to the bed. Kitty cowered on the bed. He spit on her. "You're a whore. You hear me? A whore."

Then he was gone, leaving Kitty alone on the blood-spattered bed. It doesn't really matter, she kept telling herself. None of it matters. She crumpled the two hundred-dollar bills in her fist. Nothing matters. Nothing matters. Nevertheless, she could not stop crying.

XIII

Kitty, sad Kitty, sat in the cocktail lounge at Caesar's Palace, desperately unhappy, alone. Her eyes were still blackened from the punch Angel Amato had thrown at her. He had cracked the bridge of her nose, and there was still swelling and some pain. She wore a pair of butterfly sunglasses to conceal the damage.

She had made up her mind: she was finished with Porter. For three days she had lain around the Excelsior, her eyes swollen almost shut, her whole body bruised and aching, waiting for Porter. She had lain there whimpering like an animal, frightened, confused. He had not appeared, nor had he called.

There was no reason she could think of why Angel Amato had beaten her, but she felt she deserved it. She deserved everything that came her way in this life. Old man Pepik, then Porter and the System, now this. Deserted, called whore, her nose broken, her eyes puffed shut—she deserved it all.

After the terror passed, she felt dead inside. She found she could not care about anyone, least of all herself. It was like operating the System: the edge went against you and you just waited it out. Caring didn't help. Caring was useless.

After three days she called Billy Ray's. Porter was not there. "You know where he is, don't you, Billy Ray?"

"I hope to meet my maker, Kitten, I don't. He don't tell me nothing. Probably went out to get some beers and chips or something."

"Well, you tell him I'm moving out."

"Where you going?"

"Where I'm going is nobody's business but my own. Just you tell him!"

"Kitten—" But she had hung up. The phone rang right back. She did not answer it.

She left Porter a note: "The way you been acting toward me is not right. Let's put it this way you been using me like an old shoe. I have had body injury because of you and you just don't care. Well Mister Big Shot I have had it. I am wishing you Good Luck tho I am sure you do not wish me same. We have had good times and we have had bad and it makes me sad to know you did not like me more." Then she packed up her things and called a cab.

She moved into the South Seas Motel and paid her first week's rent out of the money Angel Amato had thrown at her.

Her room at the South Seas, though not elaborate, was, nevertheless, pleasant. It had a green flowered rug and green furniture. The wallpaper had a pattern of palm trees, sand, water, and sky. There was a large double bed and a small kitchenette. She had color television.

She felt isolated, yet somehow proud that she had managed to break away from Porter. She was coming to realize how used she had been by men most of her life, beginning with her stepfather, who, when she was twelve years old, had crawled into bed with her one drunken night. She had awakened to feel his terrible, rubbery weight pushing down on her, pressing the breath out of her, smothering her. Her whole life, since that time, it now seemed to her, had been an unbroken line of outrages committed on her by men. She would never be used again, she vowed. From now on she would be the one doing the using.

226

Her first evening at the South Seas she dressed up in her red satin dress, glued on her false eyelashes, and attempted to cover the purple bruises under her eyes with makeup. She put on her butterfly sunglasses and took a cab to Caesar's Palace.

Now, she sat in the cocktail area sipping a stinger.

A man moved into the table next to her. He was a large man with short-cropped gray hair and a round, reddish face. He was not bad looking, Kitty decided, and when he looked over at her, she smiled. He smiled back, then picked up his drink, and moved to her table. "Do you mind if I join you?" He had a thick Southern accent.

"No."

"What's a pretty little thing like you doing all alone?" he asked, easing into the chair next to her.

"I like being alone."

"My name is Charlie Smith."

She smiled. "They call me Kitty."

"I'm a food broker. You know what a food broker is?"

"No, sir, I'm afraid I don't."

"Work on 3 percent commission, deal in nothing but trailer loads."

"Oh."

"Beautiful set-up. Took me twenty-seven years to get there, but now I can enjoy it. If I want to come to Vegas or go to Puerto Rico or the Bahamas, my customers just place the orders with the secretary. I don't handle cases, like your fifty cases or your seventy-five. Trailer loads, that's the only thing I handle. Everyone in Atlanta, your food chains, your supermarkets, and the like, they all know Charlie Smith."

"That's terrific."

"Sure is. I handle my four items exclusively—my mushrooms, my pickles, my olives, and my hearts of artichoke, which is what we call a luxury item. Want to know something?"

"What's that?"

"I do almost a million dollars a year on my mushrooms alone. At 3 percent, you figure it."

They had several drinks together while Charlie Smith explained to her the intricacies of the grocery business. It had something to do with National Foods and how they had fired him twenty-seven years ago with not even a week's notice, how he had taken his customers with him, how he had started out dealing in cases, and how now he only handled trailers. He spoke about his wife, dying of a cancerous kidney, of a son who was born megacephalic. "He has an immensely large head and no brain to fill it." Another son was thirty-five and couldn't keep a job. "*Handsome*. You never met a man so handsome—"

"Good-looking, huh?"

"Not good-looking. *Handsome as the day is long* and just as damn lazy. Would you believe he has thirty-five pairs of shoes and yet he has to call his father to borrow the rent money? I said to him, I said go take a flying jump in the lake."

He told her he was staying in the hotel at Caesar's; didn't she want to come up and see his room?

"What's in it for me?"

Charlie Smith laughed. "Oh, is that the way it is!"

"I'm big losers gambling," Kitty lied.

"I guess I could make up some of your losses. How much?"

Kitty had no idea what to ask. She felt ashamed, not over what she was doing, but at her lack of expertise. She shrugged. "How much do you want to give?"

"I never give more than thirty-five dollars," Charlie Smith said.

It didn't seem like much to Kitty, but she didn't really care. It would be a start. "All right," she said.

His room was decorated in bright red: red rug, red drapes, red wallpaper, red coverlet on the large circular bed. He sat on the bed. She sat next to him. She didn't know how to pro-

228

ceed and just sat there. She could feel that Charlie Smith was becoming uncomfortable.

He removed her sunglasses. She was embarrassed at how she must look. "I was in an automobile accident," she said. "That's too bad."

Suddenly the whole idea lost its appeal; she regretted having come up here or at least not drinking more. She was cold sober, and the idea of going to bed with this man filled her with revulsion. She looked toward the door, hoping in some stupid way it would swing open and Porter would enter. She wanted to be with Porter.

"Take off your clothes," Charlie Smith said, vaguely irritated.

She undressed. She stood before him naked, unable to bring herself to the bed. She was conscious her body was covered with bruises where Angel Amato had beaten her.

Charlie Smith looked at her with what she felt was boredom and began casually to take off his clothes.

He was very fat, fatter than he looked with clothes on, and his body was covered with wiry gray hair. His stomach sagged in rolls of fat that almost concealed his penis. She felt as though she would throw up but steeled herself and came to the bed.

She lay out on the bed next to him. He mounted her and drove into her with a furious, grunting motion. She was completely dry, and the pain was excruciating. She pretended she was enjoying it and masked her pain with fabricated moans of pleasure. He huffed against her like a pig, squealing ridiculously. She pressed her chin against his shoulder and attempted to count the red flowers on the opposite wall. His skin smelled sour. She prayed he would come quickly and forced out long false screams of delight to hasten him. The weight of his body felt as though it would crush the life out of her; the unrhythmic jab of his penis slashed like fire between her legs. The time stretched to an excruciating eternity and tears came into her eyes.

At last, with a ferociously awkward driving motion, he came. He got up without a word and walked to the dresser where he began to thumb through his wallet. She rose, went into the bathroom, cleaned herself out, and returned to the room. Her insides were raw.

"You're not the best lay I ever had," Charlie Smith said glumly.

"It's the end of the day for me. I'm usually better in the morning."

She began to dress. He handed her two ten-dollar bills. "That's all the money I have on me," he said.

"You told me thirty-five—"

"I pay for service—in life as in the food business. I don't call what you did there service."

Filled with anger and disgust, she put the twenty dollars in her purse. She attempted to force a smile, but she felt as though she would break into tears. She hurried from the room.

Downstairs she went to the drug counter and bought a jar of vaseline. Then she returned to the cocktail area. The next man who approached her, a loud-talking Texan with a tall Stetson and a blue frill shirt, she asked fifty dollars. Up in the room she demanded the money in advance. She was learning fast.

Billy Ray Walker watched a fly crawling across the ceiling. A fly's life is thirty days, someone had once told him. Be thankful you're not a fly.

He was a sick man and he knew it, but for many months now he had tried to deny that he was poised on the edge of oblivion. Now, as he lay on the stained and soiled sheets of his bed in the Sultan Motel gazing up at the swirling, dirty-cream of the ceiling, the excruciating rattle of the air conditioner grinding painfully in his ears, fighting a desperate battle to get air into his lungs, he knew for certain how close death was. Death was whispering to him, trying to kiss his face, attempting to embrace him.

The thought terrified him that he might take a breath and the air would not come! How would it feel to die? Would everything just go black, his consciousness cut off like a severed wire, or would he be wrenched, choking with pain, into some horrible, frightening gray area before death where he would suffer each torment of his life's dissolution?

A fly's life—but then, of course, a fly does not know the meaning of his thirty days, just as he did not know the meaning of his years. When you die, all the time that has gone before becomes meaningless. . . .

He was cold with perspiration. A raw pain seared his chest. His hands trembled. The room pressed on him like a heavy weight.

He did not want to die like this. He cursed the collapse of his world, the smell of his room, the chaos around him. When he had to go, he prayed, let death catch him unaware, let it be at the blackjack table, let him be lost in the beauty and perfection of the Four-Deck System.

And he realized now that was the System's ultimate function: it was a grand, fantastic narcotic to screen out the awareness of life's fragility, to ward off the immense presence of death.

He shifted on the bed and groaned softly. Damn his clogged heart and all that contributed to it, the booze and cigarettes, the women, the anger and anxiety, and, most of all, the terrible frustration of having won big then lost it all! The fly continued to crawl across the ceiling, moving toward the bare light bulb at the center.

"You feeling any better?" Porter was sitting in the chair opposite Billy Ray. He had been sitting there quite still for a long time, a smoldering stogie held loosely in his hand, watching without a show of emotion. I'll die and he won't change expression, Billy Ray was thinking. Sitting there just watching me die. Then he quickly gave thanks that at least *someone* was there. At least he will not die alone. For that would have been the most horrible of all possible fates: to die alone.

Billy Ray took in a deep gasp of air and nodded his head. "Is my stogie bothering you?" Porter asked. Billy Ray shook his head; the smoke did not bother him: he could not bring in enough air to taste the smoke.

"Do you want some more pills?"

He shook his head, no, once more. "Maybe I better call you a doctor—" And again Billy Ray signaled no.

It would pass. He knew now it would pass. He had come this way before. There would be a time, of course, when he could not turn back, but not this night. Even as he realized he was back from the abyss, the pain in his chest abated, and he could feel the blood once more coursing through his veins. "Damn," he said softly, raising himself up on one elbow. He glanced at the ceiling. The fly was gone. "Old ticker's like a goddamn soggy sponge."

Porter puffed on his stogie and remained seated in the chair. "Billy Ray, we're a piss ant's ass away from our stake. You got to keep that ol' ticker going," he said.

"Yeah," Billy Ray said.

"I'm working on my connections, you know?"

"Yeah, yeah."

"So don't you worry now."

Connections! He was working on his connections! Did he have any connections that could tie his heart together?

Billy Ray smiled wanly. He hefted himself up to a sitting position. His breathing had evened out. "I damn right know it, we're going to get our stake." He reached over to the night table and picked up a half-can of warm beer and drank from it. "Goddamn! Three years ago the doctors told me that damn ticker of mine was clogging up and should be spliced up in some way. I had the money then, but, damn, the System was going beautiful and I couldn't stop."

He swung his legs around and sat up on the edge of the

bed. "The worst damn thing isn't the pain. It's just the fear," he said.

"You all right now?" Porter asked.

"Yeah, I'm all right."

"You sure?" Billy Ray nodded and dug around for a usable cigarette stub in the overflowing ashtray.

Porter rose and stood above Billy Ray. "I'll check back with you later tonight," Porter said.

"Where you going?"

"I got a mission to accomplish, Billy Ray. I got to get us our stake."

"Your connections?"

"You got it, Billy Ray," Porter said. Billy Ray was staring up at Porter. Behind the thick lenses of his spectacles there was still a hint of fear in his eyes. "You want me to bring you back some ribs or something?" Porter asked.

"That would be nice. Bring me back some ribs."

Billy Ray got up off the bed and shuffled toward the bathroom. It shocked Porter to see how frail and old he seemed at that moment.

He heard the sound of Billy Ray's urine flowing, then the flush of the toilet, and Billy Ray appeared once more in the room, buttoning up his trousers. And it seemed sad to Porter that he should be wearing trousers without a zipper.

His face had some color now and he was grinning. "I'll tell you, Don, the worst damn thing is for your heart to act up when you need to take a piss. Damn near pissed my pants."

Porter began to laugh and Billy Ray laughed, and they both knew, at least for a while, everything would be all right.

"Kitty called before."

"What she want?"

"She says she's moving out."

Porter paused at the door, feeling suddenly immeasurably lost. His life had been a series of irrevocable blunders. He had wounded and he had destroyed. He was isolated. He had the

233

System and he had Yolande, but he was isolated. "She'll be back," Billy Ray said.

"Who needs her?" Porter said, and departed, leaving Billy Ray alone in the room.

The air conditioner rattled on. Billy Ray gazed up at the ceiling. The fly was back.

Porter drove with Yolande to a small Italian restaurant on Charleston. His mood was somber. Kitty's departure had cut deep into him.

He didn't love her, he didn't need her. Why was he disturbed at her leaving?

They sat in a darkened corner of the grottolike restaurant. A thick candle burned on the table, dripping wax into a saucer beneath it. They ordered ossobuco with side dishes of linguine. They had a nice white wine with the meal.

"You're depressed," Yolande said. She was in a good mood. Her face had lost some of its puffiness and signs of fatigue since Porter had been spending time with her. They had been making plans.

"It'll pass."

Why did he feel so desolate inside? Kitty had moved out. Well, what of it? That simplified things for him, didn't it?

He had treated her badly, that's what was bothering him. All his life he had treated somebody badly. It wasn't that he wanted to. It was just that nothing mattered deeply to him. He was missing some essential element of humanity. Only the cards, only the System . . .

"I think we should live in Europe. Would you like Europe?" Yolande gazed at him across the candle flame, her eyes shining with happiness. She had never looked quite so lovely, Porter found himself thinking. It disturbed him that he was undercutting her mood with his grimness. He fought to shake off his stupid despair, but it would not leave him alone.

"Europe's fine."

234

Lately, the idea of the two of them running off had grown in their discussions. What had started out as a wisp of a dream had begun to take on the proportion of a reality.

"I've been thinking. We should discuss it with Matt."

"Do you think that's smart?"

"I don't know."

"You said he wouldn't like it. That he'd—"

"I think if I prepared him—"

"I don't know. I mean—"

"Yes?"

"We ought to do it right, you know."

"You don't have to go through with it. I don't want you to go off with me unless you want it."

But what about her husband, her child, Angel Amato, Kitty, Billy Ray Walker, even Eddie MacRae? What about them? Would they just disappear, leaving a dull tear in so many lives? He did not speak for a long time. The restaurant was almost empty. A busboy with long black hair and sleepy black eyes swept the floor. "I'll do whatever you say," Porter said at last.

She smiled. She slid her hand across the table. There was a large Manila envelope in her hand. The envelope contained two hundred crisp hundred-dollar bills.

Eddie MacRae, standing at the check-in desk of the Paradise Hotel, had spotted Kitty walking through the lobby. She was with a short, dark man with black, greasy hair and a pockmarked face. He called out to her, and she turned and saw him, but continued on. She entered the elevator with the man. The doors slid shut. She was staring straight ahead, her face a pale, sad mask.

The bellhop said to him: "What's wrong, Eddie?"

"I just saw a friend of mine—"

"Yeah?"

"She just looked on by me."

"You mean the girl just got on the elevator? The hooker?"

"What?"

"She's a hooker."

"She is not."

"She been coming in all week with different tricks. Benny, the night man, got a deal with her. You'll see. In a half hour she's back down, unless this is an all-night job."

Eddie MacRae sat waiting in one of the lobby chairs, deeply shaken. Kitty, a hooker! It isn't true, he told himself over and over again, it isn't true.

In four days he would be fighting Julio Martinez, and he was *afraid*. He needed Kitty and Porter at the fight. All week without success, he tried contacting them. It was absolutely necessary for him that they be at the fight. . . .

And now this! A hooker! The idea caused him to go sick inside. How? How did she get into it? How? It isn't true. It isn't true. . . .

After a while Kitty came back down on the elevator. She saw Eddie and attempted to hurry past him. He rushed after her, catching her at the steps leading into the casino. "Didn't you see me before when I called out to you?"

"I saw you," she said. She kept glancing around the lobby as though she were looking for someone.

"I'll buy you a cup of coffee."

"I can't. I have an appointment." Kitty did not look directly into his eyes. Her head moved from side to side as she scanned the lobby.

"I'm fighting this Wednesday."

"So soon?"

"I want you and Don there. You're my good luck."

"I'll try."

He did not speak for a moment. His head twitched sharply. Kitty fidgeted. "Was there something you wanted to say?" she asked.

"I heard a story about you."

"What kind of story?"

"A story."

"There's all kinds of stories about people. People is always making up stories about other people. What kind of story did you hear about me?" There was a note of anger in her voice. Eddie MacRae could not bring himself to speak. "What kind of story did you hear about me? Did you hear I was a whore, is that what you heard?" He did not speak. "What if I am? Everybody's a whore in one way or another. What does that prove?" Her eyes were cold and hard, and Eddie suddenly felt as though he didn't know her at all, as though he had never known her. "I do what I want from now on. I'm no one's sucker. Don had no right to treat me the way he did. He had no right."

"I don't know about nothing, Kitty, that's the truth. I'm just a fighter, you know. I'm just a fighter. I just think you're good people—"

He couldn't continue. His head twitched violently as he tried to formulate his thoughts.

Kitty was staring beyond Eddie MacRae. Benny, the night man, a thin weasel in a blue and red bellhop's uniform, was standing near the house phones. "I have to go now," Kitty said, her voice suddenly soft and tinged with regret. "Everything will be fine, Eddie. Don't worry." She smiled at him and winked.

She followed Benny back toward the elevators.

It was early evening when Eddie MacRae arrived at the Sultan Motel. He learned from the clerk which room belonged to Billy Ray and knocked. Billy Ray answered the door dressed in a pair of baggy gray trousers and his pajama top.

"I'm looking for Don."

Billy Ray opened the door wider and admitted Eddie MacRae into the incredible squalor of the room. Porter was sitting cross-legged on the bed. Playing cards were spread all about

237

him. The poster board containing the Four-Deck System was propped up against the wall behind the bed.

Porter seemed surprised and not entirely pleased to see Eddie.

Billy Ray flopped into a chair opposite the bed, placed a fresh cigarette in his holder, and lit up. Eddie stood awkwardly in the center of the room. "Would you like a beer?" Billy Ray asked. His voice was hoarse and weary; he looked frail to Eddie, frailer than he had remembered him. His face was a pasty white. His eyes behind the spectacles seemed unnaturally large in his pinched face. "No, thank you," Eddie said. "How you been, Don?"

"Busy."

"Busy, huh?"

"Billy Ray's Four-Deck System is something else."

"Good, huh?"

Billy Ray Walker leaned forward, rubbing his hands together. When he spoke, it was without enthusiasm. "It's fantastic. The possibilities are fantastic. We have our stake now—" He trailed off, staring down at the floor.

"We have our stake, Eddie, and we're really going to move," Porter said. "Billy Ray's been a little sick the past few days. As soon as he comes around—"

Billy Ray laughed dryly. "We're going to grab this town by the ass!"

"Damn right," said Porter.

"I come to tell you I'm fighting Wednesday night."

"That's great, just great. Eddie's a helluva fighter," Porter said to Billy Ray.

"Hmm," Billy Ray breathed, not looking up.

"I saw Kitty. She's not doing too good."

"Yeah? What's wrong?"

"She's upset about the two of you, you know—"

"Yeah, well—"

Eddie MacRae shifted his weight uncomfortably in the center of the room. Billy Ray puffed on his cigarette, still leaning forward, his arms resting on his thighs, his eyes staring down at the floor. "Gambling and women don't mix," he said, abstracted. "That's the sad truth."

"She's a working girl now. A whore."

Porter stared at Eddie MacRae a long time. All energy seemed to drain from him. His shoulders sagged and the blood appeared to rush from his face. "How do you know?"

"I saw her. She was working the Paradise."

"Ah, Christ," Porter said.

"I figured I ought to tell you. You ought to talk to her or something."

Porter's hand went to his chin, and he began absently to rub it. "Yeah," he said.

"That's what this town does," Billy Ray said.

"What are you going to do?" Eddie asked.

"I don't know."

He moved to the door. "Will you be coming to the fight?"

"If I can. With our stake now—"

"Maybe I'll see you there after."

"Yeah."

"Maybe you'll bring Kitty." Porter nodded slowly, his gaze turned inward. "Good luck with the System and all," Eddie said.

"Yeah, good luck to you. You know, with the fight."

After Eddie MacRae had gone, Porter stretched out on the bed, crushing the playing cards beneath him. He stared up at the ceiling. Billy Ray Walker rose from the chair and walked to the poster-board chart. He lit up another cigarette. He studied a line on the chart. "At Caesar's we use the top index, hmm? The top index ought to do it." Porter continued to stare up at the ceiling. Billy Ray shook his head slowly, still studying the chart. "Good luck!" he muttered scornfully. "Two dumbest words in the whole damn language."

Porter did not answer.

XIV

Eddie MacRae eyed Julio Martinez across the ring at the Silver Slipper. Martinez was large and he was flabby, and there was a twisted meanness to his face. His black eyes stared out of narrow sockets thick with bone and scar tissue. He was balding. His skin was the color of old newspaper.

Eddie could feel his heart racing wildly. His breath came through his nose in short gasps. His head jerked spasmodically, and he was embarrassed at how ridiculous he must look. He was scared.

In a short moment the bell would ring for the first round of the fight.

Frank Murphy leaned over his shoulder, massaging the muscles at the back of his neck, pouring out a steady stream of last-minute instructions. "Box him, Eddie, box him. Stick and run, stick and run. Look at that bread basket he got on him, for chrissake! Pound him until he pukes—"

Off to his right, Eddie could see Matt Nathan and his wife seated at ringside. Next to them was Angel Amato. Mr. Nathan looked gray and serious; he was staring straight ahead. Mrs. Nathan appeared bored. She held a program in her lap and from time to time would glance at it, then peer around the hall, chew at her lip, gaze up at the ceiling.

240

Eddie had not been able to spot Porter or Kitty. During the preliminary fight, he had poked his head out of the dressing area but could not find them in the crowd. They probably were not there, and the thought depressed him. He felt friendless and alone.

Matt Nathan had stopped into the dressing area just before the fight. He had put his arm around Eddie and whispered in his ear: "Tear him to pieces. Cut him up into small hunks of meat. I bet a thousand on the fight for you." He had said this without smiling, without any feeling of warmth, mechanically.

Eddie MacRae had come into the ring amid silence. A contingent of Mexicans was there to see Martinez, and he had received a nice ovation from one section of the hall.

Martinez had entered slowly, sleepily. He had removed his purple and gold robe with exaggerated slowness, then stepped to the rosin box and, with a bored, methodical motion, rubbed his shoes in the rosin. He had danced around without much energy and thrown out a few listless, shadowbox combinations.

During the referee's instructions, he had fixed Eddie Mac-Rae with a dull, bored stare. Now, waiting for the bell, he was staring at the floor.

The bell sounded with a toneless clunk, devoid of any sense of urgency. It took a split second to register in Eddie's ears, and Frank Murphy had to push him forward. "The bread basket, Eddie! Work him to the bread basket!" the trainer shouted, and Eddie MacRae was charging forward.

Julio Martinez shuffled out of his corner. His eyes were empty. The flab of his breasts and belly bounced easily as he moved; he grimaced, revealing the red of his mouthpiece.

Eddie MacRae shot rapid jabs to the head and attempted to follow up to the midsection, but Martinez caught the punches on his forearms. Eddie moved to his right, throwing out a steady barrage of ineffective punches. He felt stupid and awkward. Martinez moved slowly, slower even than In-

241

dian Sam, but had no trouble blocking Eddie's punches. He carried his gloves below his waistband, as though the task of raising them was not worth the effort. His paunchy body was a wide open target of gray-brown skin; his arms, however, moved with lightning speed to catch a punch when it was thrown. He did not waste a motion.

Eddie circled to the far side of the ring, realized he was in danger of being cornered, and attempted to come forward. Surprisingly, Martinez backed off, and Eddie tripped over his own feet. He stumbled and almost fell, and the crowd laughed.

Martinez pounded two punches off Eddie's head, and Eddie backed away. The punches were without steam, and Eddie felt good. The fear, always present, of another man's power lessened. He had been an open target, had been solidly hit, yet was not fazed. "Jab him, Eddie! Jab him!" Frank Murphy shouted from his corner.

Eddie MacRae jabbed and ran, threw an occasional combination, still did not land a clean blow.

At one point he banged a right off Martinez's shoulder. The sound of the punch exploded through the hall, and the crowd reacted with a murmur of approval, but Eddie knew the punch had been ineffectual. Martinez bounced off the ropes and grabbed Eddie around the waist. He was breathing heavily and perspiration was already pouring off him. His body smelled sour. He lowered his head against Eddie's chest, then jerked it upward, butting Eddie under the chin. The force of the butt sent a shock through him, but it did no real damage.

For the rest of the round Martinez plodded around the ring, while Eddie peppered him with punches. None landed solidly. At the bell there was listless applause.

"You're doing real good, Eddie, real good. You got him puffing like a locomotive," Frank Murphy said.

Eddie looked back and saw the Black Avenger sitting just behind his corner. The Avenger nodded his head and winked, and Eddie felt proud and, for the first time, capable of winning.

The next three rounds progressed much like the first, with Eddie constantly moving, throwing a barrage of punches, landing very few of them. Julio Martinez's pace grew slower and slower. His blank black eyes stared ahead, showing nothing. He had even given up going after Eddie and would simply pivot around the center of the ring, picking punches off with his arms, occasionally moving in to tie Eddie up.

The crowd grew bored, then hostile. An occasional voice in Spanish would scream out: "La cabeza, Julio, la cabeza!" There was scattered booing. It was a dull fight, which Eddie was winning only by his willingness to throw punches.

Before the sixth round Frank Murphy said, "You're wearing him down, Eddie. Keep up the pace. You can begin to come in on him."

In the sixth round Eddie moved in and banged away with lefts and rights, hitting to the stomach, then to the head. Martinez blocked them easily. Eddie lunged forward. Martinez lashed out.

Eddie did not see the first punch, nor the two that followed. There was a bright flash of light, then the floor seemed to have tilted, then it swayed forward, and he was looking into the eyes of a gray-haired man wearing glasses, seated at ringside. He realized he was on his knees, his head pitched forward. He heard a roar in his ears like the crash of a wave extending far beyond any break in the ocean's surf. Through it he could hear, away in the distance, Frank Murphy screaming: "Get up! Get up!" and another voice, high and piercing, counting: "Seven, eight . . ."

With a terrible effort he pushed himself up, then suddenly he was in a black cloud of dull shock. He could feel Martinez's body under his arms, wet with perspiration, the roaring still in his ears, heavy grunts cutting under it. He felt no pain. He was gazing out at the crowd now, and they were tinged with red, their mouths open in terrible grimaces. And

243

now they were splitting and flying apart, and black was splitting them apart, and Julio Martinez's face, broad, puffy, black eyes like burning dots, skimming close by, and everything collapsing like a shattered mirror.

He did not remember going down again, nor did he remember much ever after that.

They laid him out on a stainless steel counter in the dressing area. He was staring up at the ceiling, but he saw nothing. The Black Avenger knelt next to his ear, saying over and over again: "Eddie, Eddie . . ."

Matt Nathan entered the room and approached the table. Frank Murphy, standing behind the inert form on the counter, was white and shaken. He licked at his lips and shook his head. A small, gray-haired man stood holding Eddie's wrist. "I want this man in a hospital," he said.

"Eddie . . ." The Black Avenger pleaded.

Matt Nathan turned and walked out of the room.

Porter found out about Eddie MacRae from Yolande Nathan. "It's some kind of blood leaking into the brain. The doctors think he had been injured once before." She had difficulty talking about it. She had been shaken and appalled when she learned the seriousness of the injury.

He visited Eddie in the hospital, but he might just as well not have come. Eddie MacRae sat up in the bed staring straight ahead. There was a slight, steady tremor to his head. He did not recognize Porter. When he spoke, his speech was thick and slurred. "My Dad . . . someone buy him a drink," he said over and over in a voice like a small child's.

When he left the hospital, Porter went looking for Kitty. He visited all the casinos. He found her sitting at the bar at the Sahara. She was with another girl who looked vaguely familiar to Porter.

"Hello," the other girl said with a smile, as Porter seated himself.

"Hello."

"You don't remember me, do you? Adele. We met at the Paradise. . . ."

"Yes," he said.

Kitty was looking away from him. It was the first they had met since she left him. "Did you hear about Eddie?" he asked.

She didn't say anything but turned toward him. Her face was pale and drawn-looking. She had lost weight and was now very thin. Her hair was dyed a bright blond and was up in a swirling bouffant. The makeup was thick on her face.

"Eddie had a bad accident—"

"What—"

"The fight went bad for him." He paused. He had difficulty saying more.

"Bad in what way?" she asked.

"He had some kind of injury to his head."

He lapsed into silence. The bartender came over. He ordered a beer. "Is it serious?" Kitty asked.

"Yes."

"Jesus," she said. "Jesus."

"His mind, his thinking. It's gone."

"Oh, Jesus," she said. "Where's he at?"

"Sunrise Hospital on Maryland Parkway."

"Oh, my Jesus."

"Kitty, I know things worked out kind of rotten between us. I never meant you any harm—"

"I know, Donny."

"It's just that our lives could only come this far. They had to split off sometime."

"I don't blame you for anything. I have a good life."

"Do you?"

"Yes."

Adele leaned close and whispered to her. She got up from her chair. Two men were waiting a short distance away.

245

"Good-by," she said in a barely audible voice, then walked off with Adele to join the two men.

September was over. It was a week into October. The days were growing shorter. The weather was lovely, warm, but not hot, springlike; the evenings were cool; the sky was streaked with gray, the only sign it was autumn.

Porter had been waiting these weeks for Billy Ray Walker to regain his strength. They were almost ready to attack the four-deck tables again.

Yolande had been after him to go off with her. They were at her house, seated on the patio. It was early evening. Her son, Stephen, was playing tennis with his instructor. "You have the money now—" There was a desperate urgency in her voice. Her face was tight with anxiety.

"Give me a week."

"I'm going out of my mind here. I hate this place. I hate everything about it."

The last month Porter had spent more and more time at Matt Nathan's house. Often he had made love to Yolande in her bedroom with Nathan and Angel Amato playing gin rummy or watching television downstairs. Nathan accepted the arrangement. Never overly friendly toward Porter, he was, nevertheless, always cordial.

Porter had ceased to care. Yolande possessed him in a way he had never dreamed anyone could hold him. His involvement with her had become the dominant theme in his existence. Even the System had lost its power over him.

"In a week I'll make my move again. When we go off, we'll be able to get by in style."

"How we live is unimportant to me. I just want to get out of here."

"Soon."

They sat for a while without speaking. The pong of the tennis ball resounded through clear evening air. A light breeze stirred the mesquite and palm behind the patio. The

246

chirr of crickets was so constant it seemed like silence amplified. A rotating garden hose went whoosh, whoosh, whoosh on the lawn beyond the trees.

Matt Nathan, followed by Angel Amato, moved out onto the patio. He was dressed in a pair of powder-blue golfing trousers and a blue sport shirt. Angel Amato was dressed in white. Matt Nathan stood staring for a moment out over the brightly lit tennis courts. "How long has he been playing?"

"About an hour."

"Did he have dinner?"

"He said he wasn't hungry."

"Stephen!" Matt Nathan called out. "Time for dinner!" He looked at Porter. "I think you ought to be going now," he said quietly. Porter rose. "Too bad about Eddie MacRae," Matt Nathan added.

"Yes."

"He was instructed not to punch it out with Martinez." Porter shrugged. "I liked him," Matt Nathan said. "He was a good boy. With the right break he would have done all right."

Stephen arrived breathless from the tennis courts. He ran to his father and embraced him around the legs. Nathan picked him up and held him under the arms. "How are you today, little bug?" Nathan asked.

"Lyle cheats when he plays with me," Stephen said.

"Well, we'll put a stop to that!" Nathan swung the boy around, holding him under the arms. The boy laughed. His thick spectacles slid down on his nose. His gaze was hopelessly wall-eyed. "Now, run in the house and shower up. We'll be having dinner in fifteen minutes."

Stephen ran off, his awkward feet flopping in a clumsy lope. "Did you play golf?" Yolande asked.

"Yes."

"How was it?"

"Not bad," Nathan said without looking at her. He turned

and moved into the house. Angel Amato waited on the patio.

"I hate to see a guy get scrambled up like your friend," Angel Amato said to Porter. "They should have never matched him with Martinez."

It was the first expression of feeling Porter had ever seen him exhibit. "Yes," Porter said.

"It's a crying shame. A boxer's life is lower than nothing." He stared out over the lawn for a moment. Then he turned back to Porter. "Mr. Nathan said you better go."

Yolande's face flushed with anger, but she remained quiet. "I'll talk to you later," Porter said to her, then moved off.

When Porter entered the room at the Sultan Motel, Billy Ray Walker was seated in the chair staring at the wall. He was in the same position Porter had left him. He had no doubt been sitting like that all day, staring at the wall. "How are you feeling?"

"I'm feeling fine."

"When do you think we can give it a try?"

"Any time now."

Kitty stood at the end of the hospital ward talking with the doctor. It was evening and the ward was bathed in gloom. The doctor was a young man with thin blond hair and freckles.

"He can leave any time. There's not much we can do with him."

"I want to take care of him," Kitty said.

"That's up to you. Are you a relative?"

"A friend."

The doctor led her through the ward, past beds filled with men suffering from lung disease, kidney disorder, broken legs, heart ailments. The smell of the hospital nauseated Kitty. A loudspeaker repeated a doctor's name over and over, reminding her of the casino call systems.

Eddie MacRae was seated in bed in a faded maroon terrycloth robe. He had lost weight. His face was pale.

"A friend of yours to see you, Eddie," the doctor said brightly. Eddie MacRae did not respond.

Kitty moved to him. "Eddie," she said softly.

His eyes blinked several times. A steady tremor ran through his head. "Buy . . . my . . . father . . . a drink," he said with great difficulty, like a record running down.

Kitty lifted his hand and held it in hers. It was moist and cold and without strength. "She's going to take you home, Eddie. How would you like that?" the doctor said.

Eddie MacRae said nothing.

XV

"But why the Paradise Hotel?"

"Number one, the P.C. is a shade better, number two, they know you there—"

"Billy Ray, that's the best reason for *not* playing there."

They had been arguing all afternoon. Porter had wanted to make their comeback at Caesar's Palace, while Billy Ray had been pushing for the Paradise Hotel. "The fact they do know you makes it fine. They're going to bend a helluva lot before they crack down on you."

Billy Ray sat before the bureau mirror, chain-smoking cigarettes, working on the evening's disguise: trim blond mustache and goatee, blond wig, dark glasses. He had purchased a lime-colored sport jacket with matching trousers of a lighter green, and a bright yellow ascot. He was busy now experimenting with hair styles on the wig. He looked bizarre and ridiculous.

Porter paced the motel room, puffing on a Marsh Wheeling. The air was stale with cigar and cigarette smoke. Porter's nerves were wire-tight.

Billy Ray did have a point. Porter certainly could get away with a good deal more at the Paradise Hotel than anywhere else. But if the System clicked as they anticipated? How would Matt Nathan react to being taken for a couple of hundred thousand? And then to run off with his wife! To hit the Paradise was an idea wholly practical in its conception, totally insane in its possible consequences.

One thing was certain: it all had to work this time. Billy Ray was a sick man. If this push failed, he would never have the strength to make another one.

Billy Ray lit up another cigarette. He adjusted the wig on his head. He pinched his cheeks, trying to get some color into them. "Don, we need every friggin' element going for us. If they just let us play, I know we can beat 'em! They're going to let us play at the Paradise. You know that!"

If the System clicked right off from the beginning! If they could just pull it off *fast*, then disappear for parts unknown! It could work at the Paradise if Matt Nathan gave them the slightest leeway.

The idea of striking at the heart of Matt Nathan's kingdom frightened and, at the same time, held a perverse attraction for Porter. He would succeed or go down in style: beat Nathan for his money, then take him for his wife. But if he failed?

"All right," Porter said.

"Now you're talking some sense!" Billy Ray said.

Porter phoned Yolande. "We're going after the Paradise—"

There was a pause. "When?"

"Now." Another pause. "If it works, you know—"

"Yes."

"We just go!"

"Oh, yes, my darling, yes . . ."

"Can you keep Matt away from the casino?"

"I'll try." Her voice soft: "Do you love me?"

"Yes."

"Do you?"

"Yes."

It was late when they reached the Paradise Hotel. Porter wore a pair of chino trousers, blue work shirt, his Stetson, and cowboy boots. Billy Ray, looking outlandishly spiffy in various shades of green and yellow, carried an ivory cigarette holder. He spoke with a passable English accent.

The casino was almost empty. Porter looked around for Matt Nathan or Angel Amato. They were not there.

It was three A.M. and a deep night gloom hung over the tables. Sound was muted. Dealers, box men, floormen, and pit bosses displayed the same bored, unhealthy, gray look that seems to come to all workers when business is slow and the hour is late. The place was heavy with dead air and dead hopes—the graveyard shift.

There were perhaps a half dozen blackjack players at the tables. Porter and Billy Ray chose a deserted center table. Porter took out ten thousand dollars and purchased twenty stacks of hundred-dollar chips. He split the stacks with Billy Ray.

"The shoe," Billy Ray said to the dealer, a small, dark, foxy-looking man with heavy eyebrows and close-set eyes.

"Four decks?"

"Four decks, my friend, four decks. Quadruple fortune!" Billy Ray declaimed with Shakespearean orotundity, performing small, elegant flourishes in the air with his cigarette holder. "There are tides in the affairs of men, even as there are tides in the flow of the cards! Hazard all, win all! If one can catch the tide at its flood—well, sir! Let the waves of *beneficent luck* swamp me! Hmmm." The dealer, looking infinitely bored, cut and shuffled the cards together.

The play seesawed for the first hour, the edge falling evenly between house and player. Billy Ray started out with a strong line of patter, spinning out a skein of pseudoclassical aphorisms, but quickly ran out of steam. As the hour wore on, his talk grew more and more desultory, petering out at last in meaningless "hmmms" and "ahs." Porter could tell he was desperately tired. He refused to show his fatigue, however, and sat stiffly erect, puffing on cigarette after cigarette through his ivory holder, while sipping slowly from a large glass of bourbon.

There was a change of deal. The new man might have been a twin to the first, dark and beetle-browed, perhaps a bit stockier, with the same narrow black eyes. "You're a Slav or Italian," Billy Ray said to him.

"Albanian," the new dealer replied.

"A combination of both, hmmm," Billy Ray said.

The edge began to shift to the player, and Porter and Billy Ray bet the limit. There was a desperation to their play. They would win it all or throw it all away. The graveyard shift . . .

The cards fell for them. Hand after hand, the cards fell for them. Billy Ray Walker's Complete Four-Deck System, beautiful beyond all imagining, a flame in the night, consuming great chunks of the dealer's edge!

Porter played without strain now, an instrument of the System, wholly detached, observing himself, observing the fall of the cards as though in a dream.

Billy Ray Walker sat erect, unsmiling. Beads of perspiration stood out on his brow; his breath had quickened; his complexion was chalk-white.

It was a night Billy Ray had often dreamed about. Betting the limit on every hand, they covered the table and seemed immune to loss. The stacks of chips in front of them grew with incredible rapidity, erupting into great piles of winnings, heaping and spilling across the edge of the green felt table. Hundred-dollar chips fell at their feet, and they ignored them. At the end of the second hour they had won more than sixty thousand dollars.

Nervousness spread through the casino crew. The floorman, standing next to the dealer, was joined by the pit boss, then the casino manager. A small crowd gathered behind the players.

The casino manager began to panic. He summoned Red

Polikoff, who arrived at the table with a husky, balding man in a black suit—Caputo, the casino detective. Both men had no trouble recognizing Billy Ray.

They observed the play for a short while, then Red Polikoff hurried away. He entered the office and poured himself a drink. Then he called Matt Nathan at home. Yolande answered the phone. "I have to speak to Matt," Red Polikoff said with some urgency.

"He's asleep."

"Your friend is here with a man by the name of Walker. They're wrecking us. I need Matt to tell me what to do."

"Wait a minute."

On the other end of the line Yolande Nathan set the phone down on her bedstand. She counted to twenty, feeling her heart racing wildly. "It's all right. Let them play," Yolande said, when she picked up the phone.

"Matt said it's all right?" Red Polikoff asked incredulously.

"Yes."

Polikoff returned to the casino, glum with misgivings. Caputo was sweating. He looked with alarm over at Red Polikoff. The casino manager had provided chip holders for the players. The holders, each containing ten thousand dollars, were lined up between Porter and Billy Ray. They had now won almost eighty thousand dollars.

Polikoff considered calling a halt to the play, then decided it was not his place to do so. Perhaps Matt Nathan was in on it; perhaps it was part of an elaborate scam to siphon off money for him. No, it was not his place to question Matt Nathan's decision.

"Let them play," Red Polikoff said to the casino manager. And they all stood silently by as The Four-Deck System devastated the house.

It was dawn when Billy Ray and Porter cashed in. In less than four hours they had won a hundred and eighty-two thousand dollars. Red Polikoff had provided them with a black satchel to carry the money. The money was stacked inside in ten-thousand-dollar bundles.

They stood in the parking lot gazing up at a gray sky. The morning was cold. A harsh wind blew sand all about them.

Billy Ray Walker leaned against the car and sobbed. "Oh, mama, sweet mama," he said over and over again. His body was wracked with sobs. Tears streamed down his face; the false mustache, soaked with tears and perspiration, pulled loose from his face and dangled ridiculously from the side of his mouth. "I knew it," he said. "I knew it."

In the motel room they divided the money. "What are you going to do now?" Porter asked.

Billy Ray, surrounded on the bed by stacks of money, said: "I'm going to rest for a long time." He gathered up a handful of money and kissed it. "My ticker. I'm going to get my ticker fixed."

"That's a good idea, Billy Ray."

"I most assuredly am going to do that. Yes."

Porter took his cut of the money, ninety-one thousand dollars, and placed it back in the satchel.

"How about you? What are you going to do?" Billy Ray Walker asked.

"Leave town."

"Where will you go?"

"I don't know. I just know it's not smart to hang around here no more."

"You're right. I'm going to Reno. Or maybe Puerto Rico. Come with me, Don. We could make millions."

"No, that's all for me. I have what I have and that's enough."

He called Yolande. "We took them," he said. "One hundred eighty-two thousand dollars. We took them!"

"My God!"

"You and me—we're leaving now. I'm through with all this. I just want to be with you."

"Oh, yes," she said.

"Pick me up as soon as you can. When your husband finds out what happened—"

"I'll be there in a half hour."

Porter entered the bathroom while Billy Ray began to take off his wig. He showered and shaved, then gathered up the few items of clothing he had in the room.

"You best get out of here fast, Billy Ray."

"Yes."

Billy Ray was deathly pale. His eyes were dull as though a veil had descended over his gaze. "Are you all right?" Porter asked.

"I'm fine," Billy Ray said with a small smile.

"Good luck," Porter said.

"There ain't no such animal."

They shook hands. Billy Ray's hand was cold and clammy.

Porter left the Sultan Motel, carrying his clothes under one arm, the satchel in the other.

After he had gone Billy Ray stared at the closed door. He lifted a cigarette from the bureau and lit up. He walked to the window and peered out of a corner of the curtain. Porter was climbing into a car. A woman was at the wheel.

Billy Ray Walker sat on the bed and giggled stupidly. He kicked his wig across the room. He could not stop laughing. He laughed and laughed and laughed.

Porter drove with Yolande back to the Excelsior where he hastily packed the rest of his belongings. In a drawer he discovered the charts he had made up when first teaching Kitty the System. He looked at them for a short moment, then ripped them into little pieces and threw them in the wastebasket.

"Where are we going?" Yolande asked back in the car. Her face was drawn and anxious.

"I figure we jump down to L.A. first off, then make plans where we want to end up."

256

"I'm afraid."

"Don't be."

They drove in silence to McCarren Field. The day was gray. Porter tried to think of something cheerful to say. All he could think of was they had ninety-one thousand dollars and were running. They, of course, had each other, but Porter couldn't bring himself to mention that.

In a little more than an hour they were in Los Angeles. At the airport Yolande had an attack of nerves. "He'll know we're here. He'll come after us. He'll never let me get away with this—"

They decided to keep moving. Porter bought two tickets for New York.

On the flight to New York Yolande spoke very little. She stared straight ahead at the seat in front of her. Her eyes were wide with panic. "Are you sorry about this?" Porter asked.

"No," she said softly.

"We can always give it up."

"No, no. I don't want to give it up." He squeezed her hand. It was cold and tense.

"I love you," Porter said. "You know that, don't you?"

She nodded her head but did not speak.

It was raining in New York. It was a hard, cold rain that fell in slashing diagonals and gave the city a bleak, deserted look.

They checked into the Edison Hotel just off Broadway. Yolande looked tired and old, and for a fleeting instant Porter regretted having run off with her.

Her nerves were drawn almost to the breaking point. Every sound in the hotel caused her to flinch. "We have to get out of here. He'll know we're in New York." He embraced her. She was trembling like a frightened animal.

He set the satchel down on the bed and opened it. He lifted out several packs of money.

Suddenly, inside he grew cold. Everything seemed to freeze

within. His hands began to tremble violently. He couldn't stop the trembling and he couldn't move.

There was a thin layer of money on top, perhaps two thousand dollars in all. The rest of the satchel was filled with magazines.

"What's wrong?"

"He took my money," Porter said. "When I was in the bathroom, he pulled a switch. That son-of-a-bitch! That no good son-of-a-bitch!"

Yolande looked at him and did not understand. She tried to speak but couldn't. He flung the satchel against the wall. Magazines and money spilled out over the floor.

He told her to remain in the hotel. She tried to stop him, but it was impossible. He would see her the next day. He was going back to Las Vegas.

After a while, after Porter had been gone some time, Billy Ray Walker got up from the bed and removed the money from under the coverlet where he had concealed it.

He moved quickly now, realizing that Porter could discover the switch at any time. He removed the beard and cleaned his face of the gum that had attached it. He packed the money into an old leather valise.

He was running out with Porter's share, and he couldn't exactly tell why. It had something to do with the nearness he stood to death, to Porter's indifference to his dying. Yes, he had stayed with him during his attack, but he hadn't really cared. He had watched him, that was all. Why should Porter care? He had his life, his health.

And, after all, it was his system. He had worked and suffered all these years. What gave Porter a right to the fruits of his labor, when he had youth, when he had life?

He pushed back the memories he had of other deceptions. He had long ago justified *them*, but occasionally they came back to haunt him. All his life he had done in those people closely involved with him. Why? Because of survival. Life was a game of survival. You had to maintain the edge.

Even Monty. But Monty, of course, never discovered that, never knew that Billy Ray Walker had turned him in. Well, the man was a desperado and a murderer. You couldn't travel with a man like that. A man like that deserved to be locked up, just as Porter deserved a satchel full of magazines. Neither of them had proper respect for the *sanctity* of human life. Porter had looked down on him as he was dying, talked about his "connections," viewed Billy Ray's life as no more important than a fly's. . . .

By the time he reached the airport he had almost come to terms with his actions. What he had done to Porter was the only right thing to do, the only *possible* thing. A man who will sit there and watch you die with no more concern than if you were a bug on the wall deserved whatever happened to him. . . .

He boarded a plane to Reno. He had no idea why he was going there. Reno. He smiled to himself. Perhaps he would do a little more gambling. Nothing extravagant. Just some gravy play.

The plane banked over the pink-purple mountains surrounding Vegas. At the tilt of the plane the flat, blue, disc-like surface of Lake Mead pivoted gracefully into view below, exposing momentarily its smooth promise of coolness in a wilderness of harsh desert rock. Then the plane was climbing up, heading north, rising into a sky shredded with long streams of fluff and haze.

It came to Billy Ray Walker now, in the steady drone of the plane's engines, with cotton clouds scudding the window, that he was alone once more. No family, no friends. Alone as he had been these many years; as it seemed he had always been . . .

Alone. Ever since he had left a dust-shack on a dry East Texas plain so many, many years before. He was twelve years old, and he had gone simply because there was no food.

The youngest of a dozen children, no one had thought to feed him. No one even looked at him. His mother would keep her eyes to the ground and pray. She would pray night and day. His father was long gone.

What had his father looked like? He couldn't even remember now. Just a man with skin like leather, who smelled of sweat all the time, a man who always seemed more dead than alive, a small, parched, yellow corpse crouched in a corner of the shack, sucking on the rot of his teeth. One day he got up and walked away and was never seen after that. Billy Ray had spotted the direction in which he had gone— west toward the red rim of the dying sun. Some time after, he, too, wandered off.

The years of all-night card games through the Southwest. Hold 'em had been his game in those days, and it had been his meal ticket for more than thirty years. Then he had come across the System.

The System had justified his life. The lack of a woman, of a family, of a home, of friends—all were justified by the System. He went to sleep dreaming of the System and woke to pursue it. The System had become his existence and now, even in the pain and sickness of the last few weeks, it had made everything worthwhile.

He saw himself staring over a vast, gray plain, the plain of his youth, and ached momentarily at the sense of monumental aloneness. With an effort of will, he shut off that dream and began another. Reno. He would get himself a fine room and a girl—the best hooker in town. He would drink champagne and eat filet mignon once more. No, he would not gamble for a while. He would sleep with the money under his pillow. It would bring him enormous solace. . . .

The hum and gentle pitch of the plane lulled him into a soft half-sleep. Forgotten were the pain and trembling and fear of death that had haunted him in Vegas. The sky was filled with enormous possibilities.

His chin sank down against his chest. His glasses slid partway down his nose. A loud snoring sound escaped through his nose, and he slumped sideways against the wall of the plane.

Now he dreamt he was dying and it was not unpleasant. Death was sleep, nothing more. A vague thought stirred, his last. What would become of the money?

The stewardess shook him to remind him to fasten his safety belt. His face was chalk-white, his lips tinged with blue. His glasses fell to his lap. He was indeed dead.

XVI

Why was he going back? Porter, on the plane to Vegas, sought within himself one more answer, not so much because he really wanted to know, but to divert himself from the agony of the journey.

A fat woman, seated next to him, was asleep. Her enormous bulk had him trapped in his seat. His nerves felt scraped raw. He was soaked with cold perspiration.

Why go back?

Billy Ray Walker was no doubt long gone. His money was gone. Then why?

He was grabbing at straws and he knew it. He *had* to go back; he had to see it himself, the empty motel room, the detritus of their time together. Would the chart still be there, The Complete Billy Ray Walker Four-Deck System? And the goatee and wig? The four-deck dealing shoe? He had to view those blasted shards of his existence.

Yes, these past few hours his life had exploded. Now, when he had a *chance* for happiness, it had turned out a sham and a delusion.

What would he do now? Return once more to the System? He could take Yolande to Puerto Rico or the Bahamas, Great Britain or Monte Carlo. The System was in his head.

It was as natural to him as breathing. He could pull it off again. Billy Ray had bequeathed to him that much: The Billy Ray Walker Complete Four-Deck System.

But he knew in his soul he couldn't go on with it. The attempt at the Paradise Hotel had been a last-ditch effort. The need for the System had died within him.

And what of Yolande? What about his relationship to her? Now that they had at last run off together, he had lost his passion for the idea. He felt trapped. She seemed old and used and empty to him. Would he be forced to carry her with him the rest of his life like some desperate, irreversible disease?

And what about Matt Nathan? Did he realize she was gone? What would he do when he found out?

His whole life had been like this—jumping from one prison into another. Always, he supposed, trying to break out of the prison of his *self*, that small, tired, tight confinement of self, that mean, tawdry spirit somehow crippled, somehow incapable of spontaneity or joy.

He had to admit. it. With Yolande, there was no joy, as there had been none with Kitty nor with his wife nor with any woman he had ever been with. And with Yolande there would *never* be joy; he knew it. They would cling together, bitter and barren, their future sapped by regrets, accusations, wounds—two dry husks trying to suck life from each other.

He thought of Eddie MacRae staring vacant-eyed from his hospital bed. Was that the answer? Had Eddie found that point of zero comprehension that Porter hungered for, that lack of awareness of self?

The System for a while had been his savior. It had brought him out of himself and given purpose to his life. He had discovered energy and dedication and the ability to forget his arms and hands and eyes and skull; the ability to forget the terrifying passage of time.

Time. A boxer had once said of his opponent, *he can run,*

but he can't hide. Perhaps that's why he was going back: to confront *time.* . . .

And now he realized some terrible truth about his life. He would always go back. Winners talk—and losers? They go back. Over and over again. Despite charts and systems and love and money and the absolute certainty of final defeat, they go back. They are crucified. The cross is their eternal return.

The woman next to him snored softly. She smelled of a sickening, sweet perfume, which did not completely mask an acrid, animal odor, an odor of something dying. He felt as though the presence of her, the odor of her, that ugly combination of sweet and sour, would suffocate him. He felt as though he were about to scream. . . .

The FASTEN SAFETY BELTS sign flashed on. The plane began its descent. It seemed an interminable length of time before Vegas appeared.

There it was, at last, beneath him, a vast carpet of coruscating light, a dizzying pointillist construction, an electric fantasy. As the plane dipped lower, reds and blues and yellows swirled novalike out of the white light, and it seemed to Porter he was entering some inverted galaxy, a minor, uncharted, imploding Milky Way, generating neon values unsuspected in the wide expanse of the universe.

This sense of unreality persisted. He moved out of the plane, down the Strip by cab: it clung to him. The world appeared to him altered and strange as though he had leapt the absolute boundary of physical law and had entered a bizarre, refractive dimension, a subtle approximation of the real world, but a counterfeit nevertheless, whose curved laws and slanted values gaped snarelike to hook the unsuspecting into an insane, obverse universe, a desert mirage, offering everything, surrendering only illusion and emptiness.

The Sultan Motel, where the cab driver had just deposited him, did it really exist? He knew the place, of course, yet it seemed somehow altered and unfamiliar. Had that *particular*

264

spot of neon been dark, had *that* chunk of stucco been missing? And the swimming pool: it was filled now with water.

He had retained his key to Billy Ray Walker's room. The lights were burning inside. For a moment a spark of hope flashed up within him.

He let himself in. The room was occupied. Angel Amato and two men he had never seen before were waiting for him.

The men were short and dark, chunky, but not fat. They had long, black, greasy hair and broad, flat Indian faces. They wore tight black trousers and flowered sport shirts. Angel Amato said something to them in Spanish, and one man moved swiftly behind Porter and slammed the door to the room shut. The other man stood up. As he rose, his hand flashed, and there was a soft click, and a long silver knife-blade caught the light and gleamed in his grip. Angel Amato remained seated on the bed. "Where is she?" he said without smiling.

"What do you mean?"

Angel gestured with his fist, a short uppercut, and the man behind Porter hit him in the kidney. He fell forward onto one knee, and Angel Amato kicked up at him, catching Porter on the side of his face with his boot.

"I want to know where she is."

Porter put his hand up to the side of his face. It was swelling already, although he was not aware of any pain, just a thick numbness. He tried to draw himself up to his feet, but Angel Amato kicked him again, and he fell back sprawling. The force of the blow drove him into a floor lamp, and the lamp crashed against the wall, the bulb exploding in a bright flash of light, and now the room was gray and shadowed, and he could feel blood pouring from his mouth.

He did not want to cry, but realized he was whimpering stupidly, not from fear, but embarrassment. A foot smashed again and again into his ribs, and the pain was excruciating. "She's in New York," he said.

"Where?"

"The Edison Hotel."

"What room?"

Before he could answer, one of the men ripped his jacket up over his head. Now he felt himself yanked forward. His stomach rebelled, and he began to vomit. He could see at his feet small drops of blood mixed in with his puke. The jacket was pulled off him, and one of the Mexicans was tearing at the pockets. He came up with the key to Porter's hotel room in New York. He tossed the key to Angel Amato.

Angel Amato moved to the telephone and put through a call to New York. Someone came on at the other end of the line, and Angel Amato repeated the room number. Then he heard Yolande's voice, faint, tentative, "Hello . . . hello . . . is that you, Don? Don?," as Angel held the receiver out in front of him, then replaced it on its cradle.

They forced Porter out of the room to a car parked in the darkened drive of the motel. The two Mexicans sat with him in the back, while Angel Amato drove.

They drove up Las Vegas Boulevard to Bonanza, turned left on Bonanza, and soon the lights along the road, the gas stations and hamburger stands and drive-in liquor stores thinned out, and they were driving along a road of black. No one spoke. The two Mexicans, one on either side of him, gazed out of the car; great mounds of black, looming against the gray sky, rushed past the windows. Houses? Hills? Trees? Porter could not tell. They were speeding through nothingness.

They drove for a long while. One of the Mexicans lit up a cigarette. Angel Amato flicked on the radio. Porter was aware of music but through the static could not distinguish the melody. Angel adjusted the dial. The song was "Just a Closer Walk with Thee."

The car turned off the deserted highway onto a dirt road. Off to his right Porter could see a long, thin necklace of lights in the distance. The lights hung in the dark, glowing magically.

Now the car came to a stop, and one of the Mexicans yanked Porter out. The other hurried around the car and grabbed him by the arm. Angel Amato rolled down his window.

"What's your real name?" he demanded. "Porter's not your real name. What's your real name?"

"Monty."

"Monty what?"

"Just Monty."

Angel Amato looked away in disgust. "That's not your real name."

The night was cold. There were no stars in the sky. The desert air was musky with the smell of dying mesquite and yucca. Porter stumbled as the two Mexicans pushed him through the rough desert foliage. He fell to the rocky ground. It was covered with shards of glass, rusted cans, shreds of tire, orange peels, rotting condoms. The Mexicans pulled him to his feet and pushed him further into the desert. He was not afraid. The necklace of lights appeared unimaginably beautiful to him.

He was standing in the desert looking out over the gray-black toward the lights, thinking how excruciatingly lovely they were.

He did not see the gun, nor did he feel the shot that killed him.

Angel Amato led Yolande Nathan across the casino floor toward the office where her husband awaited her. She was dry inside, broken.

Matt Nathan did not look up when she entered the office. He sat toying with the ears of his poodle, Princess.

Just off the casino floor, between the blackjack tables and the circular cocktail bar, Kitty stood with Eddie MacRae.

Eddie MacRae stared straight ahead and saw nothing.

Kitty would be with him for a long, long time. She would lead him into the future. They would stand together on the edge of the casino day and night, day and night, and none of it would make any difference.

Occasionally she would interrupt their vigil to fulfill an assignation, to earn a buck.

David Scott Milton

David Scott Milton was born in Pittsburgh, Pennsylvania, in 1934. He attended Taylor Allderdice High School there. He is a playwright and screenwriter, as well as a novelist. He wrote the film Born to Win, *released in 1971. His first novel,* The Quarterback, *also appeared in 1971. He resides in Santa Monica, California.*